# TAKE
# THE LEAD

## JOHNNY DIAZ

*Dreamspinner Press*

Published by
Dreamspinner Press
4760 Preston Road
Suite 244-149
Frisco, TX 75034
http://www.dreamspinnerpress.com/

Take the Lead

Cover Art by Catt Ford

ISBN: 978-1-61581-956-0

Printed in the United States of America
First Edition
June 2011

eBook edition available
eBook ISBN: 978-1-61581-957-7

This book is dedicated to all those people who bravely battle Parkinson's disease and other degenerative conditions in their daily lives. May a cure soon loom on the horizon.

# chapter One

*I'M GETTING too old for this. What am I doing here?* I should have outgrown the club phase in my twenties. *Is there a support group for aging men who can't stop hitting the bars?* These thoughts invade my mind as I sway to the left and pelvic thrust to the right, coaxing my body to follow the beat. I wave my hands in the air and twirl them in a circular motion. Lights flash like indoor lightning and briefly illuminate everyone's face. The pounding bass from the latest hip-hop music gets everyone (mostly guys in their twenties) to bump and grind on the dance floor. Me included, but I'm a member of the VH1 demographic, not the YouTube generation.

My blue jeans sag at my waist, and my *Star Trek* T-shirt with a floating image of the Starship *Enterprise* is drenched with sweat. I briefly remove my black baseball cap, comb my fingers through my short, dark-brown hair, and then smush it down with the cap. It makes me look a little younger and boyish, or at least that's what my friend Nick tells me. He's around here *somewhere*, dancing the night away and pretending that he doesn't have to teach grammar to his class of eighth graders tomorrow morning in Somerville.

"Just dance!" I holler to another dancer, a sculpted Brazilian guy with a shaved head, tanned body, and piercing hazel eyes that resemble two small cups of honey lit by invisible sunlight.

"Yeah, shake it, just like that!" the Brazilian cheers me on. I smile and then abandon him as I continue to orbit the dance floor to find another dance partner. Along the way, I nod my chin up at the other club revelers. I shimmy with a twentysomething girl who backs her bum up my way and then dry-humps me as she bends over. I playfully spank her and giggle. I mosey over to the other side of the club, where I join a dancing train of three Asian guys and a girl. Like a centipede, we flow forward and back with our arms waving up and down.

"Move forward, and now back! Whew!" I shout over the music, leading the dancers as everyone high-fives me and booty-shakes me on the side. I continue to circle the dance floor and jam from one song to the next. The latest tunes from the pop princesses and hip-hop kings blare overhead with their addictive musical beats and catchy hooks. The entire club is an explosion of music and movement, a choreographed Boston dance party, and I'm glad to be one of its regulars.

As I absorb the frenetic music, a slight, baby-faced guy shimmies my way and flashes a wide smile. He gyrates and crunks like a wind-up Latino doll. His gelled, short-cropped black hair reflects the bright strobe lights. I quicken my pace to match his beat. Is he old enough to be in here? Not a wrinkle in sight. He barely has any facial scruff. With each step that I match, the guy torques it up a notch. I do my best to keep up. So far, so good. No cardiac arrest. The image of the Puerto Rican flag on his black shirt blurs with his every move.

"What's your name?" I shout over the club's soundtrack.

"Pedro! You're hot… for an older dude," he says.

Gasp! I scowl and my eyes widen in disbelief. Older dude? He might as well toss me a cane or a walker to dance with. "Um, thanks, I think. I'm Gabriel, and my nurse is outside waiting for me with my portable oxygen tank," I greet him. He grins at my joke. As we shake hands, he moves closer toward me. Our faces are *thisclose*. I smell the mint gum he chews. He could easily be one of my students, a college freshman. I decide to forgive him for his immaturity.

"Are you Puerto Rican?" I ask, my hands moving up and down while my hips swivel side to side like a Zumba dance student.

"Sí, viva la patria," he gushes, his hands rising with pride.

"Well, I'm Cuban-American, so I can keep up with you. Dance as fast as you want," I egg him on. "In fact, my nurse has two oxygen tanks on standby, in case you need one yourself."

"Oh yeah?" he says, considering the dare. "We'll see about that."

Okay, big mistake on my part. My big mouth and sensitive ego can get me into trouble sometimes. Within seconds, he unleashes a burst of boundless energy. He jumps in place; his hands fly in all directions as if someone activated his inner fast-forward button. I stand there and wonder, *What the hell did I get myself into?* Again, I do my best to live up to my dare. Right now, I feel like I am watching a movie of someone else's life. Again, my mind wonders, *What am I doing here again?*

The more I keep apace, the faster Pedro the jumping bean moves. He smiles and laughs as I maintain his groove—well, just barely, with my nineties' dance moves, but the lights help me look cool. After a few minutes, my heart feels like it's about to burst out of my body and flop around on the dance floor like a goldfish sans water. I imagine myself chasing my bouncing heart around the club. I need a break before I break a body part.

"Okay, you win. I gotta catch my breath," I say with labored breaths as I place my hand over my heart to make sure it's still there.

"No problem. Come back when you get your strength back, old man!" he says with a mischievous grin. I narrow my eyes and pretend that they're shooting laser beams that eviscerate him. I imagine the starship on my T-shirt is firing backup photon torpedoes at him as well. I stalk through the crowded dance floor and wipe the beads of sweat away from my forehead. The words *old man* replay and sting in my mind. That little bastard. I'm not old. Or am I? Actually, I think I could use an oxygen mask right about now.

I decide to cool off (and catch my breath) by scurrying to the bar, where I order a Red Bull with vodka, my third of the night. The tonic arms me with liquid courage to keep dancing, even though I have a class to teach in a few hours. Thomas Jefferson College is literally around the corner and five flights up from Estate, this alley dance club/bar.

By the way, my name isn't "old man." It's Gabriel Galan, although my parents call me Gabrielito. Some people in Boston recognize my face from a great article that appeared in the *Boston Daily* newspaper. The story focused on the lack of Latino college professors in Boston. There I was, my smiling face plastered on the front page of the newspaper as I stood before my Covering the News class. My students still tease me about the article. One student, Angie, even asked for my autograph to show to her mom in Texas. She was kissing up to me so I would overlook her late paper. Not a chance!

Before I arrived in this capital of academia, I worked briefly as a newspaper reporter in Fort Lauderdale, my hometown. I covered extremely local government news in the cities of Pembroke Pines and Weston, where most Miami Dolphins players own majestic homes with intimidating high gates and spewing decorative fountains. Although I garnered several bylines a week, I felt that something was amiss in my professional life. I wanted to educate and inform people through my articles on government and everyday neighborly issues such as the lack of funding in local schools or the increases in property taxes. But over the years, as my old newspaper reduced its staff and shrunk its page size in an attempt to reinvent itself on the Internet, I realized that I could have more of an impact as a teacher. So at twenty-eight, I returned to Florida International University, my alma mater, and pursued my master's in education with a focus on creative writing.

Through my student-teaching courses, I was hired as an adjunct professor for writing and journalism. From the beginning, I liked the mix because I'm able to discuss current events as well as teach a new generation of journalists how to cover news and write short stories. The combo allows me to marry my two passions. I love reading about culture, style, trends, and stories of broad interest, but I also love to pen short stories about family and friendships. Only two of my stories have been published in anthologies, but that's okay. I write them for myself, not the greater public.

Two years into my burgeoning teaching career, I met a recruiter from Boston's Thomas Jefferson College at an academic fair in Fort Lauderdale. She flew me up for an interview, and that's how I literally landed in Boston. So yes, I am far away from the radiant sun-kissed tropical life of Las Olas Boulevard and AIA beaches, and yet I don't miss it all that much. I always yearned for stimulating conversations with fellow academics, and Boston offered plenty of that. Also, being the only Hispanic associate professor at Thomas Jefferson College, which everyone simply calls Jefferson, has awarded me some mental job security. My presence adds to their diversity quota, but it also enhances my resume. When I was offered the job, I couldn't say no. It was a great opportunity to cut my South Florida-Cuban umbilical cord and embrace a new way of living. I was also able to usher in my long-sought independence, something that eluded me in South Florida, where I shuttled back and forth between my parents' homes—something I've become accustomed to since they divorced my senior year of high school.

My father, Guillermo Galan, is a hard-working exterminator despite having Parkinson's disease, which he's been able to keep at bay over the years. The disease's assault on his body has been a slow but persistent march, from what I can tell. My mother, Gladys, is strong and healthy, too, thanks to the Shaklee products she sells and swears by. Whenever she calls me, she reminds me to take my daily vitamins, which she ships to Boston in large care packages. I adore my parents even though at times I feel like I'm in a perpetual tug of war between them. That's one of the reasons I chose to move away and be on my own in New England. I wanted my own home. I grew tired of being caught between two.

While working in Boston's cosmopolitan metropolis of college students, professors, and medical institutions has been a beautiful blessing—a gift—it has also kept me from my family, but that's what frequent-flier miles are for. And there's one thing I enjoy as much as reading and writing in Boston, and that's dancing, one of the reasons I stop by this club every week. As much as I love to dance, my father never cared for the art form. It wasn't the manliest thing to do, he would often say. That was one of our stark differences, and we have many, even though I am a genetic clone of him but forty years younger. I have the short-cropped dark-brown hair combed to the side, thick black eyebrows, a big smile, and an even bigger appetite for iced caramel coffees from Dunkin' Donuts. (Caramel swirl and black coffee, please.) At seventy-five, Papi is thinner than me, although some people (my mother, for one) would say I'm slight like a coconut palm waiting for a Boston nor'easter to knock me over. The lack of a home-cooked meal and good Cuban food in Beantown will make any South Florida native shed a few pounds. Plus, I sometimes forget to eat because I lose track of time when I grade my students' papers. I burn off the calories and stress with my daily runs along the beach in Quincy, the coastal town of American presidents that I live in and that borders Boston.

My father and I differ in other ways. I'm more liberal and open. I stood in the Boston Common to fight for local gay marriage and equal rights. Papi is a staunch conservative, stuck in the old-world ways of his native Cuba, which is trapped in a time warp. Another difference between us: I would never cheat on my partner if I had one, which is a whole other story. Papi cheated on my mother when I was in high school. That led to a divorce and the current state of my fractured family. Papi's betrayal continues to sting me emotionally, but he is my father, my one and only. I can't be mad at him forever, especially with his Parkinson's. At times, you have to overlook the flaws of your loved ones and love them unconditionally.

And we also differ in our views on dance. Papi has zero interest in the artistic expression, while I always viewed it as a form of recreational escapism. Dancing always felt natural and liberating, an extension of my creativity. My body funneled the beats and rhythms into coordinated movements and steps. I sprung to life whenever I jammed at high school dances in Fort Lauderdale, at sweet sixteens and *quinceañeras* for my cousin and friends in Miami Lakes. Later, in college, I wildly danced at South Beach clubs, which became another home away from home; I flung my sweaty shirt in the air as I partied topless with a sea of fellow young, tanned, and sculpted revelers.

My father, on the other hand, would do just about anything to avoid the traditional dance floor. If my mother began twirling and swaying in our kitchen to Celia Cruz or Shakira while preparing our lunch or early-evening dinners—when we were a family—Papi disappeared by finding an excuse to run an errand to avoid being dragged onto my mother's makeshift kitchen dance floor. I always served as her dance partner at family gatherings and wedding receptions while my dad sat glued to his chair, watching us with a cool Corona bottle clenched in his hands. No matter how hard my mother and I tried to pry my father away from his chair, he wouldn't will himself to the dance floor. He was the poster man for the I-can-do-it-all father, but he didn't think dancing was a macho thing to do, even though his wife loved it as much as whipping up her favorite sweet flan for us. I miss those moments when we were a trio, the Galan family.

As I wait for my drink at the bar, my train of thought is suddenly interrupted when a finger flicks the back of my right earlobe. This annoys me the same way a mosquito might—it invades your personal space and you want to swat it.

I turn around and I see that the annoying finger belongs to a friend with a big old dirty grin. "You know I hate when you do that, Nickers!" I say, calling Nick by his nickname.

"Oh please, GG. If it had been any other hot guy, you'd be giggling and flirting and acting all shy like a little girl... *not*! You're Boston's naughty professor."

"I wish! I'm more like the nutty professor," I joke.

"Or a slore!" he sputters. We're playing our usual name-calling game.

"A slore? What's that?" I rub my finger against my chin out of curiosity as if trying to decipher a clue in one of Dan Brown's novels.

"A slut and a whore. A slore. Get it?" Nick says, proud of his word invention.

"Is that something you learned from your middle-school students?"

"Nah, I made it up. I thought you'd appreciate the play on words."

"No, but I appreciate your effort, Nickers. I'll give you a B plus for that," I say, patting him on the shoulder.

"What am I going to do with you, GG?" Nick says, rolling his eyes.

"The more fitting question is, what would you do in Boston without me?"

A few words about Nick. He has been my wingman since I moved here. With his black spiked-up straight hair, emerald green eyes, and olive skin, he personifies the gorgeous Portuguese-Irish men of Rhode Island. Okay, he's one of the few but proud good-looking ones from there. He also comes with a thick, butch Providence accent that I find intriguing and, yes, a little sexy. We instantly clicked as friends the night we met here at the club as we both stood in a long line of guys, girls, and drag queens waiting to pee. I accidentally bumped into Nick and apologized. He noticed my FIU T-shirt and struck up a conversation. He had dated, okay, more like hooked up with, a college student at my alma mater during a spring-break trip to Fort Lauderdale. Immediately, Nick and I started comparing my hometown to Boston and Providence and the guys each city seems to attract.

I learned right away that Nick majored in education in Boston and works as a middle-school teacher. He still complains that his students are a pain in the ass, yet I know he misses them every summer. From that night on, we've been buddies. Nick even indulges me by watching old episodes of the original *Star Trek* series, my favorite. (That's the hallmark of a true friend.) I know Nick is not the biggest fan of the sci-fi show, but he knows that I am, and he boldly goes where no other friend of mine in Fort Lauderdale had wanted to go: a night of reruns with me in my condo at least twice a month. Nick is game as long I serve him his preferred drink and venture out with him to the bars to man-hunt, or more like boy-hunt, in exchange. He believes in emotion-free seductions, and he usually has penis on the brain. I guess you could say that I'm the Cuban Spock, the sensible and more logical one, to Nick's gay Kirk, who is always on the prowl and looking for new adventures in bed. He sets his phaser to "hooking up."

I must admit that I do enjoy watching Nick chase guys ten years younger than him. Nick is thirty-two, but his thin, tight, muscular build (size twink) and some makeup help him pass for twenty-five, and he knows it. Tonight he's wearing a dark-green T-shirt that reads "Hit It!"

"So are you going to treat me to a drink, Mr. Professor? You know us public school teachers don't make crap," Nick says, flashing those beautiful green orbs of his like a seductive vampire so he can persuade me to buy him a drink. It usually works. I'm a sucker for green eyes, even if they belong to good friends.

"Yeah, yeah, yeah, just as long as you stop the poor teacher act. You've been teaching for ten years. You should have some money put away. Don't go blowing it on alcohol."

"I couldn't agree more. That's why I am asking you to buy me a drink," he says, punching me in the arm. He quickly puts me in a headlock, pulls off my cap, and starts to rub my hair with his knuckles. It kinda tickles. I let out a full-on belly laugh. Once Nick lets me loose, I smooth out my *Star Trek* T-shirt and flag down the bartender to add Nick's beer to my order. Nick thanks me by spanking my ass, which makes me jump.

"*Oye*, stop that. People are going to think we're together or something, not that they don't already."

"No offense, Gabriel, but you're not my type. I like twinks... *old man!*"

I gasp and feign offense. This is the second time tonight someone has called me—I can't even say it. "Oh, you want to go there, huh? I'm not the one who dyes his hair with Miss Clairol number 130 midnight-black every month to hide his gray hairs."

"Shhh, Gabriel. Don't say that too loud. Someone might hear you," Nick whispers as he looks around us.

"And speaking of twinks, Mr. To Catch A Predator! Watch out for those hidden NBC cameras when you hook up with one of these younger guys. Whenever I turn on *Dateline*, I keep thinking I'm going to see you on there with your pants down and trying to explain your way out of a *sticky* situation," I provoke him.

"Fuckin' A. As long as they're cute and cuddly, I'm game. I like being single. You avoid crazy drama that way," he jokes. "I'm not like you, Gabriel—a sensitive Cuban Care Bear. One day, you'll meet that special guy when you least expect it. Until then, have fun, have an affair or two. Be happy, get laid! Remember, he who procrastinates, masturbates."

Okay, so Nick isn't always the most socially appropriate person, but in his classroom, he's the consummate professional who wears a dress shirt, tie, jeans, and nice dress shoes and a pair of black-framed Clark Kent glasses. One time when I visited him at his school for lunch, I noticed that he had the most disciplined group of students. The girls—and at least two boys—seemed to have a crush on him. I was impressed.

Whenever I need someone to talk to about my parents or issues with dating (or the lack of it) in Boston, Nick is there to listen. So I can excuse him for his sometimes-weird behavior and foul mouth. (Have I mentioned his underwear fetish? More on that later.) Good friends are hard to come by in this town of impenetrable cliques where gay men act like they are surrounded by invisible force fields that only come down for a select few. Boston can be its own private tea party: admission by special invitation only.

After the muscled bartender with the hairy chest hands me my overpriced drink ($10) and Nick's (a $7 beer), I hand over a twenty-dollar bill and leave the change as a tip. If the bar overcharges for drinks, I under-tip. Fair is fair. Besides, there's a ten-dollar cover just to get into this place.

"Thanks, Professor Galan," Nick says, sipping his beer. "You're my... *hero!*" He feigns admiration and puts his hand on his smooth chest.

"Yeah, yeah, yeah, whatever. It's funny how I'm always your hero when you want a drink. I know how it goes, Nickers." But Nick is not paying any attention to what I say.

His eyes are trained on the Brazilian stud I was dancing with earlier. I should just let Nick have him, because I don't hold a candle to Nick's boyish dark Irish looks. Once the guy sees Nick, he'll want to go home with him instead of me. I can't compete with Nick's tight body or green eyes. I do have some good qualities working in my favor. My best feature is my honesty, then my resume, followed by my cheesy humor and a head full of thick, short-brown hair. Someday some guy will find those qualities endearing, wherever he may be. *Cupid, if you're out there, I'm here and waiting to be struck with one of your arrows. Facebook me!*

Nick then turns to me. "God bless Brazil! Look at that guy's ass. I am going to take a loop."

"Yeah, a fruit loop! Catch you later, Nick."

And with that, he returns to his spot on the dance floor and introduces himself to the guy. I smile and raise my glass from a distance. It doesn't take long before they start kissing. Nick has found his—well, you know—for the night.

I stand along the grooved edge of the bar and watch this Boston twilight circus of partiers. Why am I here again? It's a question I ask myself each week, and the answers don't come easily. Why are these people here, anyway? Oh yeah, because they are young and this is what you do when you're in college and in your twenties. A rite of passage. It's one that I have relived repeatedly since moving to the college capital of the world, where the median age is thirty-one, according to a recent article I read in the *Boston Daily*. This is a town where the colder it gets, the more people pack the bars and clubs. Each week I declare that I am not going to go out as much, and each week Nick calls me and I then find myself dancing and drinking like I used to when I was a college student.

Tonight, I'm surrounded by many younger guys, mostly college imports, students who study here for two or four years and then boomerang back to wherever they came from. Boston is known for this perpetual brain drain, but every year, a crop of newcomers arrives, and that included me three years ago. As a professor, I meet them firsthand in class, which can create some slight complications in my professional life. It's hard for me to date when I see some of my students out and about and observing my every move so they can blog or gossip about me in the corridors of Jefferson. And any of these young guys could be a future student of mine, so I tread cautiously.

"Professor Galan! Is that you?" A voice beckons from my right as I sip my drink. I turn around and spot Craig, a former student. An aspiring broadcast journalist, he took my Covering the News class last year. He often wore a sports jacket and tie as if he were about to go live on the air at a moment's notice. He's a regular on *Jefferson Today*, the school's morning newscast. Tonight, he wears a tight-fitting blue T-shirt that frames his slight build. The shirt complements his light-brown eyes and brown fuzzy crew cut, which resembles soft peach fuzz. *Que lindo!*

"Hey, Craig! How are you?" I say, holding up my drink. He comes over and hugs me tightly, which almost knocks my drink out of my hand. I spill some on the club's carpeting. I awkwardly pat him on the back and breathe in his musky vanilla-scented cologne. I still don't know the appropriate course of action to take when it comes to touching current and former students on and off campus, gay or straight, cute and super-cute. On the last day of classes, some students, even the straight guys, hug me, which I find very moving. They say, "I love you, Professor Galan! You rock, man!" I can't recall ever hugging one of my professors in Miami, so I am always pleasantly surprised when a student wants to wish me farewell at the end of the semester with a man-hug. My female students like to wrap their arms around my waist, since I tower over them. But whenever I see Craig, who grows more adorable each year, I want to squeeze him tightly as if he were a plush doll. But again, that would be inappropriate even though he's now a senior. He may not be my student, but he remains a student at the college. It's one of the gray areas, an obscure boundary and a distance I maintain.

"I miss your class. You were the best, and you're still my favorite professor. I use your writing tips for my other classes and for writing my scripts for the morning show." He smiles and looks down. In class, he was the first to raise his hand and offer feedback on other students' papers. His enthusiasm helped pull some of the other students out of their shells. Tonight, Craig is more animated and touchy-feely. Maybe the alcohol? He clenches a Bud Light in his hand. Every so often as he talks to me, he lets his lips linger on the beer bottle's top a few seconds too long. I look away when he does that because my cheeks suddenly warm.

"Thanks, Craig. I'm glad you got something out of that morning class. I think 8 a.m. was way too early," I say, stifling a yawn. "You were one of my better students. I was just happy you and the rest of the class managed to stay awake throughout the semester. I even had a hard time staying awake," I say, feeling a little flirtatious, but I can't cross the line, although I really wouldn't mind doing so. Maybe when he graduates in the spring? Nah. By then, he will have landed a TV job in a small or midsize market in Somewhere USA with a fellow handsome broadcast-reporter boyfriend by his side.

*What am I thinking?* I must be drunk. This guy is twenty-one. I am thirty-five years old and dressed like someone trying to pass for Craig's age. (The doorman did ask me for ID, so that made my night. It must be my baseball cap and the bad street lighting from the city gas lamps.)

Every year, I grow more embarrassed to be out drinking and dancing in Boston's nightlife scene. I become more uncomfortable and feel increasingly out of place as the crowd looks younger and I don't. I need to find other things to do than be an old poser.

Craig leans closer toward me and offers to toast my drink. Perhaps he read my thoughts.

"To handsome hottie professors in Boston!" He unleashes his killer toothy smile, which reminds of actor James Franco. In fact, Craig looks like him but with a crew cut. That endearing smile will serve Craig well in future job interviews, especially with the network news.

"Um, yeah, wherever they are!" I tease back. "To the next Brian Williams!"

He glances down again and smiles. He seems embarrassed by my compliment. We take mouthfuls of our drinks, our eyes lock, and we smile. I break the spell by looking at my watch. I notice that it's almost two in the morning, last call in Boston, which still runs on Puritan time. I promised myself that I would leave early because of my morning class. It's difficult for me to be completely focused if I don't get a full eight hours' sleep. Being a professor is akin to performing. If you are off, the class will know, and these kids—*did I just call them kids?*—are paying forty thousand dollars a year to attend this liberal arts and communications school. I owe it to them to be prepared, alert, and on time. But they also like it when I veer off the syllabus and delve into the day's news and celebrity gossip. It engages them after long lectures on writing leads, online reporting tools, and how to make your words shine.

"Are you hungry, Professor Galan? We can get pizza around the corner or something on Tremont?" Craig offers with his puppy-dog eyes. He smiles and looks away as he takes another sip of his beer. The thought is tempting like a cigarette to a smoker trying to quit, but the invite also sobers me up.

"Thanks, Craig, but don't you have an early class tomorrow or something? I need to get going myself. I'm teaching the same class you took with me last year."

"Oh, the way-too-early news class?"

"Bingo!"

"Alright, I can take a hint. I'll see you in school," Craig says, his eyes slightly disappointed.

I pat him on the shoulder. "Drink some water. It'll help flush out the beer from your system. And be careful driving."

"Driving? I live in the dorm down the street."

"Ah, okay. Be careful walking, then. I have a twenty-minute drive home to Quincy with the rest of New England's late-night set of drunk drivers."

He winks at me. I turn around and start to navigate through the crowd of guys who are standing like lost cattle waiting to be herded somewhere else. I notice that Nick and his trick for the night are hopping into a cab on Boylston Street. I guess I'll hear about this tomorrow, if he wakes up on time for school in Somerville. He always does, though. I've always admired Nick's work ethic. No matter whom he is with or how late he's out the night before, he remains the polished professional when it comes to his eighth graders.

I scurry over to the twenty-four-hour convenience store and buy a bag of those delicious peanut butter M&Ms and a bottled water for the drive home. I stand outside the store, eating and drinking while watching the crowds dissipate along the Boston Common as manhole covers leak steam along city streets. A nippy breeze tickles my face as I stare up and dread thinking about having to be fresh and chipper for class upstairs in six hours. I begin to walk toward my parked car, a newer model Nissan Sentra, and I notice a slip flapping on the front windshield wiper. Great, a parking ticket. Damn it! But when I remove the paper from the glass, I realize it's not a ticket but a note from Craig.

*Great seeing you tonight, Professor Galan. You looked as handsome as always. Sweet dreams and see you at Jefferson*, the note reads.

I smile as I fold the note and stuff it in my back pocket. Just another student crush. Once Craig graduates, he'll probably forget about me. The boy crushes always do, but I don't. Sometimes, I hear from them when they need a recommendation for an internship or when they land jobs in TV stations or at big newspapers around the country. When they visit Boston to see their families or friends, I bump into them at the clubs, like tonight. They seem a little older and more mature, but not like me, the old man of the bar with the sore legs from trying to dance with a young Puerto Rican. But still, seeing Craig tonight was a nice surprise. Thoughts of Craig fill my head, and I don't know why.

# chapter Two

*DOES this stuff really work?* I ask myself, standing in front of my bathroom mirror. I apply a dollop of Rogaine on the crown of my head. I carefully smear it at the top of my skull and rub it in. Then I style my hair and comb it from left to right. The sides are closely shaven, like a military look. I still have a lot of hair, but I have noticed in the past year or so that the top has thinned… just a little. At times, I notice some gaps, especially when I step out of the shower or when I begin to dry my hair. Every time I do that, I realize once again that I'm no longer the youthful-looking guy I have always been. I am gradually morphing into Papi, who always enjoyed bragging to everyone that I look just like he did. With time, I resemble him more and more.

I've been using Rogaine for a few months, and the top of my hair feels thicker, but I'm not sure if that's because the mousse-like Rogaine is actually working or because I *think* it's working. It could all be an illusion, psychological follicle comfort. I also started taking the anti-hair-loss pill. My doctor tried to talk me out of it, claiming that I didn't need take the pill or use Rogaine, but I've always believed that the best defense is a good offense. So I am packing a double-punch against my war with hair loss. I've seen too many guys my age walking around with huge bald spots or receding hairlines or, even worse, *hair pieces*! I don't want to look like Captain Picard from *Star Trek: The Next Generation* anytime soon. I want to hold onto every follicle for as long as I can.

*Is this really me?* I continue to study myself in the mirror, and I frown at the passage of time. I recognize my eyes, but I notice that my crinkles are more pronounced, and the thin lines across my forehead are more visible, like lines on a sheet of paper coming into focus. *When did this all happen?* When did the lines—er, wrinkles—begin to deepen like tiny roads in my face? How much more pronounced can they get? Actually, I do know. All I have to do is look at my father, whose crinkles I inherited. *Thanks, Papi!* I dab some moisturizer and some anti-wrinkle cream by my eyes. I smile often, and that has resulted in these laugh lines that aren't making me laugh too much right about now.

I glance out my bathroom door and momentarily look at the framed photograph of Papi and me that hangs in the hallway. My mind begins to page through a backlog of fond memories. It's a picture from my college graduation, when Papi draped his arms around me and plopped a kiss on my cheek. The photo makes me smile. Next to that photo is a similar one with my mom. I had to take separate photographs for each of their homes.

I remove my teeth-whitening strips and suck on the rim of my upper teeth, which creates a pucker sound. I wink at myself. Perfect. Before I leave, I recite a passage I wrote years ago that always boosts my spirits whenever I feel stressed or down: *Gabriel, you are a beautiful man with a good heart who deserves the best in this world and nothing else. You are going to have a great day.* Now I'm all set for another day of teaching college students how to report and write. Thomas Jefferson College, here I come.

THERE'S nothing more humbling than teaching a group of young, energetic, and baby-faced college students with heads full of thick hair, small waistlines, and high metabolic rates. At thirty-five, I'm not that much older than them, which is why I suspect I was recruited to teach here. My department chairwoman, Alisa, said she believed that our students would connect with someone like me, who has had experience in journalism and isn't jaded like the over-fifty-year-old tenured professors who began teaching after they accepted early retirement offers from their newspapers because of cutbacks. She also likes that I'm a minority in a school that houses a mostly ultra-white faculty and student body. That's Boston for you. The city is a majority-minority population, although the professional work force remains Anglo. In my initial interview a few years ago, Alisa told me, "We want our minority students and those of color to know there are professionals who look and talk like them. You would be a great example of that, Gabriel. You would be a great addition to our faculty. Of course, your experience and references speak volumes about your teaching abilities."

She was right. I still get e-mails and postcards from former students who have pursued careers in journalism across the country. They thank me for being an inspiration. I keep those letters with me in a manila folder in my work office. Whenever I'm stressed about my job or feel that I'm not reaching a particular student, I reread those letters, and I am instantly inspired and reminded why I became a teacher. Speaking of teaching, I'm going to be late for my 8 a.m. class, one of two morning classes today.

I grab my windbreaker, double lock the doors of my one-bedroom apartment, and sprint half a mile to catch the Red Line in North Quincy. With their old-world charm, Quincy and Boston have become my second chapter in life, and I'm proud and happy to report that I'm still writing that story. My career continues to bloom here like the daffodils and tulips that burst in the Boston Common and Public Gardens in spring. I live in Quincy, which is one of the more diverse zip codes, from Asian business owners to the region's old-school Irish. I was drawn here because of the multicultural milieu the city offers. The various languages I hear at the supermarket or on my daily subway rides serve as my personal cultural soundtrack, music to my ears.

I live along Wollaston Beach, where I have a view of an aging seawall and the cluster of Harbor Islands in the distance. This area reminds me of a New England version of Hollywood or Fort Lauderdale because of its waterfront properties. From my bedroom window, I hear seagulls caw and planes hum overhead as they descend into Logan International Airport. And like one of the early explorers who arrived and never left this area, I—the resident Cuban-American—feel welcomed here in a town named after one of our American presidents. I like to think that I fit right in with my Chinese and Vietnamese neighbors and the Irish workers who inhabit the stately triple-deckers and Cape and Victorian homes in my blue-collar bay-front neighborhood.

As I bound to the subway stop, I bop rhythmically to "Brown-Eyed Girl" by Van Morrison playing on my iPod. Within a few minutes, I'm clutching the support pole inside the subway train as it rumbles and charges out of Quincy. The train glides onto the bridge that runs over the Neponset River and Dorchester Bay Bridge. From this vantage point, I catch my favorite morning view: Boston's sweeping downtown skyline against a bright blue sky. My students await.

As the train surfaces in Dorchester and then South Boston, my cell phone vibrates. The caller ID reads "Mom."

"Hola, Gabrielito! How are you today?"

I hunch down in my seat, look down at the black linoleum floor, and speak softly. I don't want all the other morning commuters to hear me babble to my mom. Actually, when my mom calls, I rarely get a word in, because she tends to hog the conversation with her daily list of imaginary ailments.

"I'm good, Mom. I'm on my way to work. On the subway. Can we talk later?"

"Ay, of course. You never call, though. I always have to call you. I bet you call your father more."

"Please, Mami, and no, I don't call Papi more. I'm just busy with my students and their papers. I will call you tonight, okay?"

"Bueno, don't forget your familia. There is more to life than working and going out with your, ahem, amiguitos," my mother says, using her code word for "gay guy friends/boyfriends/hookups."

"And are you taking your multivitamins, the ones I sent you from work? You need to eat more. The last time I saw you, you were too thin, hijo. Did I tell you that my lower back hurts again? Probably from picking up the cat too much. Celia eats too much, just like me. And my knees are still bothering me, especially when it rains outside, and—"

I jump in and cut her off or else I will never get off the phone or the subway. "Ma, I gotta go. I'm at my stop!"

"Okay, I love you, Gabrielito!"

"Love you too," I respond, feeling slightly embarrassed as I am surrounded by tight-jawed, stoic morning commuters (*are these people robots?*) who clench their lattes and newspapers with intensity.

Half an hour later, the subway slowly screeches to a halt at the Park Street stop, right in the heart of the Boston Common, the city's majestic mini-Central Park. I emerge from the darkness of the subway into the radiant morning light. I gingerly criss-cross the park toward Thomas Jefferson College, my home away from home. I stroll by former students who wave and smile at me. I pass rows of homeless people who slouch on the benches as bushy squirrels scurry up and down the grand oak trees. I drop a few quarters into a homeless man's empty Dunkin' Donuts cup. The seasonal actors who play patriots and old-world Bostonians greet tourists and take them on a small tour of historical spots. Fall blooms brightly, and the park makes me feel like I'm strolling inside a little kid's drawing; the air is crisp and cool, and the scene is filled with bright yellow and scarlet leaves that plunge everywhere like Mother Nature's confetti. I smile because I never tire of fall's comeback; it's my favorite season.

Before I know it, several students and I are packing into the tiny college elevator like lobsters in a tank at a local seafood restaurant. I ride the elevator to the fifth floor to my class. As I exit the elevator, I see Rosa, one of the college's cleaning ladies. Her back is turned, but I know that it's Rosa because I recognize her long, straight black hair, which she pulls into a bun. At five feet, three inches tall, Rosa is also shorter than the average student here, so she stands out in the crowd of backpacks, messenger bags, and Apple notebooks. Her cart, which is topped with cleaning supplies, also announces her whereabouts.

"Hola, Rosa! ¿Cómo estás?" I say, standing in front of her cart.

"Muy bien, Professor! Your room is all ready for today. I used that special strawberry deodorizer that you like so much," she says in her thick Spanish-accented English. Whenever I see Rosa, I stop and chat for a few minutes. She's one of the few employees here who speaks Spanish, and I know that she appreciates when someone tries to reach out to her in her native tongue. The other professors, who are mostly locked away in their offices or in their classrooms, don't really interact with the help. They tend to reflect the conservative clannish city culture, something I still don't quite understand.

"How is your daughter Laura? Is she still having trouble with math?"

"Ay, sí. I don't understand Algebra," Rosa says, putting her right hand on her forehead to convey her frustration. "I am looking for a tutor. Mi hija is too smart for me. I can only help her so much, Professor." I smile and tenderly look at Rosa, who has this job and also works at Taco Bell so that her daughter can have the life that she didn't have back in her native Honduras. Her work ethic reminds me of Papi's.

"Bueno, if you need help in finding her a tutor, I can ask around."

Rosa's eyes fill with gratitude. "Ay, thank you, Professor. We need to find a tutor in Somerville."

"My good friend Nick is a teacher at a middle school there. I can ask him and get back to you."

"¡Gracias! I will tell Laura as soon as I see her tonight at home."

I put my hand on Rosa's shoulder. "Rosa, you can call me Gabriel, you know. Forget the professor stuff."

Her face erupts into a warm smile as she wheels her cleaning cart toward the women's bathroom.

Meanwhile, I amble toward room 542, where my sixteen students welcome me. "Good morning, Professor Galan!" some of them announce. I wave and reciprocate the greeting. I drop my messenger bag behind the desk, and I begin to prepare for today's class: ethical issues in the media. I load up my lesson plans onto the projector. I lower the window shades to block out the view of the park and shafts of sunlight.

"Good morning everyone. Happy Monday! For those of you who are here mentally or physically, welcome back. I hope you guys had a nice weekend."

"How about you, Professor Galan?" asks Alex, one of my brighter and more ambitious students. Although he looks like one of those rich white kids from a CW network show, Alex has the chops for broadcast television, his major. I call him "Anchorman" because he always wears a dress shirt and slacks. His head, full of thick, straight brown hair, was made for TV news or at least future shampoo commercials. In fact, most of my students come well dressed except for the five or so who come in their jammies since their dorms are upstairs. They literally come here after rolling out of bed.

"Well, I spent most of the weekend grading your papers, which I have here in my hand. You guys made two hours of grading fly by with your fantastic work. I don't know if I'm making this class too easy or if you are actually taking what I say to heart."

Missy, the girl with the long black hair pulled into a ponytail, chimes in. "Oh no, Professor. You make us work. This is not an easy class. Trust me, but it's my favorite," she says, flashing her blue eyes like a cartoon character. She's buttering me up.

"So do you guys want your papers back now or after our discussion on ethical issues?"

Hands shoot up, and I hear a chorus of, "Now!"

"Okay, you win. Here are your papers." I loop around the three rows of workstations and return the papers.

"Now don't freak out when you see all the purple ink. It's just *feedback... feedback...* like that old Janet Jackson song"—and I mimic one of her dance moves from the 2007 video. The entire class groans and rolls their eyes in unison.

"Not cool, Professor Galan!" Alex says from the front row.

"What? You don't like my cool moves? Okay, bad joke. But consider the feedback as good criticism. I want you guys to learn how to make your writing more muscular, so look at my suggestions in purple. Overall, you did a good job."

As I walk around the room, my cell phone vibrates in my pocket. I pull out my phone, look at the number, and I see "Aunt Cary" displayed. I decide to call her back after class. As I begin my discussion on ethical issues, my phone vibrates again to alert me that there's a voice mail message. That's strange. My aunt never calls me in the mornings. I wonder what's on her mind.

Throughout my whole discussion of recent conflict-of-interest cases with young journalists, my mind meanders back to her phone call. I decide that as soon as my students exit the classroom in an hour, I'll step into the stairwell and dial my aunt.

# chapter Three

IT'S 9:15 a.m., and we're wrapping up a lively discussion involving the ethical complications of an attractive education newspaper reporter who had an affair with a top school official while covering his office.

"I still think she was asking for it. You're not supposed to be sleeping with the guy you report on your beat, no matter how much she liked the dude," Missy announces with her right hand under her chin.

"Yeah, but the guy was pretty hot," interjects Alex, sitting in his perfect anchorman pose and using his hands to emphasize his point. "I wonder who leaked their personal e-mails. That's what exposed them. What a juicy story!"

"On that note, more news at eleven," I say, dismissing the class.

Everyone gathers their bags. They rummage through their papers and books and log off from their classroom computers and laptops.

"See ya Wednesday, Professor," Missy says as she exits the hallway, combing her hands through her hair and walking with purpose. She reminds me of a raven-haired Elle Woods from *Legally Blonde.*

"Bye, Professor Galan!" Alex says, adjusting his tie. He must be preparing for the midday newscast for *Jefferson Today.*

I lean over the podium and wave and smile as everyone pours out of the room.

"Remember to read the *Daily* and the *Tribune* for Wednesday's current events quiz!" I quickly remind them.

As the classroom empties out, I wipe the white board clean of my notes and sling my messenger bag over my shoulder. I pull out my phone and dial my voice mail.

"Gabrielito, it's your Tia Cary. I need to speak with you. Please call me later today. It's about your father." I press "End" on my phone and stare at it for a few minutes. The words *it's about your father* replay in my mind. I have a half-hour break before my next class begins, so I scurry down the five flights of stairs as I weave between the parading students, some of whom linger in the stairwell. I finally reach the ground floor and venture outside into the sunny fall day. At a quiet spot outside the front of building and away from the pack of chain-smoking drama student smokers, I dial Aunt Cary and find out what's going on with Papi.

I pace back and forth in my small corner of Boylston Street while the phone rings on the other end. Aunt Cary has always been the family insider, the one who knows the scoop on everyone else. She's not a gossip in the negative sense of the word. She means well and looks out for everyone, including my mom, despite the divorce. Aunt Cary proves that just because someone isn't legally part of the family anymore, that doesn't mean you should stop caring about them. She calls my mom every now and then to gab about medicines, Mom's Shaklee products, and their favorite Spanish soap operas.

Another thing that I always admired about my aunt is the fact that she was one of the few Cubans in Miami who actually learned how to speak English fluently when she came to the United States on one of the Freedom Flights in the 1960s. When she arrived with my late Uncle Jose, she landed a job as a cashier in a pharmacy in Miami Lakes. When Walgreens bought the store a few years ago and renovated it, the new managers promoted her to assistant manager because of her hard work ethic and friendly communication skills. The job keeps her busy and focused, especially since her husband died of a heart attack six years ago. My aunt must also work, because she couldn't make ends meet if she were to retire. Social Security doesn't stretch as far as it used to, people tell me. I'm glad she lives and works near Papi, because she likes to look after him. She acts like the elder sibling even though she is twelve years younger than Papi. She's the only family my father has left, because my paternal grandparents passed away when I was in elementary school.

"Hey, Tia, I missed your call earlier. I was in class. How have you been?"

"Gabrielito, I'm so sorry to call you in the middle of work. I know how seriously you take your classes."

"No hay problema. What's going on? I always have time for my favorite aunt."

"Bueno, I'm a little concerned about your father, but you can't tell him that I told you this, okay?"

"Got it. My lips are sealed. What about Papi?" I say helpfully.

"I think his Parkinson's is beginning to affect his walking. The other day, he had some difficulty getting up from the sofa when I visited him. And he doesn't want you to know this, but he fell while picking mangoes in my yard. You know how much he likes mangoes."

"What? Was he okay?" I say with alarmed concern.

"Yes, he had some scratches, but he's fine. I think it's the Parkinson's, Gabriel. It's aging him."

"But that could be because he's old. The more we age, the harder it becomes for us to do the things we used to," I say, leaning against the brick rear wall of the college. Ahead of me, students and office workers dash on Boylston with the Boston Common in the background.

"No, Gabrielito, it's not his old age. I told him that he should schedule a visit with his doctor, but you know how stubborn he is. He may need to adjust his medication for a stronger dose. His right leg seems to be weaker. He isn't walking as fast as he used to. Other than that, he's good, still exterminating part time, and he always has a Corona at night when he gets home."

"Thanks for the update. I'll call him tonight after my last class."

"But don't mention that we talked, okay? I don't want your father to think I am spying on him or that I'm una chismosa."

"I promise. I won't say a word. And no, you're not a gossip. Thanks for letting me know. How are you doing? You like to care about everyone else, but what you about you?"

"I'm good, nephew. I can't complain. Thank you for asking. I was employee of the month, and Jessica visits when she can from the university. But it's a six-hour drive from Gainesville. I talk to her every day," she says, referring to my younger cousin, who is a sophomore at the University of Florida. I wrote her a letter of recommendation for her college application. Jessica is the closest thing I have to a sibling. I've noticed that among Latinos, cousins are like second siblings. And being an only child like Jessica, it's nice to have someone whom I can relate to family-wise. Jessica and I are close because Aunt Cary and Papi are close and talk often.

"I know the feeling. Papi and Mom call me several times a week," I tell my aunt.

"Because they love you and miss you, Gabrielito. You are all by yourself in Boston. When are you coming to visit your favorite aunt?" she says coyly.

I chuckle. "For Thanksgiving. The semester is going well, so I don't like to be away for too long. But now that you're telling me this about Papi, maybe I should use one of my free tickets and come down next week for Columbus Day weekend. Then I can see how Papi is really doing."

"Okay. I'll make your favorite Cuban sandwich with extra pickles when you come. Jessica will be down here for Thanksgiving, and then we'll have the whole family together."

"You got a deal. I can already taste the sandwich. Anyway, I gotta get going. My next class is about to start."

"Go to your class, and we'll talk soon. Just talk to your Papi tonight and let me know if you come down sooner than Thanksgiving. I love you, Gabrielito."

"And I love you too, Aunt Cary. Say hi to Jessica for me," I say before ending the call.

I emerge from the alley and head back onto busy Boylston, where throngs of students, mostly artsy drama kids, smoke and gossip about their weekend. I smile as I walk by, remembering when I was a college student at FIU in Miami, where I commuted between two campuses and Papi and Mami's homes. By the time I graduated, I had logged 140,000 miles on my little Toyota hatchback.

As I walk into the building, my cell vibrates again. The display screen reads "Papi." His ears must be ringing. I return to my corner on Boylston to chat.

"How is my son, el professor?"

"Your son is about to head into class. How are you doing, Papi?" I say, standing near a pack of students. I cover my left ear with my hand to block out their chatter.

"I just finished exterminating the Holiday Inn in North Miami Beach. Talk about cucarachas. There was an army of them. It's the heat, Gabriel. They multiply like raindrops." Papi always enjoyed sharing his adventures in roach-hunting as if they were episodes in his own reality TV show: *The Roach Hunter, starring Guillermo Galan.*

"I'm sure you got them all. You're the Exterminator... you'll be back," I joke, channeling Arnold Schwarzenegger's *Terminator* character.

"Hijo, you need better material," he says, laughing along with my joke.

"Well, then, come up with new stories, Papi," I tease. "How are you feeling, Papi? How is your Parkinson's today?"

"Parkinson's? Por favor. I'm strong como un caballo. I work, I drive. I mow your aunt's yard. Why?"

"Just asking, Papi."

"Hmmm. Did you speak to your Aunt Cary?" Damn. Papi is good. He can read me from 1,600 miles away.

"Um, no."

"Gabriel…."

"I just wanted to know if you're okay. I saw a story on TV about a new drug for Parkinson's patients." Total lie. I'm such a bad liar.

"Gabrielito, soy tu papa. You're talking to your father. Did your aunt call you?"

"Well…." *Busted!*

"I knew it. That's your aunt for you. She sees me having trouble getting off the sofa and she thinks I'm in trouble. She doesn't know when to mind her own business. She's un busybody," he says in annoyed tone.

"Well, since you brought it up, how is your right leg?"

"It gets weak sometimes, son, but that doesn't stop me. I did fall the other day in the yard, but that can happen to anyone. I lost my balance," Papi says defiantly, as if to spite the disease that is robbing him of his movement and control. He won't let it, though. Good old macho stubbornness.

"Dad, you should have told me. When was the last time you saw your doctor?"

"More than six months ago. I hate going to the doctor in Aventura."

"Well, I'm coming down soon, and we'll go together."

"Don't worry about me. When you come here, you should see your mama and your aunt, Jessica, and your friends. I can go to the doctor myself." Again, that macho pride.

"Papi, I've decided to come down for the long Columbus Day weekend. I am taking you to the doctor myself. End of discussion. ¿Comprende?"

"Wait, when did you start telling me what to do? I'm the parent."

"When you started ignoring your health and keeping me in the dark. I need to get back to class. We'll talk later, okay?"

"Go. I'm sure your students are waiting for the best writing professor in Boston." Papi always likes to end a conversation with a compliment.

And with that, I say good-bye and begin to stroll back to class and finish up the rest of my workday. As I bound up the stairs up to the fifth floor and pass streams of students on the way—*don't they have class?*—I reflect on how it hasn't been easy watching my strong-willed and muscular father slowly decay because of this cruel disease.

With each trip I make to Fort Lauderdale, Papi appears older. He looks more like my late grandfather than the father I grew up with, the one whose image weighs in my mind. Papi still has the dark, thick hair combed back and the strong shoulders and arms from lugging around all his exterminating equipment. In my mind, he walks swiftly and with purpose. When I see him on my return visits, I notice he walks more cautiously and slower. His arms are more sinewy. Gray continues to raid his black hair. At times, Papi doesn't show much facial expression. I've read that Parkinsonians have a particular masklike facial expression because of a lack of facial muscle control, which I have seen increasingly in actor Michael J. Fox in TV interviews. In the last photos I took with Papi for his birthday, he didn't smile except with his eyes.

I love my father with all my heart, and if I could yank that horrible disease out of his body, I would. I'd fight it and win. But it's Papi who is quietly engaged in his own private battle with his body. I would use every bit of my strength to help him. But with me being in Boston and him living in Fort Lauderdale, I'm at a disadvantage. I need to do more for my father because he has done so much for me, like working tirelessly for forty years in a blue-collar job so Mami and I could have the home he always dreamed of in Cuba. My mother got that house in their divorce, and Papi has his own apartment, where he lives alone.

Slightly out of breath, I reach the fifth floor of the college. I walk down the brightly lit hallway, its walls lined with bulletin boards about upcoming student events. Once again, the narrow hallways are jammed with students as they casually walk to and from class. As I walk around them, the rumbling sounds of several falling books interrupt my thoughts. I peek through the crowd of shoulders and backpacks to see the source of the commotion. A few feet away, I see a plump, blonde, curly-haired young woman with black-framed glasses kneeling on the floor. She looks like a newbie, a freshman. Everyone moves around her like a stream flowing around a rock. Just as I'm about to step in and help, Craig suddenly comes into focus. He bends down and collects her books.

"Are you okay?" I overhear him ask her.

She sheepishly smiles. "Yeah, thanks. I'm okay. I just slipped. It can happen to anyone, you know," she says, her eyes blinking and her cheeks blushing. Then her eyes widen. She recognizes Craig. I back up a little, and I stand just a few feet away by the entrance of another classroom. I watch them and eavesdrop some more.

"Oh! I know you. You do the morning news for *Jefferson Today*. You're Craig, right?" she says nervously as she uses her right hand to tuck her blonde curls behind her ears. She adjusts her glasses back into place and ruffles the back of her hair.

"Yep, that's me. That makes you one of our two viewers. We're up there in the ratings with *American Idol*. Not!" he deadpans as he finishes gathering her books off the floor and hands them to her.

"Like, please! You're the cutest guy on that newscast. You *make* the newscast!"

Now Craig blushes back. I tilt my head, fold my arms, and lean against the doorway, smiling and quietly admiring Craig for helping this girl out. As he talks to her, Craig's eyes radiate a certain tender kindness that moves me and piques my curiosity at the same time.

"Why, thank you. You're too sweet. Anyway, I gotta get to my own class. Be careful walking these hallways. I've seen some nasty spills with people rushing to class," Craig tells her as he quickly rushes off.

Once he's gone, I emerge from the entrance of the classroom and head back to my own. I do so carrying the sweetness of the scene with me. While most students walked by and hustled to class, Craig was nice enough to stop and help this girl out. It shows that Craig isn't just willing to help people but also to help someone feel welcomed. That warms my heart, and it allows me to see another side of Craig. Not that I didn't think he was a nice guy before. He was a stellar and ambitious student, but I am beginning to see him in a different light, as if I put on a new pair of glasses and am discovering him in a whole new way. Before this morning and the night at the club, Craig was just another attractive aspiring young journalist. Today, I feel as if I know him a little better, another layer of him peeled back. Yet there are many layers to him that remain, and I'm curious. I admit that I'm growing more attracted to him than I want to—or should.

I charge into my next class, where my next group of students awaits and greets me with big smiles. "What's up, Professor?" they ask, some waving, a few yawning. But in the back of my mind, my thoughts are with Craig and also with Papi.

# chapter Four

IT'S late Friday afternoon, and I'm riding the subway's Red Line back to Quincy. I lean back in the plastic chair and hold onto the metal support bar as the train charges ahead. It's rush hour, and the subway is packed with other commuters who, like me, are traveling outbound. I lean my head back against the window. I close my eyes and reflect on the long week of teaching.

Fifteen minutes later, the subway pulls into the Wollaston Beach stop and the electronic voice overhead announces our arrival. I open my eyes and rub them with my knuckles. I loop my messenger bag over my shoulders and step onto the subway platform with the crush of hurried passengers. I begin the mile or so trek to my bayside condo at Ocean Cove Apartments. This short stroll is my way of decompressing. My thoughts wander benignly while I watch little Asian and Irish kids pedal bikes on the sidewalks, play ball in their front yards, or scurry about. Couples walk their dogs, and homeowners rake the rainbow of fallen, crinkly dry leaves that litter their yards and cake their sidewalks. In the distance, along the seawall, joggers run, and in-line skaters roll along the beach not far from the choppy waves. I'll join those folks once I change out of my preppy professorial clothes.

When I approach my four-story bricked building, which is ribboned by a verdant lawn, I exhale deeply and smile. I embrace the end of the day, the end of the week. Home. I swiftly climb the stairs to the second floor and fidget with the lock to open my front door. Once inside the kitchen, I toss my keys in a big blue bowl shaped like a whale. Walking toward my bedroom, I peel off my bag, strip off my dress shirt and blue jeans, and throw them on my bed. I slip into a pair of blue sweatpants and a loose-fitting white T-shirt. Back in the kitchen, I munch on a chocolate and peanut butter protein bar for a much-needed energy boost. I then walk on my creaking wooden floors and approach the balcony's sliding glass door. I open it and step outside, where sprouting red and orange flowers fill a handful of small IKEA pots.

The sunlight bathes the rows of Victorian and Cape houses across the bay in hilly Squantum in a dimming golden light. Nick likes to tease me by calling the neighborhood "Squat-um." So Nick. A cool beach breeze greets me and serves as a gentle reminder that winter is not too far away. I lean over my balcony, take a few deep breaths, and release my tension. Down the boulevard, an older gay couple saunters along the seawall hand in hand. One man is bald with a beer belly. The other is slight with a sun-spotted face and snowy mane. They look at peace together, happy. I wave at them, and they reciprocate. Nearby, another elderly couple tosses pieces of bread at the cawing seagulls. The woman has gray hair pulled back in a short ponytail. Her companion sports a Boston Red Sox cap that hides most of his wisps of gray hair. They bend over and laugh as the birds swarm their feet. They remind me of the sweet couple in the beginning of the Pixar computer-animated movie *Up*.

Sometimes, I wish I had someone to come home to. Someone I could share my thoughts with about school, concerns about Papi's condition, how I sometimes envision my parents being together again, and I imagine having my own special person to come home to. I do have Nick to talk to, and then there's my cousin Jessica, but it's not the same as having someone waiting at home for you who is excited to hear all about your day. I want to have a partner who shares similar interests and dreams of being together unconditionally.

I don't have the best track record in love. The men I've dated are either cute but not ambitious in their careers or, if they are ambitious, then I'm not physically attracted to them. It's always one thing or another, and I haven't been fortunate enough to make commitments stick even though I've desperately tried. Other times, the men I like are too old for me and we don't have much in common. Being a professor, most of my colleagues are well into their late forties or fifties. Then there are my students, who are too young for me, and they're in a phase of their life that I was done with thirteen long years ago.

That's why I don't feel that getting involved with Craig is a good idea. It can only lead to disappointment, although I do relish the way he looks at me with his big light-brown eyes. His youthful energy is infectious. The note he left on my car was a nice touch. And why am I even considering this? I must be getting desperate.

Whenever I feel lonely or down about such things, I escape by reading my romance novels, cycling in my neighborhood, or watching my all-time favorite *Star Trek* episodes. The original series, not *The Next Generation*. I enjoy getting lost in space with Captain Kirk, Spock, Bones, and the rest of the *Enterprise* crew who keep me company in this condo.

Maybe that's why I've been single for so long. I'm a closeted Trekkie. I remember last year, I met this cute firefighter named Kevin at Club Café. There was a charged, lust-filled attraction between us. He had thick salt-and-pepper hair combed back, mesmerizing hazel eyes, and a sculpted body. Just looking at him sent waves of tingles throughout my body. We left the bar, and I invited him over to my place. When I showed him my *Star Trek* DVD collection, he looked at me quizzically, as if I were an alien that the *Enterprise* crew had just encountered during one of their voyages. I recognized the look, which read, "Um, you're weird, dude." I don't think it helped matters that a huge framed poster of the inaugural crew hung over my sofa and that another poster of Captain Kirk was displayed in my hallway. So I tend to keep the *Star Trek* fandom mostly on the down low, which is hard when I have the occasional guy visit. I remember how much Papi heckled me about my Trek fix when I was in high school.

"Oye, Gabrielito, let's go. I need your help picking up some pesticides at the warehouse," he said to me one time. But I couldn't peel myself away from my TV. I loved watching the crew tease each other and banter. They were a family connected by friendship and loyalty despite not having any shared bloodline. Whenever I watched the show in reruns, I felt that I was a part of their extended family, even though mine was fracturing at the time because of the looming divorce. Sometimes, I wished I had been a member of the *Enterprise* family instead of my own.

So if I'm not grading papers or scaring guys away with my *Star Trek* memorabilia, I really enjoy meeting up with Nick and listening to stories about his latest trysts with young men. He has encouraged me to date more often, but I just haven't met a guy I'd want to see more than a few times (or who has wanted to see me and my *Trek* collection on a second visit). Someday, I will find my personal happy ending. The guy is out there somewhere, I hope.

As these thoughts fill my head, I decide to snap out of it and join the crush of Quincy residents enjoying the fading daylight. I grab my keys and prop my green bicycle onto my shoulders as I lug it into the elevator to go down to the ground level. Once downstairs, I hop on my bicycle, zip across the street, and ride along the seawall with the rest of my neighbors.

Twenty minutes later, I pull into Marina Bay, an upscale Quincy community that has always reminded me of Miami and Fort Lauderdale because of its waterfront condos, docked sailboats, and views of downtown Boston. During the summer, the neighborhood brims with wedding parties posing for photographs along the marina. As I cycle, my phone vibrates in my pocket. The display window reveals that it's Nick.

"GG, what are you doing tonight?" he says, calling me by his nickname for me. It sounds like something you'd call a dog or cat.

"Hey, just relaxing. I'm riding in Marina Bay."

"Well, it's Friday. You know what that means, slore!"

*Oh no, he probably wants to tear up the town with a bar crawl.* "Um, that you want to hang out and look for cute young guys?"

"You got it, boyee! Let's hit the city."

"Not tonight, Nick. I have a lot of papers to grade this weekend, and I really don't want to bump into any of my former or current students." I lean my bike against a wooden bench in the marina and watch the sailboats and fancy yachts bob in the water like trinkets on a charm bracelet. The horn of a passing boat echoes in the distance.

"Oh come on, Gabriel! We could use a good night out, and you could spend some time away from the crew of the *Enterprise*," Nick urges. He's probably just horny and doesn't want to be seen alone at a bar.

"Nah, you go ahead. I'd rather stay near my place."

"What's wrong? You usually love to go out. Is everything okay, dude?" Nick asks with concern.

"Yeah, just a long week. I have a lot on my mind, that's all. I got a call earlier this week from Aunt Cary. She thinks my dad is getting worse from the Parkinson's."

"Sorry, dude. You wanna talk about it?"

"Actually, that might be good for me. Instead of hitting the gay clubs, how about if we go to a small pub and just get some drinks?"

Nick's voice brightens audibly at the idea. A small pub would most likely have more straight men and bisexual men who don't frequent the usual gay haunts. "Hey, as long as we don't have to watch the *Enterprise* fight off the Klingons again this month, then you got it. Maybe we'll go to Harp & Bard in Dorchester. It's not that far from you. I'll come over and pick you up."

"Cool. See you tonight."

"See you then, GG. And one more thing," Nick offers before finishing the conversation.

"What's that, Nickers?"

"You're gonna be fine, and so is your dad. I'm here to listen. I'm your, as you Latinos would say, amigo, or as I like to say, your fellow slore."

I smile into the phone. "I know, I know, Captain Cock. Thanks."

IT'S five minutes to ten o'clock, and I'm gently popping my contact lenses into my eyes. I almost drop one of them when I hear a car honk loudly three consecutive times from the open sliding glass door of my balcony. It's Nick. I spritz on some cologne, dab some Rogaine at the crown of my head, and wash my hands. I flash two thumbs up at my reflection in the bathroom mirror. I'm ready to go out and start the weekend.

A few minutes later, I'm in Nick's bouncy pickup truck heading to…. "Nick, destination, por favor?"

"Uranus. Just kidding… I thought we'd do something different. Instead of Harp & Bard, how about we go to Marina Bay?" he says as he drives, fidgeting with his iPod adaptor.

"Well, that would be different, even though I was just there on my bike earlier. But remember, it's not Marina Gay, it's Marina Bay—very heterosexual, Nick, and it's a five-minute drive. If you meet someone, which you probably will, I could just walk home. Can I tell you something, Nick?"

"Yeah, GG."

"You're my hero…. Does that sound familiar?" I say sarcastically, placing my hand on my chest.

He punches me hard in my left arm with his right hand, and I start to laugh.

A few minutes later, we pull into the long, winding road that leads to a small community of luxury townhouses with pristine lawns. We pass them on our right and then turn onto Marina Bay's Victory Road, where restaurants, cafés, and gift stores sit shoulder to shoulder under a grand old towering town clock. The businesses all face the twinkling lights of the marina and bay. We stroll to Marina Bay Beach Club, a popular straight bar with outdoor seating. We perch ourselves on the bar stools and scan the menus. The bay's breeze brushes against my face and makes Nick's spiky black hair move slightly despite all the gel he doused it with.

"Ahh, this reminds me of Fort Lauderdale," I say, looking at Nick over the rim of the menu.

"Yeah, I figured this might be something different for a change instead of going out in Boston. And besides, we have parking and a great view of the city from here."

A cute college-age waiter greets us with a big smile that highlights his bright white teeth. He is fair-skinned with a black crew cut and soft brown eyes. I order a Red Bull with vodka. Nick orders a light beer and fried calamari as our appetizer.

"So let it out, what's on your mind? It's written all over your face," Nick says, folding his arms as he leans back on the stool. His bulging veins map his strong forearms.

I tell him about Papi and what Aunt Cary said.

"That can't be easy, Gabriel. Your dad is alone down there. It's not like with me where I have my sister living with my parents in Providence. She keeps an eye on them, and I know I can always drive down there in less than an hour. I feel for you, dude. But at least your father is still active, and it sounds like he's not letting the Parkinson's overwhelm him."

"Yeah, things would be so much easier if my parents were still together and if I had a sibling to share the responsibility."

Nick extends his right hand and places it on mine. "You know what you have to do. Go with him to the doctor the next time you visit and see if there are any other medications he can take to help him regain more controlled movement in his right leg."

"That's just it. There are only so many medications out there. Luckily, the doctor started him off with a low dosage so he would have more to work with if he had to increase the dosage. Parkinson's is a progressive disease. It's only going to get worse."

The waiter brings our appetizer and drinks. I twirl my red straw to mix the elixir.

"Well, GG, here's to finding more advances in Parkinson's, and to your father." Nick holds up his beer bottle and clinks it with my glass.

"To Papi!" I say before slurping the rim of the glass.

"Gabriel, I have an idea. What if you started looking at hospitals and clinics up here? This is Boston, the medical Mecca of the world. I bet there are new programs and research trials happening here right under our noses. Have you thought about finding a local doctor for your father for a second opinion? It can't hurt, dude."

"You're right. Maybe I can do some behind-the-scenes work here and share it with my father and his doctor in Miami. There has to be something in Boston that could help my dad."

"And you can bring him up here for a few days. That way, you can monitor him better and really gauge how he's doing. We can even take him to Club Café for a guy's night out."

"Ha!" I smile at the image of my father drinking a Corona surrounded by twinks at Boston's most famous gay bar.

"Besides, I'd love to meet your dad. You're always going down to Florida. It's time your dad and mom visit you."

"It's just easier for me to visit them. Besides, I am planning to visit for a quick trip over Columbus Day weekend, which is right around the corner," I say, cradling my cool drink with my right hand.

"That's great. But if you got him up here someday, I think your dad would really like your condo and living so close to the beach. When you're at work, he can walk along the seawall and explore your neighborhood. It would be a nice break for him from South Florida."

"Thanks for taking me out, Nickers. I have a lot to think about, and getting out tonight is just what I needed."

"Me too. Besides, I've been hearing that gay guys are going to more straight bars like this place lately. If you think about it, why do we have gay bars anymore? Everyone is blending in and hanging out in other places. Even the South End has more families than gay couples. If you want to hook up, you go online. The bars aren't what they used to be. People are more accepting and open in general."

"I read an article about that: the loss of the gayborhood," I say, munching on some crispy calamari.

"Well, I think the gayborhood is right here at this bar, Gabriel. Look at the guys at the bar. They look like those straight Southie guys, with the fuzzy hair, big blue eyes, and Irish-flag tattoos on their arms, as if they just walked off the set of a Ben Affleck Boston movie. One just looked at me and winked. See what I mean? The more masculine and cuter gay guys are the ones who don't go to gay bars as much. They meet up with their straight friends at straight bars, which are the new gay bars."

I laugh at the irony. "You might be onto something there, Nick. I don't recognize any of these guys."

"And wouldn't it be nice to say that you met someone at a regular bar instead of the local gay watering hole where everyone knows your entire biography and sexual history?" Nick deadpans, his eyes locked on the Southie guy who winked at him. The bar's speakers blare the latest booming pop songs, adding to the party vibe. I tap my right index finger along to the beat. The breeze carries the salty scent from the bay.

"I know. We all know way too much about everyone. That's why this is a nice change of pace tonight. I believe we meet someone when we least expect it. Serendipity. When you're at a gay bar, it's obvious why you're there. It takes away from the spontaneity. I know it was nothing like this for my parents back in Cuba. They met through a mutual friend at a house party. No bars. No online hookups. It was just meant to be, or so I thought it was." I lean my face against my right hand and continue twirling my straw in my glass, creating a mini twister of Red Bull and vodka.

As we chat at the bar, couples walk by and gaze at the boats in the marina. Others sit on benches and share spoonfuls of ice cream from the nearby ice cream parlor. I lean back in my chair and feel the alcohol swirl in my system, warming me from within. I order another round, and we swap stories about our classes. I tell him about all the cute young guys at Jefferson, mostly closeted broadcast students. He tells me about his students' hot fathers, whom he met during a recent parent-teacher night.

"I swear, I was flirting with Mark Levine's father so much that one of my co-teachers, Lindsay, had to pull me away. He looked like a taller Tom Cruise. I think he's bisexual," Nick blurts out, his eyes widening at the thought. When Nick is buzzed, he becomes more animated and hyper like a cartoon character.

"Oh, one of those! They want to play, but they don't want the sticky commitments because they're married or have girlfriends. Just be careful, Nick. You don't want to end up being a stepmother to one of your students." I stick out my tongue at him. Nick tosses a wadded-up napkin at me.

"And while you're at it, tell him to send his son to Jefferson when he's older. I'll take care of him there," I tease.

As we gossip about work, a familiar voice calls my name. "Professor Galan!"

I look over my left shoulder toward the boardwalk. A handsome future broadcaster smiles at me. Craig. He happily waves and begins to walk toward us.

"Isn't that your former student from the other night, the one you told me about?" Nick asks, raising his right eyebrow and flashing me a devilish expression.

"Um, yes! The one who left me a note on my car."

"Stalker! It's the stalker!" Nick teases a bit too loudly. I hush him up before Craig walks over.

"Hey, Professor, how's it going?" Craig greets me with a handshake. I introduce him to Nick, who offers a firm handshake. "What are you guys up to?"

I tell him that we wanted a quiet non-Boston night out.

"And you, Craig? You're kind of far from Jefferson."

"Me and some guys from the dorm wanted to hit the bars here."

"Dorm?" Nick interjects.

"Yeah. I'm the only gay guy on my floor of the dorm. My dorm mates are cool with it. They're over there, flirting with the girls at the other bar," Craig tells us. As he talks, Craig stands two inches away from me. He's wearing a tight polo shirt, and a few light brown chest hairs poke out from the buttons. I want to nuzzle my head against his chest and hug him.

"That's great that your dorm mates are so accepting," I say. Nick continues nursing his beer and watches as the conversation unfolds.

"Yeah, you'd be surprised. When straight guys drink too much, they get all affectionate and lovey-dovey, but they respect me. I'm just another guy to them. I even told them about this certain handsome writing professor. They all knew it was you. They took one of your creative writing classes as an elective. They thought it would be an easy A."

"Um, thanks, Craig, for the inside scoop, I think. I guess I have a reputation as being an easy professor."

Nick then looks over to me and silently mouths, "Slore!" I narrow my eyes at him, silently firing back with, "Dick!"

Craig, oblivious to the private exchange between Nick and me, continues rambling. "I wouldn't say you're easy, but your class is so much fun, and you keep us so engaged that it feels easy. You're one of the more popular professors among students. I bet your student evaluations are always high."

My cheeks warm from the compliment. It is true; I average a 94 percent on my student evals, not that I am bragging or anything.

"Anyway, you should come and say hi. We're over there," Craig says, pointing to the bar at the other end of the marina. "I'm sure they'd love to pick your brain about the school and hear about your adventures in dating."

"Uh, maybe another time, Craig. Nick and I are just being low-key tonight and taking it easy."

"Okay, Professor, but one day, you're going to give in to me," he says confidently. "Well, I gotta get back to my friends. See you in school—or somewhere else."

"Have fun, and don't drink too much, Craig," I say, shaking his hand, but Craig leans over the table and suddenly hugs me before he takes off.

Nick shoots me a surprised look and nods his head toward Craig. "That guy is really cute, GG, and he wants you... badly! Watch out. He wants some extra credit, and he knows just how to get it, Professor Slore!"

"Um, thanks, Nick. I think. I'll have to keep my distance from that one."

"But he's not your student, right?"

"Correct. He was my student last year."

"Well, what's the issue? I have a feeling he's gonna wear you down. He's a journalist in training. They don't give up that easily."

"Yeah, but neither do I, Nick." I wink at him and we exchange a toast. "I don't want to have any problems at work. I would hate to be the butt of jokes among other students gossiping about how I look naked or what I do in bed."

Nick shakes his head. "It's college. That's what it's all about. I say just go with the flow and see what happens with Craig. He's graduating next semester, right? So he'll be off campus in a few months. If anything, get your rocks off. Have a fling. Don't be Boring Professor Gabriel for once. Craig might keep your mind off your dad—and, dare I say... *Star Trek*!"

I feign offense and laugh. "Nick, that sounds highly logical," I say in my best Spock voice.

"Live long, play long, and prosper," Nick chides. We both hold up the Vulcan peace sign before ordering another round of drinks.

# chapter Five

WELL, I was right. As usual, Nick was on a manhunt, and tonight, he locks on his target early on—the cute straight-acting guy from South Boston. Throughout our conversation, I notice how Nick often leers over at the stud by the bar.

"Hey, I'm going to talk to the cutie at the bar," Nick announces as he drains his beer. "I'll be right back, Gabriel."

I raise my eyebrows and glass and say, "Attaboy! I'll be right here."

Nick then confidently walks over to the guy and his friends, and he quickly strikes up a conversation. It doesn't take long before Nick has the guy under his spell. I don't want to interrupt Nick's groove, so I decide to let him off the hook easily.

Nursing the rest of my drink, I walk over to Nick and his new friend, who greets me with a warm smile.

"Hey, I think I'm gonna take off," I tell Nick.

"Hold on! I'll give you a ride. We can leave together," he says, putting his hand on my shoulder. Nick's new friend then momentarily turns his back as if to give us some privacy, which is difficult because we're surrounded by a noisy, mingling crowd of single young men and women who are drinking and grooving in place to the blaring pop music. As Nick and I talk, I notice how the green-eyed South Boston guy can't peel his eyes off my friend. I've never been one to cock-block, so I announce my exit.

"Don't worry about it. I'll catch a taxi. It's a short ride. I'm literally down the street," I say, reassuring Nick that his night with this guy won't be ruined and that I won't be offended if he stays with him. I'm used to this. My buddy never has a problem meeting guys, and I like to support him when he does meet a fellow whom he likes—even though it's usually for the night.

"Are you sure, Gabriel?"

"No problema! Have fun. I'll be fine. I'm sleepy, anyway."

"Okay, if you say so, GG." Nick takes the bait. We exchange hearty hugs and pat each other on the back before saying goodnight. I wave to the guy whose heart (or ass) Nick is about to break.

I leave the rowdiness of the bar and stroll alone along the marina's boardwalk, where an endless flock of boats softly rock with the tides. It's such a beautiful cool night that I decide to walk home instead. It's a two-mile trek, and the walk could help sober me up. I had three drinks, and the alcohol continues to swirl warmly in my system. With my hands in my front pockets, I saunter out of Marina Bay and onto the main road, which is lined with lampposts rimmed with small halos. Cars zip by me on their way to and from Quincy and Boston.

As I approach a traffic light, a small used Mazda pulls up on my left. The driver rolls down his window. I'm surprised to see that it's Craig, whose eyes sparkle under the streetlights.

"Need a ride, Professor?" he greets me, leaning over the passenger seat to open the door. A small smile forms on my face.

"Ha! What are you doing over here? I thought you were with your dorm mates back there?" I say, leaning closer into his passenger window. I catch a whiff of Craig's cologne.

"They wanted to stay. They can all hitch rides with each other. I was feeling beat from school. I just wanted to get out of there."

"Me too," I say, holding Craig's intense stare. The cars behind him drive around.

"But seriously, do you need a ride?"

"I'm not that far. I was going to—"

"Hop in," Craig interrupts, a huge grin plastered on his face. "Handsome young-looking men shouldn't be walking alone at night like this. You might get picked up by some wacko."

"Yeah, like right now?" I quickly consider his invitation. *Would I be violating school code? Is this unethical? He's not my student. It's just a ride! We're not even on campus. He's so cute. It's just a ride. He's being nice.* I begin to have second thoughts about the offer, and then I have second thoughts about those thoughts, which technically means that they're third and fourth thoughts, right?

"Well…?" Craig says hopefully.

"Um, sure, why not?" I say, caving in and ignoring those niggling wiggling second, third, and fourth thoughts. Maybe I am the easy professor after all.

And with that, Craig swings his door open, and I hop into the car and buckle up. As he pulls away, Craig gently places his right hand on my left knee. I leave his hand there because the touch comforts and stimulates at the same time. Thin, strong veins map his slightly hairy wrist. But then I realize that he might get the wrong message, so I gently remove his hand from my knee.

I advise him to turn left along Quincy Shore Drive, where the back porches of homes in Squantum glisten from afar. Like steel candles, the streetlights that line the boulevard shimmer against the shore. Before I know it, Craig is pulling up to the front of my complex. As we sit in the car, the bay breeze pours through his sunroof. I'm relaxed, slumped in his seat and gazing at my building. As soon as Craig cuts the engine, I hear a chorus of crickets begin to sing.

Craig turns down the volume on the radio, which is playing another song by a former Disney teen star trying to be taken seriously as an adult musician. "So this is where you live? Not bad, Professor Galan. You can't beat the views and the water."

"Thanks, Craig. I like it. It's relaxing, a great place to end my day from Jefferson," I say, stifling a yawn.

I feel like a shy schoolgirl in the car and not the energetic and outgoing professor that he knows me as.

"Do you mind if I use your bathroom?" he says, looking at me with his light-brown orbs.

"Sure. You can park on the side of the building for a few minutes. You won't get towed there."

A few minutes later, I flip on the lights inside my apartment as we walk in. I point to the bathroom and offer him some water for the ride back to downtown. But Craig is too focused on the family photos that top my corner bookshelf.

"These are your parents, right? I can tell. You look like your father." I walk over to Craig and take hold of the framed photo of Papi and me at my college graduation. In the image, we stand shoulder to shoulder, Papi's arm tightly around me.

"Yeah, that's my dad," I say proudly with a tight grin.

"Is this him too? He looks older in this photo, thinner. He isn't smiling in this one," Craig says, now focusing on the image from Papi's birthday last year.

"Yeah, it's the same guy. My father has Parkinson's, and the disease is aging him more than usual. He looks ten years older than he should." I softly take back the framed photo and let my fingers graze the glass. I frown.

"I'm sorry, Professor."

"You can call me Gabriel. I'm not really your professor anymore."

Craig places a comforting hand on my right shoulder. "My grandmother had Parkinson's too. I know what my mom, aunts, and uncles had to deal with, so you have my sympathy, Professor, I mean, Gabriel. But your father still looks like he's in good shape. He looks like a strong guy, a fighter."

"He is. He still drives and works, and he calls me every night."

"Every night? That's so sweet. My parents call me once a week, and that's a good week. We don't talk too often. I guess it's different with Latin families."

I follow Craig's eyes as they explore the other framed photos on my shelf. Some of them are with Papi and others are with my mom.

"You have a beautiful family. And it looks like your dad is dealing with the Parkinson's better that my grandmother. She was in a wheelchair and had trouble breathing. It's a horrible disease. I watched her lose control of her body. No one should have to go through that."

I turn to Craig and look deep into his eyes. "I'm sorry about your grandmother too."

"Thanks. To honor her, I wanted to do a project for my TV Images class on how Parkinson's can affect caretakers. I was thinking of interviewing my mom and our doctor and talking about what's being done to fight the disease. I know I can get video footage about Michael J. Fox from *ABC News* archives to show how much more attention the disease has received in recent years."

"I bet you'd have a lot of interest!"

"Hope so!" Craig says, placing his hands on his waist to emphasize his point.

We stand silently in the corner of my living room, the lights from the street slanting through my balcony's sliding glass door. I lose myself in Craig's eyes as I study where the pupil and brown shades intersect. His eyes bore right back into mine. Craig tilts his head slightly to the right and suddenly uses back of his hand to brush my cheek softly. I close my eyes and surrender to the touch. Through the veil of my eyelashes, I see Craig's soft lips grace mine.

As we kiss gently, I feel the small, fuzzy hairs from his crew cut tickle my face. I begin to giggle, which makes Craig burst into a wide smile. I forget about school and my parents and allow myself to flow with this moment. Craig intrigues me, and I don't know why, but I am drawn to him. I just don't see him as a former student. I see him as a young man with a lot of possibility. My heart melted like warm butter after hearing about his love for his late grandmother and how he wants to honor her. But I don't want this moment to go too far. I want to get to know him some more. He's like a promising new and exciting story that continues to unfold and write itself.

"Bueno, Craig, this has been nice and all, but I think you should use the bathroom and get going," I say. I need him to leave before I do something stupid such as jump his bones in my alcohol-induced fog.

"Professor Tease!" he remarks, walking toward the bathroom down my hallway, which is decorated with posters of *Star Trek* and classic Cuban tourist advertisements.

"Hmm. I see you're a big *Star Trek* fan," he says, pausing in front of the poster of the *Enterprise* crew that hangs on the wall across from the bathroom door.

"Yeah, something like that."

"Remember the episode with the Tribbles and how they invaded the ship?" he says, his voice echoing from inside the bathroom.

"Yeah, that's one of my favorites."

"Mine too," he says, flushing the toilet, which is followed by the sounds of the running water. He then reappears in the hallway and approaches me.

"Well, we'll have to have a *Star Trek* date night. There's more to you than meets the eye, Prof. And here I thought you were just a very nice, handsome professor. I had no idea you liked *Star Trek* and that your dad has Parkinson's. We have so much in common. I want to hear more about your family, more about you."

"Same here," I say, caressing his right arm. I start pitching a tent in my pants.

He kisses me long and deep, and his touch charges me like electricity. I savor the moment and then walk him to the door. "Do you remember how to get out of here?"

"Of course, this is Quincy. Just over the bridge from Boston." He winks and happily waves as he heads toward the elevator. When he's out of view, I close my front door and lean my back against it and look at my empty apartment. I start to wonder, *Who is this Anchorman, and more importantly, what am I getting myself into?*

# chapter Six

PARKINSON'S disease. I punch the words into a computer in the research pod in the third-floor library at Thomas Jefferson College. Between classes, I've been trying to arm myself with the latest articles on the disease.

I know the basics of the condition as a result of Papi's first diagnosis years ago. In my mind, I thought if he took his pills, remained active, and ate well, that he'd be able to manage it as he has been since I moved to Boston. Perhaps I've been in denial that this disease will slowly take my father away from me. Deep down inside, I believed that it was a manageable condition that he could live with and still remain active in his everyday life.

I've noticed in my last two trips to Miami, Papi's voice has grown softer. He walks in shorter steps and he stands more hunched. Yet whenever I see him, he puts his best face forward, which makes me think that he's fine. Macho pride. The phone call from Aunt Cary served as a catalyst for me to take Papi's condition more seriously than I had before. I've been a passive son. Now I must be an active one and take more of a hands-on approach with Papi's health. If I don't, who will?

I'm sitting in the middle of this brightly lit library where students lug research books, articles, and magazines from the reserve desk to the rows of wooden desks, where they read and type. While they do homework, I delve into the history of the disease, advances, and breakthroughs.

One article says that symptoms of Parkinson's disease can be traced back to medieval times, but the disorder wasn't officially recognized until 1817, when a British doctor named James Parkinson penned *An Essay on the Shaking Palsy*, which highlighted symptoms of six people who had the disease that would eventually bear his name. Another article details how, in the 1950s, a Swedish scientist named Arvid Carlsson documented the biochemical changes in the brain of Parkinson's patients. He was credited with publishing reports of improvements in patients who took levodopa, the drug that has become the standard for treating Parkinson's.

I spend an hour Googling different organizations, support groups, and various definitions of the disease. I learn that despite all the research, there's still no cure for Parkinson's, which afflicts more than 1.5 million Americans. Like Papi, most patients take a daily mix of pills that slow the progress of the disease, which occurs when brain cells that produce dopamine die off. Dopamine is a naturally produced chemical that transmits the signals that control muscle movement. When dopamine-producing cells are destroyed, people start to lose their balance, coordination, and muscle control.

*Papi.*

The articles reinforce what I already know, but they serve as good reminders. I can never learn enough about something that is aging my dad and slowly stealing his flexibility and self-control.

I rest my eyes from all the research, and I lean back in my chair and glance around the library. Students dash in and out, whispering about their classes and weekend plans. Others hunch over their books and sit by the large glass windows that offer a stunning view of the Boston Common and the historic buildings that hug Tremont and Boylston streets. The sun pours into the library, making it slightly stuffy. I peel off my forest-green windbreaker and loop it around the back of my chair.

I stretch and yawn loudly, which momentarily disrupts the students sitting near me. When I return to the article I was reading, a familiar sweet voice interrupts my concentration.

"Hey, Professor!" I turn around and see Craig's handsome face. A tingling sensation fills me. He's a great sight for eyes that have been buried in Parkinson's literature.

"Hey, you! Doing some research?" I say, yawning again.

"Yeah. I was reading some of the papers and news magazines for an assignment for my Beat Reporting class. I saw you deep in concentration and just wanted to say hi. So, hi!" he says, standing next to me. I'm at eye level with his abs, which I imagine are lean and tight. Craig wears his trademark navy-blue sports jacket, a white dress shirt, and blue jeans. Mr. Anchorman. "So what are you up to, Professor?"

"I'm on a break and doing some research on Parkinson's. Just seeing if there's anything out there that can help my dad when I visit him in a few days."

"Actually, you'd be surprised how many research studies have been done, but there are no long-term results yet. Exercise seemed to help my Grammy, I mean, grandmother. That's what we used to call her. She felt better after some working out, but she started doing it after she was placed in a wheelchair. At least the arm exercises put a smile on her face, Professor. It was cute watching her lift two-pound dumbbells." As he smiles at the memory, tiny lines form around his eyes.

"Craig, you can call me Gabriel, remember? I'm not your professor anymore."

"Yeah, sorry. My bad. Speaking of… when are we going to hang out? I have some projects I'm in the middle of for school, but I'm hoping we can get a bite to eat and chat and maybe watch some old *Star Trek* episodes," Craig says with interest.

Sitting in my chair, I look up at him and lose myself in his beautiful light-brown eyes. The fluorescent library lights highlight his brown fuzzy hair and add a twinkle to each eye. Besides his looks, what I really like about Craig is hearing him talk about his grandmother. He obviously loved her very much. We have a common bond because of Parkinson's.

"How about when I get back from Miami?" I say.

Craig's face brightens. "You got it, Prof—I mean, Gabriel," he says, catching his error. He puts a comforting hand on the top of my back. "Well, I'll let you get back to work. I have to get to my next class."

"Me too. Talk to you soon, Craig."

"Ditto," he says, with a wink. With his messenger bag looped across his torso, he bounds out of the library.

I use the extra few minutes before my class begins to read some more articles. I find one from a medical journal that states that there are no exact causes of the disease but several working theories. One of them holds that Parkinson's may result from a combination of genetics and a vulnerability to environmental toxins, along with exposure to these toxins. *Toxins?* I wonder what kind. I continue reading. The suspected toxins are found in certain pesticides and in metals such as iron or manganese.

My eyes pause on the word "pesticides." Papi has been an exterminator for the past thirty years. When I was younger, before the divorce, I had noticed Papi mixing the chemicals in the garage, but he always wore gloves. Years of spraying in the hotels and apartment buildings and breathing in the toxins could have affected his nervous system. It's something to consider and to ask his doctor about.

All these thoughts rumble in my head over the next few days, which pass uneventfully, making them feel longer. I follow my routine: my classes, the gym, and running along the seawall in Quincy. When I bump into Craig in the hallways at school, we chat briefly and exchange flirtatious grins that remind me of the night we kissed. Even in the bustling corridors at Jefferson, I want to steal a kiss from him, but I can wait.

I also keep tabs on Papi over the phone until my trip home, which is just around the corner. In the meantime, Mami continues to call me nightly, and I tell her what's been happening with Papi and in my daily life. Our conversations always begin with the weather.

"Gabrielito, is it cold up there?" she says, using her speakerphone in the kitchen. Her small kitchen radio plays tropical pop music in the background. Whenever she calls me, her voice sounds muffled as if she's using one of those walkie-talkies because she speaks too loudly into the phone. You'd think the phone was in her throat.

"Not yet. It's cooling down. I have to wear a jacket or windbreaker when I leave the apartment," I say as I stroll in my neighborhood after work later that week. "You'd really like Boston in fall, Mami. I know how much you love flowers and colors. I have to get you up here sometime."

"Bueno, not when it's cold. I can wait for spring. I don't want the cold weather to affect my sinuses, hijo."

We move on from discussing the weather, and I quickly tell her about my classes and that yes, I took her Shaklee vitamins this morning. I also tell her the latest about Papi's recent medical issues and how I'm surprised that he doesn't do a better job of keeping me up to date with his Parkinson's.

"Bueno, I'm not surprised. Guillermo is un stubborn pig. He's not going to tell you how he's really doing because he doesn't want you to worry, mi amor," my mother says. As we talk, the sky is a smear or reds and oranges. The sun begins to set earlier with each passing day. I walk and step on the damp, colorful leaves that dot the sidewalks.

"I've always been puzzled why Papi has Parkinson's. No one else has it in the Galan family, right?"

"Ay, hijo. No. Your aunt and your father's cousins and abuelos never had anything like that, just high blood pressure. We don't know why Guillermo has this terrible disease," she says, her voice laced with concern.

"I was doing some research the other day at the college, and an article stated that chemicals like pesticides that affect the nervous system might be partially to blame."

My mom sighs on the other end of the line. "Bueno, Gabriel, when Guillermo and I got married in Cuba, we applied for a visa to leave and to meet up with the rest of the family in Miami. Your Papi was forced to work in the fields for six months because we applied for the visa. We had just been married. It was very hard, hijo. We were newlyweds. I saved as much money as I could from working as a waitress at a coffee shop while Guillermo sent me letters from the farm where he was assigned to work."

I remember Papi telling me about this a long time ago. But what does this have to do with Parkinson's? As Mami continues her story, I squat down on the cool sand along the bay.

"Guillermo worked in the tobacco fields, and he mixed the chemicals for the pesticides. He used his hands. They didn't use gloves or precautions. Things were different back then."

I'm stunned by the revelation. "He used his bare hands to mix the chemicals, Ma?"

"Sí, but everyone did in those days. Remember, this was Cuba in the 1960s. Who knows what damage that could have caused to Guillermo's system?" Mami says. Despite her strong I-don't-care front toward Papi, I know she still cares deeply about him. It surfaces whenever I bring up his health.

"He was thirty years old. Guillermo never had any health issues in his life. It wasn't until his right hand started shaking a few years ago that we knew something was wrong. That's when Dr. Reyes told us he suspected that Guillermo had the early signs of Parkinson's." When my mom pronounces the word, it sounds more like *Pahr-keen-son's*. Her accent is endearing and reminds me of home.

"Ma, that may explain how he got it. If those chemicals are intended to kill insects and bugs, imagine the effect they can have on a person in the long run? I'll keep doing some research. Thanks,

Mom. We can talk about this more when I get to Fort Lauderdale. I'll be there before you know it, and I'm looking forward to seeing you too. I miss your flan. I've tried to replicate it, but it's not the same."

"That's because you don't add enough evaporated milk, mi amor," she says, her voice lifting with pride as she talks about her sweet concoction, which is always a hit at family gatherings. "I can pick you up from the airport and bring you home. I want you to spend your first night here, okay? You have the rest of your stay to see Guillermo."

There she goes again, putting me in the middle of her and Papi. Whenever I visit, I have to split my visit between her house in Fort Lauderdale and Papi's apartment in Miami Lakes. Mami gets jealous if I spend too much time with Papi.

"I'll prepare all your favorite foods, and the bedroom is just as you left it. Sometimes I walk in there and think I'll see you sleeping in there like you used to before you moved to Boston." I remember Mami knocking softly on my door to wake me up each day for classes at FIU or, later on, for work at as a cub reporter. She always greeted me with a cup of café. She enjoyed doting on me, especially after Papi moved out. I also believe she feels safer with me at the house even though she has a high-tech alarm system and lives in a middle-class suburban development slightly west of Fort Lauderdale.

"You got it, Mami. I'll talk to you and see you soon."

"I love you, Gabriel!"

"Love you too, Ma," I say before hanging up and completing my neighborhood stroll.

# chapter Seven

IT'S two o'clock in the afternoon, and the American Airlines flight hums and hovers over the South Florida coastline. The pilot announces that we'll be landing shortly. With the few minutes I have, I gaze out the oval window and soak up the view. I marvel at the colossal beachfront condos and high-rises, the golden sandy beaches and the white-tipped waves that lick them. In the distance, the Sun Life Stadium, where the Miami Dolphins and the Florida Marlins play, beckons. Farther west, the Everglades shimmer with golden marshlands, murky waters, and a sea of sawgrass.

The plane gently swerves west, and the pilot slowly descends into Miami International Airport. Before I know it, we land and thump along the runway. Once on the ground, everyone begins to clap. I never understood this, but the passenger applause only seems to happen when I fly into Miami.

I dial Mami from my cell phone.

"I'm already here, by the Versailles cafeteria in terminal C. See you soon, mi amor," she says excitedly.

I then dial Papi and tell him that I've arrived.

"Bueno, spend time with your Mami. I know how she gets. And stop by my apartment whenever you want, Gabriel," Papi says with similar enthusiasm marked by a raspy voice. "Your Aunt Cary helped me set up your room. We're all set for your visit."

"Thanks, Papi. I'll see you soon. I gotta go. Everyone is getting off the plane."

Shortly after, I navigate through the maze of wide corridors of the brightly lit terminal and finally emerge through security. Immediately, I spot my mother standing near the mini Versailles restaurant. She wears a big smile and waves at me.

She rushes to greet me with a big, tight hug followed by a kiss on each cheek. Her gray-flecked straight auburn hair is fashionably cropped and frames her sweet face. She looks as if she just stepped out of the salon. Her purse hangs off the middle of her right arm. Her coral earrings dangle and shake whenever she moves. She wears a casual light-pink blouse and white capri pants with flat shoes and, of course, her Jackie Onassis sunglasses. Mami is so cute.

"Mi amor, welcome back to Miami. I missed you so much!" she gushes. Her fingers comb the back of my hair as she sizes me up.

"Look, I brought you something to eat," she says, pulling out a wrapped Cuban sandwich from her large purse. I can't get a word in. "¿Tienes hambre, Gabrielito?"

"Thanks, Ma. Yeah, I'm pretty hungry. The only thing they give you on the plane is half a can of diet soda. I'm starving." I rub my growling stomach. As we exit the terminal, Miami's stifling October heat wraps around me like gauze. I wipe the sweat beading on my forehead while Mami fans herself with a copy of the *Miami News* that she bought for me to read on the drive back to Fort Lauderdale.

Walking toward the parking garage, I slow down so as to not rush Mami. She's in her early seventies, and while she remains active and healthy, I don't want to make her walk faster than she has to even though she's a ball of energy with a sharp mind. Throughout our stroll, she keeps her hand on the small of my back and rubs it affectionately.

"We'll be at the house before you know it, Gabrielito."

"Thanks, Mami, for picking me up. I would have flown into Fort Lauderdale, but all the flights on Jet Blue were taken, so I went with American. Sorry for the long drive."

"That's okay. It will be easier for your Papi to drive you back to Miami when you leave," she says, looking up at me with a sweet grin.

My mother lives about twenty minutes or so from Papi, and that short commute always made it easy for me to dash between both homes. For each trip, I stay with my mom one or two nights and then stay with Papi on alternating nights. Commuting back and forth can get crazy. Sometimes, I wish I could splice myself in half and leave one part of myself with each parent. It would make life easier during my visits. My only downtime is when I go out to the bars in South Beach, when I meet up with my cousin Jessica, whom I see during the holidays, or when I grab a good romance book or a stack of student papers and grade them along the Intracoastal off East Sunrise Boulevard, where I sit on a city bench and watch the flotilla of yachts coast by.

Twenty-five minutes later, Mami pulls up to my childhood home. She lives in a suburban development called Emerald Estates, where all the homes were constructed from the same cookie-cutter mold. They are Mediterranean homes flanked by palm-lined winding roads and pristine sidewalks. In the middle of the development sits a lake with a fountain that spews water three feet high. Ducks and geese bob in the water and roam on the grassy areas that blend into people's backyards.

Our house sits at the end of a cul-de-sac where, like the rest of the neighborhood, every hedge is trimmed and every newspaper is plucked from the driveway. Mami's house is a modest two-bedroom beige home with the signature Spanish-tiled red roof, one-car garage, and driveway. Mami's colorful red and orange flowers dot the cement walkway to the front door, where a sign reads *Bienvenidos a Casa Galan.*

Once I step inside the house, the sweet scent of my childhood welcomes me with a strong, invisible embrace. Fresh roses and carnations from Mami's garden fill the house. The flowers' scents perfume and mix with the lingering aroma of the Café Bustelo that Mami must have brewed earlier in the day. I am flooded with a sense of warmth and love, which is lacking in my life in Boston. As I venture deeper into the house, a familiar meow catches my attention. It's Clara, Mami's cat. I gave this fluffy gray cat to my mother as a gift after the divorce. I thought Clara's presence might cheer her up and give Mom something to take care of besides me and her flowers.

"Clara, remember your Uncle Gabriel?" Mami says as the cat squats before us and stares up at me with her big green eyes. I scoop her up into my arms and massage her tummy's fur. She tucks her head into the crook of my arm and purrs like a mini lawn mower.

As I walk with Clara nestled in my arms, I notice how immaculately clean the house is, as it always is. Mami always says that a house must always be clean, because you never know when a relative or neighbor might suddenly drop by. It seems to happen a lot in our family. The cream-colored Mexican-tiled floor shines with a blinding sheen. The dining table sparkles against the slanting sunlight. The central air conditioner hums and breathes cool air throughout the house.

I gently drop Clara to the floor and walk to my old bedroom, which is also perfectly clean and smells like gardenias from a plug-in device. I glance at my childhood photos, my old *Star Trek* posters, my framed graduation diplomas, and my former news articles from my previous employer. I drop my bag by the foot of the bed.

I stretch and flop myself on my old bed and fold my hands behind the back of my head. A wave of memories, buried in this room and house, bombards me. I remember the family vacations to Marco Island, where Papi would fill his cheeks with air as he floated in the ocean. I recall how Mami would sit under an umbrella with her Jackie O glasses and fan herself with the latest Spanish-language magazine. I remember our drive to Key West, where Mami convinced Papi to let me drive the whole way with my learner's permit, although she freaked out whenever I tried to pass a car in the no-passing zone. Then there's my fifteenth birthday gift—this comfy bed. The memories are bittersweet. As my thoughts drift, I begin to doze off. Then I hear a soft tap on my door.

"Gabrielito...," Mami whispers.

"Yeah, come in."

She slowly opens the door and steps in. Clara scurries in and hops on my twin bed, which still has my favorite light-blue comforter.

"I made some of your favorite flan. Do you want some?" Mami says, holding a small slice on a plate. Clara hops on my chest and makes herself at home there. Damn, she's heavy.

"Yeah, you can leave it on my desk. I'm just tired from the flight," I say.

"Bueno, get some rest, and I'll make you some dinner later before you visit Guillermo."

"Thanks, Ma." After she puts the plate down, she slowly walks over and plants a kiss on my forehead. She rubs my head with affection like she used to when I was younger. She also pats Clara's head. Mami then tiptoes out of the room and slowly closes the door behind her as if not to wake me up, even though I can't sleep now because I have a ten-pound fluffy cat purring on my chest. I pick up Clara and gently throw her to the side of my bed. We both fall asleep.

# chapter Eight

MY STOMACH bulges like a woman who is six months pregnant. That's because I just devoured a tender breast of chicken along with a bed of yellow rice that Mami cooked. It's her signature dish and one that I desperately miss in Boston. I don't cook much in Boston, unless one counts assembling a turkey or chicken sandwich for dinner. Sometimes I think my mother tries to bribe me with these delicious meals as a way to lure me back to South Florida.

With my heavy stomach leading the way, I carry my empty plate to the kitchen. I grab the extra set of keys to Mami's Honda Accord, which she lets me borrow during my visits.

"Have fun with your Papi!" she says as she picks up the rest of the leftover food from the dining room table. I kiss her good-bye on the cheek and then walk out into the stuffy, dimly lit garage. "And don't stay out too late," she says, her voice trailing through the door. "I need the car in the morning to deliver some Shaklee products to my customers. Say hello to Guillermo for me."

"No problem, Ma." I smile back, knowing how much she still cares for him.

After navigating the winding roads of the development, I hop on Interstate 75 and gun the car to Miami Lakes, on the Miami-Dade and Broward county border. Whenever I get my hands on my mother's Honda, which has a peppy engine, I transform into a speed demon. The wide interstate invites me to floor the gas, something I can rarely do on Massachusetts's Interstate 93, which is about half the size of Florida's typical highways.

I enjoy these drives because they inspire introspection, automotive meditation. I lean my head against my left hand and look out at the shoulder-to-shoulder developments, the sprawling suburbia that hugs the highway and extends to the seemingly boundless Everglades. I think about Craig and his soft brown eyes, the way he dashes to and from his classes like a reporter determined to get a story. I remember the smattering of light-brown chest hairs and how they poke out from the top buttons of his shirts. The memory stirs a slow, tickling burn in my belly. I want to smell him, taste him, and touch him again. A boner sprouts in my shorts at the thought.

Once I get back to Boston, I'll definitely call him and take him out, even though I have some nagging reservations as to whether this is a good idea. Words like "professor" and "former student" flash in my head like those blinking neon signs on a Las Vegas boulevard. He's not my student, but still, this could create some complications if things were to get out of hand. He's young, twenty-two. I remember what that was like—you feel like you're on top of the world, invincible, and whatever crush or emotion you feel is multiplied because of a lack of experience. Again, those warning signs flash in my mind like the upcoming road signs on the highway. Another one appears in my head and reads, *Be careful, Gabriel.*

Overhead, clumps of clouds look like sweet puffs of meringue and fill the bright blue South Florida sky. My cell phone vibrates in my pocket. When I pull it out, I don't recognize the number. It's a text message.

*Hey, prof! I hope you have fun in Miami with your mom and dad. Get back to Boston soon. I can't wait for our Star Trek night. XOXO, Craig!*

The message tickles my heart, but I'm puzzled as to how he got my number. I never gave it to him. Hmm. If he called my office number, a recording leaves a message with my cell number in case of an urgent matter. Perhaps that's where he got it.

Minutes later, I descend the exit ramp to Miami Lakes, a small city that is true to its name, with twenty-three lakes nestled within the neighborhood. But I like to think that the town got its name another way. When it rains, the town becomes one giant Miami Lake because of rampant flooding. Whenever a South Florida rainstorm rolls in, I ask Papi, "Did you swim to the grocery store? Did you hop on your raft?" For that reason, I also tease Papi that he lives in Land O'Lakes. He laughs every time even though the joke is years old.

Papi's neighborhood used to be a 3,000-acre dairy-farm, home to hundreds of cows that grazed on various parcels. Some cow patches remain, but today, large trees provide constant shade over the curving streets that hug parks and tot lots every few blocks. The fading sun filters through the trees and creates shadowy shapes on cars' windshields.

I pull onto Papi's street, Cow Pen Lane, and then into his development, which is marked by a small, spewing fountain at the entrance. I've never told my mother this, but I am more partial to Miami Lakes than Fort Lauderdale. Miami Lakes feels like a small suburban slice of Miami hidden away from the traffic and chaos of downtown and South Beach. Plus, I always enjoy running along Main Street because of the steady shade and the distant soundtrack of mooing cows.

Papi and I have a tradition here on Main Street. When I visit, we always have a late lunch at Don Shula's Steak House in the hotel that also bears his name. As a sports fan, Papi enjoys telling people that he dines at the former Miami Dolphins head coach's restaurant. Papi has sworn to people that he has met the man, but I've never seen him there beyond his framed pictures with former players.

As soon as I pull into the visitor parking space by Papi's unit, I text Craig back

*Thanks, Craig. See you soon.*

I then see the curtains of Papi's living room swish side to side. His smiling face appears, and he waves. Before I even shut off the engine, Papi is already walking toward me. The vision catches me off guard. Papi moves slower, more carefully, than months before. I notice his right leg drags slightly. Aunt Cary was right. He looks older, weary as I happily greet him. I snap out of my thoughts and happily greet him.

"Gabrielito!" he says warmly in his Spanish-accented masculine voice. As I step out of the car, he hugs me tightly. I catch a trace of his Old Spice cologne and deodorant.

"Hey, Papi. You never let me get to the door first. You always beat me to it," I say, putting my arm around his shoulder and patting him gently on the back. We talk as we enter his apartment.

"Bueno, I don't get many visitors besides your nosy aunt. It's not every day that I have my son, el profesor, back in Miami," he declares as if he's one of those melodramatic Spanish-language radio news announcers. Papi always refers to me as "el professor" to his friends and clients. To me, that sounds old.

Once inside, a gush of cool air welcomes me. I plop myself on his old beige leather sofa. Unlike my mother's house, Papi's place exemplifies minimalism. The walls feature vintage posters and maps of Cuba. (He gave me two for my condo in Quincy.) On top of the flat-screen TV is a photo of us from when I last visited. Papi loves to take photos with his Kodak camera, not the digital kind. That's Papi—he doesn't change with the times. He prefers to drive to Walgreens and drop off the film the old-fashioned way. Plus, my Aunt Cary gives him her employee discount for photos and everyday necessities. I know she stops by his apartment and tidies up when she can. I think it makes her feel useful now that Jessica is away at college. But I'd like to think that it also gives her another reason to check up on Papi.

As we catch up, Papi escorts me to the second bedroom, which also serves as his office for the exterminating business. The room, painted a soft yellow with beige carpeting, is sparse of furnishings. A pile of invoices and receipts fills the top of his old work desk. Along the window, which faces a small backyard, is a twin bed, which I use for my visits. There's also a small closet with files and some hangers for clothes. I always leave some extra clothes after each visit because I always end up swimming laps in the development's pool.

"See, you still have a bed here. You always have a place here, Gabrielito," Papi says, looking at me with pride. His eyes radiate kindness. He's one of those good, humble Cuban men, despite the flaws that destroyed our small family.

"Yeah, I love the office, er, I mean, bedroom," I joke as we stand in the middle of the room. "You haven't changed a thing. You never change, Papi."

"I'm un viejo, Gabrielito. Once you get to my age, nothing changes except your health and property taxes," he says. "They raised my taxes again. Those politicians!" he says, raising his hand.

"Well, at least you don't live in Massachusetts. You know what they call my state?"

"¿Que?"

"Taxachusetts. My paycheck shrinks from the state taxes, the local taxes, federal taxes. We even have a car tax."

"Un car tax?" Papi says, surprised.

"Yeah, the newer the car, the more you pay for it in taxes. Be glad that Florida has tourism to negate the need for that kind of tax."

Papi always liked to complain about money, or the lack of it. After the divorce, he helped support my mom and me, even though I was an adult in college. He took on more clients to make extra income. Today, he's frugality personified. He still drives his twelve-year-old Chevy Impala, which he paid off long ago. He most likely won't buy another new car unless he absolutely must. Papi sticks to tradition. He treats his car like the Cadillac he imagines it to be. From the office window, I see the waxed white beauty parked in Papi's designated space. Despite his frugal ways, he refuses to let me pay for our lunches when I visit. When I attempt to pay, he threatens to make a scene, which cracks me up.

We return to the living room, where we talk about my trip and classes, our usual small talk. That's our way of communicating. We don't talk about my dating adventures or lack of them or about his on-

and-off relationship with Gloria, whose face I immediately spot in a framed photograph near the bulky old television set.

Her name alone conjures up stinging feelings that I thought I had buried. Gloria, the woman Papi hooked up with while he was married to my mother. Gloria, the woman who broke up my parents. Gloria, the woman who thought she had hit the jackpot when she met Papi after he exterminated her apartment building in neighboring Hialeah. Gloria, the woman who only comes around when she doesn't have another boyfriend. Gloria, the raven-haired mujer who hangs out with Papi so that she doesn't feel so alone. Gloria, the woman who has a son named Javier, who is ten years younger than me and seems to have a lot more in common with Papi than I do. They always talk about sports and cars. With Gloria, Papi has another built-in family. Another woman. Another son.

I can't blame him. He must feel lonely without having me here regularly. I hope I don't bump into Gloria during my visit. Although she has always been nice to me, she's a reminder of why my family is fractured. I am diplomatic for Papi's sake, but I don't see the point of them being together, since it's so unstable. But if Papi enjoys her company, what can I do? I no longer live here. He needs to have a life, and I have my own in Boston.

As Papi babbles about the Marlins and how the local female TV anchors on Spanish newscasts grow younger and more voluptuous each year, I think of the small family we once had and the new family he has embraced, although Aunt Cary told me that Gloria hasn't been around in the past two months. Perhaps she found another guy and she's simply distracted. Or maybe she's seeing what I am seeing: Papi growing weaker from the Parkinson's.

As Papi flips through the channels for some sports updates, I get up from the sofa to fetch a bottle of water from the kitchen. On the Formica counter in the corner, under the fluorescent kitchen lights, I notice several pill bottles lined up in a perfect row next to the jar of cookies, crackers, and sugar. I grab each bottle and read their labels. *Amantadine, twice a day by mouth. Ropinirole, three times a day with each meal.* There's a bottle of vitamin E tablets and COQ10

(Coenzyme Q10 supplements). I read and reread the prescriptions. The number of pills unsettles me.

"Hey, Papi. Are all these pills for your Parkinson's?" I shout from the kitchen as I study each bottle.

"Sí, Gabriel. Your Aunt Cary picks them up for me. She's my younger hermana, but she acts like she's my mother. She never leaves me alone. I'm surprised she doesn't call you more often."

"Well, she does, but that's another story. At least she's keeping an eye on you. My vision doesn't stretch that far from Boston," I joke to lighten the mood.

With a cool bottle of water in hand, I return to the living room, where Papi sits in his armchair and watches TV. I study him and my heart breaks. His right hand suddenly shakes up and down sporadically like a jackhammer pounding a pavement. His hand tremors remind me of skin softly hitting leather, a flapping sound. His once broad and strong shoulders curve forward. He seems smaller. Why haven't I noticed this before?

"How are you really feeling, Papi? You never talk about the Parkinson's, and I always assume that you're okay. You never tell me anything." I scoot over next to him as the TV blares the latest sports updates on Univision television.

"I'm not the way I used to be, but I manage," he says, his right hand still shaking. A long yawn escapes him.

"When was the last time you saw the doctor?"

"A few months ago. Estoy bien, Gabrielito," he says, with a tone that suggests that he wants to change the subject.

"You seem weaker than you did on my last trip. I think we should get you an appointment while I'm here and find out what's going on."

"I'm fine, chico. This is your vacation. Don't worry about me. Go to the beach, see your mama, meet up with your friends. Do what you do when you go out to those *clubs*," he says defensively.

"Oh, you mean like dance and have fun? Oh, I forgot, you hate to dance. God forbid that a masculine, okay, semi-masculine, Cuban man can go out and have some drinks and dance the night away."

"I can dance. I just choose not to, Gabriel."

"Yeah, yeah, yeah. I'd love to see you try one day, Papi. And don't think I didn't notice what you just did. You changed the subject. I used to be a reporter, and my students try this on me all the time. I know that old trick. Now back to the subject at hand, your doctor, an appointment. I'll make an appointment, okay?"

"Gabrielito…," he responds. We stare at each other. The father-son draw. Papi never liked hospitals or doctor's offices. He and many Cuban immigrants from our family seem to believe that if you check into a hospital, you won't leave. So they avoid doctors at all costs. They are superstitious. If they can find a home remedy, they will use it.

"Well, I don't think it'll hurt if I call your doctor and make an appointment. Besides, I haven't been with you to a doctor's appointment in a while. Who knows, maybe he can give you something stronger or boost your dosage. I went online at work and found that exercise can help. Are you exercising?"

For years, I've wanted Papi to retire from exterminating, but he enjoys having a regular work routine. He feels active and important when he exterminates, even though it's becoming more challenging with his Parkinson's—and he knows that all too well.

Papi shoots me a sidelong look. "I'm too tired with the exterminating. The most I do is walk around the development with your aunt when she visits, which is a lot. We need to find her un hombre so that she will leave me tranquilo," he says with humor in his eyes.

"Well, that will be another project for another day. In the meantime, I'll call your doctor and see if he can see us Monday before I leave Monday night."

Papi sighs as if he's surrendering. I inherited my stubbornness from him, and he knows that. "Whatever you say, if it makes you happy, Gabrielito, but you're driving to Aventura."

"No problem. I don't mind driving your old ass around," I say with a wink, and I playfully punch him. I suggest that we go to Don Shula's Steak House for lunch the next day.

"I can never say no to steak with my son," he says, rubbing his stomach as he lights up at the idea.

With that settled, I let Papi watch the rest of the newscasts and head back into the office, er, my bedroom, and make some phone calls on Papi's business line. I manage to get through to his doctor's assistant. She squeezes us in for an appointment for Monday morning, which surprises me because it's a federal holiday. But doctors in Miami are always working. When you least expect it, the universe works its magic.

I'm glad I came on this short trip to see my parents. I'm glad that Aunt Cary gave me a heads-up as to Papi's condition. But I'm not happy that I seem so distant, powerless in helping. How much can I help from Boston? Being back in South Florida seems to make a difference to Papi as well as Mami. I need to find a way to visit more often, but how I do I balance my life in Boston with my former one here? How do adult children care for their elderly parents from 1,600 miles away?

The voice from the doctor's assistant snaps me out of these thoughts. "Do you know how to get here?" says Rose, the assistant on the other line.

"I remember. We'll see you Monday morning. Thank you, Rose. We really appreciate this."

"See you Monday. Have a good day."

As I lean back in Papi's pleather office chair with my hands folded behind my head, I glance at the corner of his desk, where there's another photo of us. This was taken when I was in high school. Papi and I stand arm in arm in front of my first car, a used Nissan hatchback, which he and Mami bought me for my seventeenth birthday. Papi looks so strong and healthy, and I look so much thinner (and younger) with my bush of curly hair. My cheeks are fuller and my hair thicker. Sigh.

Then I wonder, *Will I turn into my father someday?* I look just like him, or at least I look the way he did at my age. We're a living before-and-after shot. Does the Parkinson's that flows through him silently sleep in me too? The questions come fast, and hopefully, Papi's doctor can shed some light on this.

# chapter Nine

SINCE Papi is such an early bird, passing out in his armchair to the latest Clint Eastwood movie on cable, I decide to have a night out on my own. It's eleven, and the crickets and nearby cows sing, the unofficial soundtrack to Miami Lakes. Their sound mixes with Papi's loud snores, which echo from the living room. I take a quick shower and luxuriate in the hot steam that fills Papi's bathroom. The hot water rolls off my body. I clean my face and pat it dry with a towel. With my index finger, I wipe a clean spot on the mirror so that I can see myself through the hot vapor.

My hair is slick, wet, and combed down, just as it was when I was younger. I grab my Rogaine from my bag and apply some of the mousse on my crown. I take my anti-baldness pill with tap water. I apply some moisturizer to my face and neck. I massage some hair gel into my head and comb it to the right. I spritz some cologne and let it rain all over me. The older I get, the more I prepare for a night out. It wasn't that long ago when I just towel-dried my hair and then bolted out the door. Those were the days. None of this cosmetic upkeep.

After I change into my clothes—blue jeans with a gray polo shirt and black loafers—I'm set to go. A night in South Beach, just like old times. I grab the keys to Mom's Honda and my adventure begins.

As I drive on Interstate 95 toward Miami Beach, my cell phone rings its *Star Trek* ringtone. I glance at the caller ID, and it reads "Nick." I answer.

"Gabriel, you won't believe who's sitting next to me at the bar."

"Who? Who?" I say, sounding like an owl.

"No one, because *you* should be here with me hanging out. When does my buddy get back to Boston?"

I laugh into the phone as I gaze at the view of a gleaming downtown Miami in the distance. I try to imagine Nick sitting alone at a bar. "I'll be back before you know it. If you really want to see me sooner rather than later, I could use a ride from the airport."

"Deal, but then you owe me a drink or two the next time we go out."

"Yeah, yeah, yeah. I'll text you with the flight information. What are you doing tonight, Nick?"

"Um, nothing, because my wingman, my compadre is MIA in MIA. It's been a while since I've flown solo."

"Yeah, but you're never alone for too long. I'm sure you can survive going out without me. You'll live, Nick, you'll live! Speaking of going out, I spent the day with my dad, and now that he's asleep, I'm headed to South Beach for some fun of my own. Wish you were here!"

"You can say that again. Anyway, have fun tonight, GG, and I'll see you at the airport in a few days."

"Hey, Nick. I forgot to tell you something."

"What, GG?"

"*Slore!*" I laugh into the phone.

"Yeah, that will be you tonight! See ya!"

Twenty-five minutes later, I pull into the frenetic public parking lot adjacent to Lincoln Road in South Beach. The pedestrian mall is jammed with night crawlers, a mix of tourists and locals who saunter up and down the boulevard of boutiques, cafés, restaurants, and bars that blare boom-boom-boom dance and tropical music into the Atlantic-whipped air.

As I walk onto the strip, I try to mix in with the crowd and soak up the scene. Younger, tanned men in tank tops or sleeveless shirts lounge at the tables outside Score, the local gay bar. They sit next to tables filled with straight couples and friends munching on vegetarian pizzas and pasta dishes from the neighboring cafés. The street is one giant carnival of models and wannabes. It's as if everyone has something to show off, a hectic swirl of humanity, an exhibition of plumped and plucked body parts. In fact, most of the population here (men too) has been surgically enhanced by science in one way or another.

Not me. Although I grew up in Fort Lauderdale, I never subscribed to this scene. I always felt thin and average compared to these guys. When I visited, I became an outsider among the beautiful people in South Beach. In Fort Lauderdale, the gay community skews a little older (read: white men in their forties and fifties with mustaches and bellies). The scene there is also more cohesive, thanks to the town of Wilton Manors, which has blossomed into the epicenter of Broward's gay community. We have two gay pride parades and we have gay politicians in office. In Miami, being gay has more to do with looks and superficiality than with advocacy and civil rights. *Then why am I here again?* Oh yes, the music, the men, an escape. A night out.

I pass the coffee shops and the dessert store that scents the strip with a sweet chocolate aroma. I stand in an eight-person line at Score as two overweight drag queens sashay in as if they own the place. *Why do drag queens get to go in first?* The bouncer with the bleached-blond hair air-kisses the pair of queens and grants them access while the rest of us paying folk wait in line.

Ten minutes later, I'm finally inside. The pounding dance music pulses inside me. I sit on a stool at the bar and order a vodka and Red Bull from the hunky Australian bartender with the sexy black goatee, which matches his thick, black, wavy, combed-back hair. He reminds me of the actor who plays Wolverine in all those *X-Men* movies. He whips up my drink, which makes his bicep bulge tightly like a basketball. I want to reach out and squeeze the delicious bicep. He serves my drink, and I leave him a two-dollar tip for the eight-dollar drink.

I twirl a red straw in my drink and study the scene. A gaggle of twinks giggles on the narrow sofa that lines the front bar window. Men linger by the front entrance and eye-fuck everyone that walks in. I'm leaning over my drink to take a few swigs when a booming anchorman voice startles me into raising my head.

"A cranberry with vodka, Dan," the voice says. I turn to my right and see a dapper man in a crisp gray suit and pink tie. He has short-cropped black hair that has been relaxed and smoothed to the side. His skin is naturally tanned—he's Portuguese, I suspect.

"Coming right up, Ted Williams," the bartender says in a friendly but serious tone as the guy perches himself on the stool next to me. He flashes his ultra-white smile and says hi. We quickly do the how-are-you, I'm-fine, nice-to-meet-you pleasantries.

"I come here every week. You'd think the bartender would know my drink by now. Geez," he says, slightly snarky. "Sorry, I'm babbling. I'm Ted Williams." He extends his right hand, which bears a shiny Rolex, and I gladly shake it.

"No problem. I'm Gabriel," I say, sipping my drink.

I take a closer look at this guy, and then it hits me. This is Ted Williams, famous reporter and anchor for Miami's Channel 7 News.

"Aren't you a TV reporter?" I ask, admiring his profile and panache. I've always had a weakness for journalists even though I'm no longer one. We tend to speak the same special language of reporting and writing. We understand each other when we talk about story ideas, coverage, media analysis, and how overbearing editors can ruin a good story.

Ted beams from the recognition. "Why, yes. That's me, the one and only. You must be one of our loyal viewers, or you've seen my billboards around town." He forms the number seven with his right hand against his chest to emphasize his station.

"I used to watch the station when I lived here, but I tune into your sister station in Boston," I say.

Ted suddenly grows more animated. "You live in Beantown?" Ted says with curiosity. "That's where I'm from, well, the Cape. I was a reporter up there before taking a weekend-anchor job down here in good old Miami. What brings you back to Miami, Gabriel?"

He leans in closer. I catch a whiff of his strong Dolce & Gabbana cologne, which perfumes the air immediately around us. The sweet, powdery scent makes me tingle. I could breathe it in all day. From my seat, I notice other guys whispering and pointing to Ted. It must be nice to be a celebrity. I wonder why he's here alone.

The bartender plops Ted's drink on the counter.

"I'm visiting my parents. My dad lives in Miami Lakes. Mom is in Fort Lauderdale. Just here for the long weekend to get away from Boston."

Ted sighs and smiles. "Ah, Boston! My dream job is to be the main anchorman at the ABC affiliate, the most respected station in New England. But for now, Miami will do. I can't complain. One day, you'll see," Ted says, with a wink. "I'll be back in Boston as the *main guy*."

We sit, side by side, with our faces toward each other. And as I sit there, thoughts of Craig slowly surface. The memory of our kiss in my apartment flashes before me. I push the thought away by asking Ted about his work.

"So what stories have you been working on?"

Ted lights up. Journalists love to talk about their work. That's why I invite them as guest speakers to my classes at Jefferson. It takes the pressure off me and allows someone else to do all the talking.

"Well… let's see. It's all a big blur by the time the weekend rolls around. This week, I covered a high-speed chase on I-95 that tied up traffic between Broward and Miami-Dade, as well as a story on how the housing market has picked up again. I did a story on how a Miami officer used crime tips for profit. Oh, I had a sit-down with former attorney general Janet Reno. She's been out of the spotlight since retiring. That story did really well on our station's website. The story was picked up by the network, so the clip will be part of my reel."

"I remember her. Didn't *Saturday Night Live* run a spoof about her years ago as if she had her own TV dance party?"

Ted laughs. "Yeah. She still has her red Ford pickup truck. The focus of my story was on her work on behalf of Parkinson's research. Sometimes, she headlines fundraisers in South Florida."

"How is she doing with it?" I ask out of concern and curiosity.

"As well as she can. She's had it for some time. Her body shakes a lot. We didn't show her too much on camera because of her condition. We cut away a lot to her years in office and the work she has done."

"Well, at least she's getting out there and doing something," I say, my shoulders slouching on the bar stool. "There aren't that many big names with the disease besides Michael J. Fox."

Ted tilts his head to the right and studies me for a few seconds. He rubs his chin with his index finger. Every now and again as Ted talks, his Rolex reflects the nearby club lights. "I take it you have an interest in Parkinson's, Gabriel. How come?" Ted asks, twirling the straw in his glass.

"It's a long story, but the Cliff Notes version is that my dad has the disease. That's one of the reasons I'm here. I'm checking up on him."

"Oh. I'm so sorry, Gabriel." Ted places his hand on my right hand. His lips tighten into a frown. I'm getting used to that expression.

"Thanks, Ted. We're going to see his doctor on Monday. He's been getting weaker, and he hasn't been telling me about it. That's my macho Cuban father for you. He holds everything inside."

"I know the feeling. My dad is the same way. I think that's why I became a reporter, because no one ever told me what was going on in our family. I had to ferret out all the information. I had to investigate." Ted smiles, which makes me smile. My face is beginning to ache from all the smiling, but I'm not complaining. I'm having fun.

"Well, I'm sure the doctor will know what to do, and he may boost your father's medicine or suggest some therapy. It's nice that you came down for him."

I look down and grin.

"Are you here by yourself, Gabriel?"

"Yeah, just wanted to get out of my dad's house for a bit."

"Well, it looks my buddy Brian is missing in action for the night. He said he'd be here tonight. You'd like him and my other friend Ray, who lives in Cambridge. He's a former movie critic, and he's taking some classes at Harvard. I'll probably be up there to visit soon with my boyfriend Jurgen, who just left this morning back to Germany. He's a flight attendant, so we see each other every few days or weeks or whenever he can get a layover."

"How's that going?" I ask, now playing reporter with the reporter.

"It's going well. I love him and he adores me. The distance and time apart is hard. I have my career here, and he loves to travel. We make it work. It's a balance. You give and take. What I wouldn't do to have him in Miami full time, but my guy has the travel bug, so what can I do? How about you, Gabriel? Anyone special in Boston? I'm sure all those blue- and green-eyed Irish boys must love you." Ted arches one eyebrow with a half-grin.

"Nah, single as a Pringle. There is this one guy that I met that I kind of like, but he's a bit young. He's twenty-two."

"And... what's the problem?"

"He's also a student at the college where I teach. Well, he was my student last year. He's not currently my student. He wants to be a broadcaster. You better not mention this in one of your newscasts!"

"I can see it now. Breaking news: Boston professor hooks up with student. More salacious details at eleven. Seriously, I like the guy already, if he's going into TV news. Like I tell my friends, don't knock it until you try it. If I hadn't given this pushy German flight attendant a chance, I wouldn't have fallen in love. You never know where one road might take you."

"He's very cute, the all-American boy, with his fuzzy crew cut and light-brown eyes. But we are in completely different phases in our life."

"Well, at least you guys are in the same city. Don't be so quick to dismiss him. You never know. Anyway, let's get another drink. I feel my buzz fleeing," Ted says, slurping the rest of his vodka and cranberry juice in one swoop.

Ted flags the bartender down for another drink. I finish the rest of my vodka and Red Bull.

The bartender returns with our drinks and plops them hard on the counter.

"We need to make a toast, Professor Gabriel!" Ted announces at the bar as he raises his drink toward mine.

"To what?"

"To Boston and up-and-upcoming anchormen!"

"You got it!"

"And to your father!" Ted adds.

I clink my glass to his. "Cheers!" We exchange a smile and gulp down our drinks.

Two more drinks and half an hour later, Ted Williams and I morph into two buzzing bar bees. We stand and sway at our perch at the front bar, where we soak up the latest dance music. We continue to exchange war stories about being journalists—his from Channel 7 in Miami and mine from community reporting in Broward.

"One time, I did this story about two women who were stuffed into suitcases left by the side of the road. Can you imagine that, Gabriel?"

I almost spit out my drink. "Were they chopped up and folded inside?" I say, intrigued by the gruesome story. It sounds like the stuff of nightmares or a horror movie. *SAW: Fort Lauderdale.*

"They were diminutive women. Actually, they were young prostitutes. It was absolutely *horrible.* I even saw the bodies at the morgue. Anyway, I found each of their mothers and interviewed them. I had the exclusives. We called the story "The Samsonite Killer," for obvious reasons. I think their luggage sales dropped after our stories ran." A hint of a mischievous grin appears on his face.

"Did they catch the guy?"

"Nope. He's still out there. What about you? What was your worst or most bizarre story, Mr. Beantown Man?" Ted's voice slurs as he removes his straw from his drink and sucks on it. My eyes bounce from my drink to Ted's dark-brown eyes.

"Nothing as serious as that. I covered more community news in Pembroke Pines and Miramar. You know, school board meetings, planning and zoning issues. But every now and then when we were shorthanded, I was dispatched on a breaking news story. The most bizarre story I worked on involved this hustler named Lance who would meet older gay men online, romance them at a bar, and then rob and beat them."

"Oh wait, I totally remember that story. What did they call him again?" Ted says, bursting with excitement.

"Romance Lance! You can't make this stuff up. Now you know where all those CBS crime procedural dramas get their ideas from— here! Our stories. We're great fodder for the entertainment world," I say.

"Well, this is South Florida, the land of tourists and fugitives looking to make value meals out of us. Without them, we'd be covering alligators named Ginger breaking into people's pools to cool off during mating season."

"We don't have these kinds of stories in Boston. Most of the news coverage is political or about Harvard. I always believed that the South Florida heat factored into the crime wave here," I say, dancing in place at the bar, my eyes trained on Ted. It's not that I am interested in Ted. I just find him entertaining in a cartoonish kind of way. He's good company.

"Yeah, there's something in the air here alright, and her name is Lady GaGa! We have to dance, *just dance*," Ted says, waving his hands and singing the hook to one of the eccentric pop singer's older songs as it plays in the background. Ted awkwardly grooves to the infectious, bouncy dance beat as if following his own unique rhythm. We're both riding high on our liquid buzz. I'm having fun, and Ted has been a great distraction. Getting out for the night was a good idea. I miss these warm South Beach nights during the frequent blizzards when I'm holed up at home with a stack of movie rentals.

Just as I plunk my drink down on the counter, Ted removes his jacket and leaves it with the hunky bartender. Ted then suddenly grabs my right hand and drags me to the grand dance floor in the middle of the club. Along with the droves of guys, we dance, moving to the left, shaking to the right. Our hands fly in the air. We bump our bums side to side. We punctuate the dance music with our laughter while leaning forward and back to the beat.

As I glance at the other dancers through my semi-drunken haze, everyone appears euphoric, carefree. The music pulsates from within, and I capture each beat with every step. It's as if another creative influence has taken over me and I'm along for the ride. I temporarily forget about my classes. My concerns for my aging parents dissipate with the soft puffs of club smoke that float through the dance floor, which now looks like a giant cloud packed with happy people. Boston, Craig, my mortgage, my lack of a love life, my loneliness—I push these thoughts away and let the music guide me. I feel free, thanks to the music and a new friend, the one and only Ted Williams.

"Welcome back to Miami, Gabriel! Woo-hoo!" Ted shouts, putting his hands on my shoulders as he jumps in his drunken state. I grin, and we dance the night away among a sea of dancing cuties. It's good to be back in Miami.

# chapter Ten

"WE HAVEN'T seen you in a while, Mr. Galan," Dr. Steinberg greets me as he walks into the small examining room where Papi and I have been waiting. I drove Papi this morning for his long-overdue appointment. I'm surprised the doctor even remembers me from my previous visits. I've been a stranger to my father's illness and care, but I am slowly changing that for the better.

Dr. Steinberg's office is in Aventura, the waterfront city better known for the giant sprawling mall that keeps expanding with new department stores and tourists every year. The doctor's office is in a five-story gleaming white medical building along the Intracoastal Waterway, which is dotted by rows of high-rises and condos in north Miami-Dade County. The city is also a few miles from Florida International University's north campus, so I know the area well.

"Hi, Dr. Steinberg. I know, I know, it's been a few years," I say with embarrassment. The doc shakes my hand and Papi's, which is trembling slightly again today. I remember this examining room and its familiar inescapable hospital-type sterile smell well. Dr. Steinberg has been Papi's neurologist since he was first diagnosed with Parkinson's. In the beginning, I accompanied Papi for his first few appointments, and the condition was kept at bay. But then I moved to Boston, and in my absence, Aunt Cary began going with Papi, and I figured things were fine.

A pang of guilt overwhelms me after I realize how much time has passed since I've been here with Papi.

As we sit back in the plastic chairs that flank the examination table, the doctor calls up Papi's file on the corner desk computer. Dr.

Steinberg performs the routine check of Papi's eyes and ears and asks him to take deep, slow breaths. He then asks about Papi's symptoms.

I look at my father, who is wearing a light-blue guayabera shirt with a few buttons left open so that his hairy chest and gold cross are on public display. I never understood why Latin men dress like this, as if they are going to play dominoes in old Havana.

"How is your hand? How have you been feeling, Guillermo, since our last appointment?" Dr. Steinberg asks, his fingers typing notes on the computer as Papi describes his symptoms.

"My hand is shaking more," Papi says, holding up his right hand. "But I feel fine." Papi makes a fist to show his strength, as if in defiance of the disease.

"Um, Papi, don't hold back! Tell the doctor what's really going on. I noticed you were weaker the moment I got back in town Saturday." Papi throws me a sidelong, annoyed look. He is not one to volunteer information unless you press him.

"Gabrielito, why don't you do the talking, since you have so much to say?" Papi says, folding his arms and leaning back in his chair. Across the room hangs a painting of a captain and his sailboat bobbing in an ocean of blue hues. I notice Papi looking at the picture, which seems to soothe and calm him as it does me. The doctor's eyes volley back and forth between me and my father as he obviously wonders who will answer next.

"Okay, so Dr. Steinberg, my aunt told me that my dad fell the other day while picking some mangoes in the backyard. He swears he just lost his balance, but I think it has something to do with his right leg. He seems to drag it a little. He seems weaker from earlier this year. Maybe you should take a look."

The doctor rubs his graying goatee with his right index finger. He adjusts his black-framed glasses and returns his gaze to Papi. "Were you dizzy right before you fell, Guillermo? Dizziness is a common symptom of Parkinson's. Sudden head movements can cause some Parkinsonians to lose their balance, as well."

"Sí, a little dizzy," Papi says meekly.

"Has this been happening often?" Dr. Steinberg asks, surveying my dad while typing at the same time.

"Sometimes."

"Any other symptoms or instances since our last visit? By the way, you were overdue by two appointments. I am supposed to see you every four months."

"I know, yo sé. I have a lot of buildings to exterminate. Mucho trabajo," Papi says, holding his hands. "This is Florida, the land of cockroaches. We never go out of business. We've been seeing an increase in palmettos," Papi says with a proud grin.

"Palmetto roaches, Guillermo?"

"Sí, the roaches that fly," Papi says, comically flapping his hands like wings.

"Yeah, they're airborne. Anyway, can we focus on the Parkinson's and not Florida's peskiest insect?" I pipe in.

At this point, the doctor tells us that he is going to run some tests. My eyes shift to Papi and then to the painting of the sailor, who now seems lost and adrift on his boat in the middle of the ocean. Maybe that is how Papi feels about this disease. It ebbs and flows with no immediate trajectory. Some days are choppy. Others are smooth sailing, and it's a journey that he can't chart, because the Parkinson's is making all the decisions. When Papi wants to go left, another force can lead him elsewhere.

The doctor's words snap me out of my stream of thoughts. "This isn't anything new. We've done these exercises before, so you should remember them," the doctor says, getting up and offering Papi help, which he politely refuses.

Dr. Steinberg instructs Papi to walk up and down the long vacant hallway that leads to the door to the waiting room.

"Walk like your normally walk. I want you to do this twice."

As the doctor and I stand in the doorway of the examining room, Papi saunters back and forth down the hallway. He walks with his head held up high and his chest forward. He's showing off. As he walks, his right hand continues to shake.

The doctor observes, nods, and takes more notes. "Very good, Guillermo."

We all return to the examining room.

Then the doctor asks Papi to write his name and his address on a sheet of paper. Using his right hand, Papi does as the doctor asks. I notice the penmanship is squiggly. I can make out the letters and numbers, but I can also tell that Papi has to really concentrate to make his hand do what he wants it to do. It's as if he is fighting with his own body, willing it do what was once so effortless.

The doctor observes and logs more notes on the computer.

A few more tests, one of which includes having my father grip a ball and squeezing it, and the doctor is done.

He scoots back in his chair and leans forward toward us as we take our seats again.

"Guillermo, this is what we're going to do. I am going to boost your dosage of Requip to three milligrams, three times a day. That should help with the loss of coordination in your right hand." He pulls out Papi's previous writing samples and compares them to today's.

"As you know, Parkinson's is a degenerative disease, and with each year that goes by, you may notice some weakening. But since we started you on a low dose of medicines years ago, we have a lot of room to work with, so I am going to increase your dosage, and that should help with the mobility. I also noticed that your right leg is stiffer, and you are slower to get up and sit down. We need to loosen your muscles and strengthen them. Are you exercising, Guillermo? Nice long walks at night and riding a bicycle, even a stationary one, will loosen some of your stiffness."

"I walk in my neighborhood in Miami Lakes. When I work, I am exercising," Papi says. His voice has become raspy suddenly.

"I strongly suggest you do some more exercise. It's not just good for your muscles. It will lift your spirits. Exercise releases endorphins, which elevate your mood. There are several physical therapy programs and classes available to seniors. I believe it might do you some good to take part in a class or have one-on-one personal training. Gabriel, can you or your aunt help your father with that? My assistant can give you a list of websites and contact information for some local programs."

"Thanks, Dr. Steinberg. I leave tonight for Boston, but I can make some calls this afternoon."

"And about the dizzy spells. I would be careful with turning your head too fast, especially when you are picking mangoes," the doctor says.

"They make for great mango shakes," Papi jokes.

"I want you to do some stretching exercises where you turn your head slowly side to side in the mornings before you go to work. That will loosen up your neck muscles," Dr. Steinberg says, showing Papi how to do the exercise.

"Do this a few times in the morning. In the meantime, I'll have my assistant call in a new prescription, and if you feel any side effects or anything, please call me right away. You'll notice a difference with the upped dosage. Other than that, you're strong as a horse. You're doing better than average, Guillermo. You've managed the Parkinson's much better than most folks."

I grin and pat Papi on the back.

The doctor then shakes Papi's hand and mine before saying good-bye. "Good seeing you, Gabriel, and don't be a stranger. Say hi to your aunt for me and tell her that I miss her Cuban sandwiches. She always brings me one when she comes with your father for his appointments."

"Yeah, that's my aunt. Always feeding people, whether they want it or not."

"And you can always call my office for anything," Dr. Steinberg tells Papi.

With that, the doctor leaves the examining room and dashes off to visit another patient. Papi and I get up and walk down the same carpeted hallway that we came through earlier. We stop at the nurse's desk, and she gives us the prescription the doctor signed off on and schedules Papi's appointment for four months from now.

With that done, we slowly walk out of the office and step into the waiting room packed with other Parkinson's patients. Two elderly women sit in wheelchairs. One of them has drool spilling from her mouth, and another woman next to her, her daughter or caretaker, I suspect, quickly dabs it with a pink handkerchief. An older gentleman wearing a gray suit sits in a chair as his left leg pumps and down like a nervous needle in a sewing machine. They all have that familiar masklike look, with their mouths half or fully open. Their jaws droop, and their eyes seem vacant. I look at them and imagine how that might be Papi one day. As blessed as he is that he can still walk, how long will it be before this cruel disease completely takes over and renders my strong-willed father a shell of his former self? I keep my hand on Papi's upper back as we wait for the elevator. The prescription slip pokes out of his front pocket.

"See, wasn't it a good idea to come here, Papi? You needed a stronger dose. You'll feel better in no time," I say reassuringly, but I don't know if I am reassuring him or myself.

"Yes, Gabrielito. More medicine. I am tired of taking these pills," he says, pulling out his small pill box from his pocket. He rattles the box to emphasize his point. "Pills in the morning, pills during lunch, pills at night. I spend my day swallowing pills," he sighs.

I shrug my shoulders, not knowing what to say. I can't imagine having to take so many pills. They are constant reminders of his condition.

The elevator dings that it has arrived, and we step in and continue the conversation. Soft, instrumental country music plays in the background as we ride five floors down to the lobby.

"Before I leave tonight, I'll get your prescription, and we'll see about you joining a gym or taking some sort of class."

"I'll be fine, Gabrielito. I will walk more in the development. Don't worry about your viejo father. I can take care of myself." Papi grins tightly and stares up at the descending numbers. His right hand begins to shake again, which makes his wrist watch jangle. Papi grabs that hand with his left hand to try and control the shakes. He stands closer to the corner of the elevator as if trying to keep his right hand from my line of vision.

My heart breaks. I try and change the subject, but I can still hear the watch rattle against the elevator's wood paneling. "So it's almost noon. You know what time that is?" I rub my stomach. "Don Shula's Steak House, Papi? My treat!"

"No, my treat."

"Papi...."

"Gabrielito...."

Again, the father-son draw. I just smile and cave in as we step off the elevator and head back to Miami Lakes for a big, scrumptious lunch.

# chapter Eleven

AHH, Boston. I'm back home. Well, almost. I am just over the city. One of my favorite things to do as the plane descends into my adopted home is to peer through the oval American Airlines window and gaze at the constellation of triple-deckers and Victorian homes below that dot the Quincy shoreline. I place my right hand under my chin and watch the plane's wings slice through the puffy clouds that linger over the city like a silk blanket.

The pilot announces that we're about to land. I sit back and reflect on the entire weekend.

After Papi's doctor's appointment this morning, and a trip to Sears, I drove back to my mother's house, where she cooked another one of her fabulous feasts. Afterward, she dropped me off back at Papi's place. At the house, she simply waved to him from the car as I got out and kissed her on the cheek. Papi insisted he was fine to drive despite his weakening leg, and he drove me to the airport.

When I visit, our understanding is that Mami picks me up from the airport and Papi drops me off. It's been our tradition for years, but sometimes I feel like a yo-yo, traversing the complicated world of parents with separate homes in two counties.

Papi promised me that he would take an exercise class per Dr. Steinberg's orders. At Sears, we looked at various bicycles. Well, at least I did. Papi, who wore a yellow baseball cap, his guayabera shirt, and shorts, was too busy browsing the latest tools in the hardware section. When he returned, I showed him an exercise bike that wasn't too expensive. As much as Papi fought me on allowing me to pay for the bicycle, I persisted and charged it on my credit card, which is already swollen with debt from my previous trips here and a shopping excursion at IKEA a few weeks ago.

"Gabrielito, this is three hundred dollars! That's a car payment," Papi exclaimed as I signed the receipt at the Sears counter.

"Yeah, but you can get a lot of mileage out of this. You can ride it whenever you want, maybe in the mornings for twenty minutes. That will get you going," I said as we walked toward the shipping area of the store. There, a studly twenty-year-old guy with a crew cut, matching thick dark-brown eyebrows, and toned, tanned arms—typical look for Miami men—fetched the box with the bicycle inside. He carried it to the car, where we loaded it.

During the drive back to his place, Papi and I continued to playfully argue about the purchase and the need for it. Back at his apartment, I struggled to get the fifty-pound box inside. Once I unpacked the bicycle, I assembled it in the living room near the television set.

"You can watch Univision or ESPN while you cycle," I said as I hopped on the bicycle and pretended I was Lance Armstrong. I bobbed my head left and right like a little kid.

"So you promise me you're going to do this a few times a week? Remember what the doctor said. You need to loosen your leg muscles. Now it's your turn, Papi. Get on the bike and test it."

He sighed and folded his arms before performing my request. "Sí, Gabriel, I will do this. I wouldn't want your hard-earned dinero to go to waste," he said as he climbed on the electric bike and slowly pedaled. I stood there and made him exercise on the bicycle for twenty minutes.

I left the apartment with the feeling that I had accomplished my mission for the weekend. I helped Papi get his medication updated. I felt better about being more educated about his medicines. I encouraged him to work out. Hopefully, he'll continue to do this on his own.

When we said good-bye later on at Miami International Airport, he gave me a big, strong hug. I felt his thin frame during the embrace.

"Call me when you land," he said

"Of course, I always do. We did a lot today. Maybe that'll help you sleep better."

As Dad slowly pulled away from the airport's curb, I stood on the departures sidewalk where other drivers dropped off their friends or loved ones. As I slung my backpack off my shoulder, I watched Papi and his Chevy recede from my view.

Walking inside the brightly lit terminal, an overwhelming feeling of guilt crept up on me. Thoughts replayed in my head like a compact disc stuck in repeat. *I should be here in Miami Lakes. Papi is getting sicker. Mom is in better shape yet alone too. How can I care for my parents as they get older and weaker? This is not going to get easier as they get older.* I tried to shake off the thoughts as I printed out my boarding pass at the airline kiosk.

Later, I stood in the snaking line in the security area, where I was required to remove my shoes and expose my socks for the world to see. Although I dozed off for half the flight, those previous thoughts of my parent's aging resurface as the plane descends into Boston.

The pilot's voice jolts me from my train of thought. The plane lands, thumping momentarily like a giant, clumsy steel dragon on the runway. "Welcome to Boston, where the temperature is a cool fifty-eight degrees. We know you have your other options in traveling, so we thank you for flying with American Airlines this evening," the pilot announces with a wicked Boston accent. I'm home, yet so far away from where I'm really needed.

The following morning I'm back to work and standing in front of my class. I fight off memories of the fun weekend—being in my old bedroom at Mom's house, dancing at Score with the infamous Ted Williams, and having brunch with Papi at Don Shula's restaurant in Miami Lakes. Whenever I leave South Florida, it's hard for me to peel myself emotionally from my life there, my old life.

I imagine that I could easily move back home and pick up where I left off, but I do enjoy my job and my life in Boston. The hub remains an educated city, ripe with opportunities in the world of academia. I find that my students are more engaged and involved, taking classes seriously because they (well, their parents or the state) are footing the high tuition costs. In South Florida, where I was a college student myself, I found that we were distracted by the bars, the beach, and the tropical air. Everyone seemed to skate through their classes. Some even came to class on in-line skates. School was a place to pass time when you weren't going out.

"Class, as I'm sure you've noticed in your syllabus, today we have a special guest speaker," I announce as students scurry in.

I write down the reporter's name on the whiteboard: Tommy Perez, general assignment features writer at the *Boston Daily*. "You *should* have read some of his recent articles online for his visit. This is your opportunity to pick a real reporter's brain. I want each of you to ask him a few questions. He took time out of his busy schedule to come here, so let's make the most of his visit," I say as I slowly pace back and forth. The morning sun softly streams through the wall of windows from the east side of the classroom.

"While we wait for Mr. Perez, I suggest you take the time to read the city's papers online, which you should have, ahem, done already before class," I say, widening my eyes to emphasize my point.

"How do you know Mr. Perez?" asks Angelica, an aspiring broadcast journalist.

"Well, Mr. Perez interviewed me for a story he wrote a few months back on the lack of bilingual Latino college professors. It turns out he's from Miami, like myself. Small world, huh? Anyway, I thought you might all want to hear about how he arrived in Boston from Miami. He's also one of the younger reporters at the paper, so I thought you all might relate to him."

As I speak, there's a knock on the door. I glance through the window and see Tommy Perez's smiling face and waving hand. I open the door. He walks in holding a can of Diet Coke.

"Hey, Tommy, welcome to Covering the News."

He firmly shakes my hand. "Thanks, Gabriel, for inviting me. I'm happy to help you out. It wasn't that long ago that I was a J-student myself, so I know how important it is to hear from people working in the industry."

I introduce him to the class, and he waves at everyone. Tommy then sets down his black *Daily* messenger bag behind the podium and places his Diet Coke on top of the desk. Instead of using the podium, he casually sits on the desk, his legs dangling.

"So, class… Tommy Perez was kind enough to stop by our class today. He's a general assignment reporter for the *Daily*'s Features section, but you already knew that because you read your syllabus, right? Mr. Perez writes about style, pop culture, local TV news, and Hispanic-related arts. Basically, a little of everything. Before joining the Features desk, Tommy worked as a reporter for the paper's City section, where he wrote about diversity and Boston neighborhoods and how the census figures showed how the city has changed demographically. And before that, he was as a general assignment metro reporter in Fort Lauderdale for the *Miami News*. Did I miss anything?" I turn to Tommy.

"Yeah, that's my bio," he says, tucking one of his curly brown strands of hair behind his ear. It's one of his habits.

"So without further ado, *heeeeere's* Tommy Perez."

The class claps and welcomes him. I grab a seat in the back of the room as Tommy begins sharing the story of how he broke into the crazy media business. He is positive and cheerful and paces back and forth as he tells his story. My students are completely focused on him. I don't catch anyone texting under their desks, which happens sometimes in my classes.

"Blame it on my ninth-grade English teacher, who read one of my essays, told me that I wrote very well, clearly, and with a certain rhythm. She encouraged me to join the school newspaper, and I did. I knew right then and there that I wanted to be a journalist. What was I thinking, right?" he tells the class.

I hear some chuckles. I knew Tommy would make a good impression on the students. He's not your jaded journalist. He remains enthusiastic about his craft, despite all the cutbacks and changes in the industry.

"Then, our high school newspaper mentor, who was an editor at the *Miami News*, came to our class one afternoon and announced that she needed a high school intern to write a weekly column for her. We all applied, of course. But I ended up getting it. I always believed that my story on condoms—I called them little preventers—gave me the edge," Tommy continues, burning bright with passion as he recounts his back story. "And that's when I started writing for the *Miami News*. I had just turned sixteen years old. I barely had a license. Then...."

Watching Tommy entertain the class with his journalism war stories reminds me of what I could have been. He's almost a doppelganger, a mirror image of myself. Mow down his thick curly hair and add a few more pounds on him and we could pass as brothers. But more so, he is excelling at the career I left behind to become a professor. I don't regret my decision, but when I see someone like Tommy, who has a similar background, being Cuban from South Florida and a journalist, I am reminded of what I could have been if I hadn't quit my newspaper-reporting job in Fort Lauderdale and moved to Boston. Who knows? I could have been a big-time journalist by now. Envy envelops me.

Twenty minutes later, Tommy is still talking about himself as if he was doing stand-up comedy. I gently interrupt and open the session to let students pepper him with their own questions. Tommy takes a sip of his Diet Coke as a forest of hands shoot up.

"Do you ever see yourself writing books or doing another kind of writing?" asks Alex.

"Funny that you should ask that. In between my *Daily* stories, I wrote a book, and it's going to be published next spring. Yay!" The class starts whispering and chatting. I hear "wow" and "oh cool!"

"What is it about?" I ask from the back row.

Tommy takes another swig from his soda. "It's like a *Same Sex in the City* or like a gay *Entourage*, you know, that never-ending show on HBO. It's about three friends who meet up at a bar in Boston called Club Café. It's a real place, by the way. The book follows their adventures at the bar over the course of a year. They're basically looking for Mr. Right. But more importantly, the book is about being a newcomer to a city and how having one or two good friends can make all the difference in the world. It's a fun, light read. Nothing too heavy, but it's all about Boston. My love letter to the city."

"And is there a Cuban-American reporter character?" Angelica asks as her chin rests on her hands.

"Yeah, someone like that." Tommy winks. "Okay, you got me. The main character is a newspaper reporter from Miami, and it's his first year in Boston. But there's also a studly Italian guy who is his friend and a reality TV has-been from *The Real World*."

"What do you prefer, writing books or news stories?" I ask.

"I like both. They are different forms of writing. One is more third-person objective. My novel is written in first-person, and I can really let loose and write words that I can never get away with in the *Daily*, like 'booyah' and 'water sports' and 'fuck'!"

The class laughs.

"So what stories are you working on now?" asks Tina from the middle row.

"Well, I'm writing a story about a special dance class for people with Parkinson's. It takes place in Cambridge. The class is designed to help Parkinsonians relax and loosen their muscles, but the dancing also lifts their spirits. You see, a lot of Parkinson's patients tend to isolate themselves and suffer from depression because of their condition. The class is one of the few in the country."

I lean forward, intrigued. "How did you hear about that class? When will the story run?" I ask.

Tommy places his right leg over his left and leans his head to the right as he explains.

"I usually get my story ideas from talking to different people when I go out. Sometimes, a previous story begets another one. I had done a story about a yoga class for people with Alzheimer's or dementia, and after that story was published a few weeks ago, someone e-mailed me about this class for Parkinson's. I get story ideas when I least expect it. They just come my way. Oh, the story runs in about two weeks. I am just getting started on it, Gabriel."

I ask the class if there are any further questions. Everyone is quiet.

"Tommy, on behalf of Covering the News, thank you again for visiting our class."

The class claps.

Tommy flashes his big, wide grin and begins to gather his messenger bag. "If any of you have follow-up questions, feel free to e-mail me," Tommy says, scribbling his work e-mail on the whiteboard. "And if you want more information about our summer internship program, just let me know."

I excuse the class, and everyone shuffles out into the hallway. I thank Tommy again and shake his hand.

"Anytime, Gabriel. I love doing these chats. It reminds me of why I got into this crazy business. It recharges me."

"Well, I owe you lunch or something. I wanted to ask you about the Parkinson's class. Where does it meet? Does it cost anything?" We casually walk out of the classroom and stand under the fluorescent lights of the hallway as students flow around us. The soundtrack of student chatter echoes throughout the fifth floor.

"It's at the Jewish community center in Cambridge. There is an admission fee for the class, but it doesn't cost much. I can send you the information or you can wait until my story runs, because it'll have all the details. I'm still working on it, though, and I have no control of when my stories run. That's up to my editors, but I can keep you posted, chico."

"Thanks, Tommy. I'll be on the lookout for your article. You've given me a lot to think about," I say, putting my hand on the back of his shoulder. "And thanks again for coming out to my class. The students got a lot out of you."

"Really? You mean I didn't scare your students away from journalism?"

We laugh as I escort him to the elevator.

"If anything, you may have inspired them, Mr. Perez."

As we walk and talk, the whole way, I think about the class and wonder if there is anything like that in Miami for Papi.

# chapter Twelve

"I'M HERE!" Craig's voice echoes from my apartment's intercom.

I punch in the code on my phone and buzz him in. Shortly after, I hear a soft knock at my door. As I open it, I'm tickled by the image. Craig stands in my doorway wearing a light-blue chambray long-sleeved shirt, a snug white T-shirt underneath, brown slacks, and matching boat shoes. His brown eyes are fixed on mine. Looking at Craig makes me feel like a mix of sunshine and honey inside—warm and sweet. Carrying this feeling, I softly kiss him and give him a hearty hug.

"Welcome back to Casa Galan!"

"Thanks, Gabriel. It feels like forever since I've been here. I've been waiting for our very first official date, señor," he says, slowly disengaging from the embrace.

I take him by the hand and lead him deeper into the condo. "I know. I've had a busy few weeks." I glance back at him and recall the kisses we shared a few weeks ago here. Oh those kisses! I can still taste him.

"How's your dad doing? How was your trip?"

"He's doing better. The doctor boosted his medication. I may go down for Christmas to check up on him again."

We make our way into the living room, where we sink into my soft brown sofa. Craig immediately leans closer to me and playfully drapes his left leg over mine. I continue telling him about the electric bicycle, my mother's fabulous cooking, and how I'm missing the

South Florida eighty-degree heat right about now. Then I realize that I've been a rude host; I haven't offered Craig a drink. It's a bad habit of mine, because aside from Nick, I rarely have guests. (I've always wondered whether my anti-baldness pill has something to do with my declining sex energy.)

"I need to get you a drink. My apologies for not offering earlier." I gently pat him on the knee, and he responds with a flirtatious slanting smile.

"No worries, man. You're a great host. Do you have beer, any alcohol?" Craig says as he begins leafing through some of the news magazines on my coffee table. They are the usual subscriptions to *Latina*, *People*, and the *Star Trek* Fan Club magazine.

I return to the kitchen and flick on the bright fluorescent lights. "Well, I have some white wine, vodka, Red Bull, diet soda. Take your pick!" I call from the kitchen as I grab two glasses from the upper cabinet.

"White wine it is!"

I pop open a bottle and peek over at Craig, who is now squatting in front of the TV and rummaging through my bookshelf of DVDs. After pouring Craig's wine, I fix myself my usual tonic—Red Bull with vodka. I carefully carry both drinks to the living room across my faux wooden floors.

"So which *Star Trek* movie or episode is it going to be? *The Wrath of Khan*? *The Search for Cock*—oops, I mean Spock," Craig says, catching himself.

"Hmm… I wonder what's on your mind. I was thinking of the Horta episode from the original series. Actually, the episode was titled 'The Devil in the Dark'," I say with sci-fi authority.

With our drinks in hand, we lie back on my plush sofa and sit close to one another. Craig softly fingers the back of my hair, which tickles. We each take generous swallows of our drinks.

"I think I remember that one. That's the one with a giant orange blob creature that starts killing a group of miners, right, Gabriel?"

"You got it! I read somewhere that the episode was William Shatner's favorite because it played on so many themes of the show. It was exciting and intelligent and thought-provoking."

"Just like you, Gabriel!" Craig says with his eyebrow raised and a grin.

I pop the DVD into the player, and the signature show introduction begins to play.

"Space… the final frontier. These are the voyages…." William Shatner's voice echoes in my apartment.

As we relax on my sofa, we take in the episode in which Captain Kirk and Spock encounter this blob and try to communicate with it. Through a Vulcan mind meld, Spock learns that the subterranean beast calls itself a Horta. It relays to Spock that every 50,000 years, its entire race dies except for one that remains behind to protect the eggs and serve as their mother. The Horta conveys to Spock that when the miners invaded her hatchery, it had to fight back by the only way it knew it could. It spewed a toxic liquid that wiped out several dozen miners.

"See, things are never what they seem," I say, nodding my head to emphasize my thought.

Craig kisses me on the neck. My right arm loops around him, and I gently squeeze and rub his right shoulder.

"Everyone thinks this thing is a killer in the caves, but it's the miners who are killing her eggs. So one begat the other," I say.

"Can you imagine being the only one of your kind and having to protect your offspring or family and not having any siblings or relatives nearby to help you? And that no matter what you do, you're it. It's all on you. It must be lonely for the Horta."

"Yeah, I know something about that," I say, looking down and taking another swig of my golden elixir, which warms and buzzes at the same time.

"What do you mean, Gabriel?"

"Never mind." I playfully swat him with my left hand. "I think the alcohol is making me melodramatic. Any minute now, I'm going to pull out a red violin from behind the sofa."

As I reach for the remote control to raise the volume, Craig inches closer to me and rubs my upper back with the palm of his hand. Like a puppy, he affectionately places his head on my shoulder.

"Gabriel, do *you* sometimes feel like a Horta?"

I spit out my drink and laugh, imagining myself as this giant roving beast wandering the cave with a drink in my hand. I can tell by the sweet way that Craig said it that he wasn't trying to be funny or insensitive. He was being sincere. It just sounded funny.

"Sometimes, I sorta feel like a Horta!" I joke, realizing the rhyme. "But no. I don't feel like one, and I definitely don't look like a Horta. But I can relate to feeling alone and having to support and protect your family. It's quite a leap, but I can sort of get that, and I can see what the show's writers are trying to say there," I explain. "You're too young to understand."

Craig rolls his eyes and puts down his wine glass, which thuds against my coffee table. "Please, Professor, ah, I mean, Gabriel. Just because I'm twenty-two doesn't mean I don't know anything about life. You'd be surprised. I helped my mom when our grandmother died from the Parkinson's, and I always worked throughout high school. The only reason I'm at Jefferson is because of my grades and my grandmother. I got a great scholarship, almost a full ride, and she left me some money for college. You think I'm dumb kid, and I'm not." His lips tighten and his eyebrows furrow. I'd struck an emotional nerve.

"I don't think of you like that, and you know that. If I did, I wouldn't be spending this time with you. You've got a lot to offer, Craig. I guess we're in two different places in our lives, and when I see you, I am reminded of how I was when I was twenty-two—the ambitious, enthusiastic, aspiring college journalist. I didn't have a worry in the world. My main priorities then were my grades and where I was going to go dancing that weekend. Now I feel like I'm caught between two worlds, one here in Boston and the other in Fort Lauderdale, and lately, I've been feeling that I'm needed more down there. I am beginning to feel the weight of having to care for my parents."

"But you're needed here too. Your students, your friends. Nick. Me," Craig says hopefully.

"I'm just a fantasy to you, a game, the older Latino college professor, someone to brag about at college parties," I say with a mix of sarcasm and truth. Isn't sarcasm truth disguised, anyway?

"No, you're the real thing, and I wouldn't brag about you unless you wanted me to. I'd only say good things. Besides, I'm a private guy. I am not going to tell the world, especially the gossipy wannabes at school, that we kissed or the details of what we are going to do later."

"And what is that exactly?" I raise my eyebrows.

Craig answers my question by softly planting his warm lips against mine. As if by reflex, my hands skim his fuzzy hair, which tickles my fingertips. As I rub his head, he cups my face and combs his fingers through my short hair. Our tongues dance sensually in each other's mouths as my body eases on top of his. I press deeper into him as we lay on the sofa.

I nudge his nape, lick the inner folds of his peach-fuzzy-ear, and slip my tongue in and out. My body erupts with insatiable tingles and heat. He wraps his arms around my back and squeezes, which cracks my bones. The sofa rocks against my Pergo floors, and I feel myself glowing from within.

A few minutes later, my cheeks are flushed from our body heat. I grab Craig by the hand and lead him to my bedroom. At the edge of the bed, I slowly unbutton his shirt, which parts to reveal a lean and trimmed hairy chest. With each hand, I make invisible circles across his chest. His nipples look like a pair of pink dimes. My tongue then travels up and down his neck while his fingers softly rake my back.

The *Star Trek* theme song plays faintly in the background over the rolling credits. I momentarily detach myself from Craig to light a candle in the bedroom. As the candle flickers to life, I hear Craig removing his pants and socks behind me. When I turn around, a beautiful young man in black briefs stands before me, silhouetted against my closet door. A smile unfolds on my face as he slowly steps toward me and swiftly pulls off my red T-shirt and jeans. He knocks me down onto the plush bed.

We ravage each other on the bed, wrestling and swapping positions. Each time we turn over, I feel as lit on the inside as the candle on my nightstand. For the rest of the night, my thoughts stray away from my concerns about my parents, my stresses from school, and the Horta. Craig is my sole focus right now.

Under the sweet buzz of my drink, I make love to Craig by the light of a flickering, sputtering candle. The flow of our sweating bodies gently rattles my queen-size bed as if invisible hands are pushing against each side. After an hour of rolling around naked, we finally pass out in each other's arms. We ease into a sweet deep sleep as if we were robbed of rest for days.

I momentarily wake up whenever Craig's crew cut rubs up against my hairy chest. When that happens, my eyes dart around the bedroom and reorient themselves to the darkness and fading candlelight. I look down at Craig, so soundlessly asleep, and I wonder how I nabbed such a beautiful guy. I look over at my own shadow, hoping it can answer that question. I know my shadowy figure would tell me that I'm not a bad-looking guy. I know that I'm not unattractive, and sometimes I do receive some extra caramel on my Dunkin' Donuts iced coffee because the young Brazilian server thinks I'm cute. But I believe that I am average compared to all these younger Matt Damon and Ben Affleck clones in Boston. I pale in sexiness next to Nick. I'm just okay-looking, and I've always been okay with that.

But being here with Craig reminds of what has been missing in my life, or at least from my bed. I've been in a slump lately and don't remember the last time I shared my bed with another guy. Maybe six months ago? That's how bad it has been. I don't know why, but I find dating in general challenging, be it in Boston or Fort Lauderdale, and I always thought I'd find my future husband at least in Boston because I was the new professor on the block. I have never allowed my parents' divorce to make me too cynical about relationships because I still believe deep down they love each other. I'm not like Nick, who is happy being single and romping around the city with every young buck he meets. I want to settle down and come home to someone, share my life with him and feel that nurturing that most couples share.

As Craig sleeps in my arms, I reflect on how men are initially intrigued that I teach in Boston. They grow more interested once I tell them that I'm Cuban-American. They are surprised to learn that I chose to move here from Fort Lauderdale, and they find that reverse migration interesting. In those initial conversations with other guys, long, piercing stares are exchanged, which leads to kissing, some heavy petting, and, eventually, sex. I rarely hear back from the guys after the first or second hookup. I've wondered if I am bad in bed, but the guys always seem to enjoy themselves throughout the sex, so I don't think that's the case. I think—hope—Craig would agree with me on this.

Other times, the guys I've met on my nights out with Nick have been sloshed—a chronic problem I've noticed in Boston since moving here. If it's not one thing, it's another. It's hard out there for a gay man in his thirties, at least in the college capital of the world, where I am well past the median age, according to US Census figures.

I've dabbled in online dating sites, but they're more directed at hooking up, even though the guys there pretend they are looking for that special someone. When an online conversation starts with "Top or bottom?" or "Do you play water sports?", you know what you're in for. My litmus test when I meet a new fellow is to ask myself, *Could I ever bring him home to see my parents?* Usually, the answer is no, especially with the water-sports inquiries.

Still, it's refreshing to know that I met someone who wasn't in a bar or online or in a park after hours. I technically met Craig at school. As my head sinks back into my pillow, I hug him tighter and think of how this was the perfect ending to a long week. In the dimming candlelight, I pass out again to the soft, hypnotic rhythm of Craig's breathing.

# chapter **Thirteen**

I'M SITTING at a corner booth at the Barnes and Noble in Braintree, waiting for Nick. I haven't seen him that much since I returned from Miami and began spending more time with Craig. So I invited Nick to meet me here to have some coffee or tea so we can catch up. As I sit by the large glass windows, drivers circle the lot in their big SUVs and small German cars. I sip my warm green tea, and I notice a young guy with a brown crew cut walk into the bookstore. He reminds me of Craig, and my thoughts immediately return to the new memories I have shared with him.

The past two weekends, when I wasn't grading papers at the bookstore, Craig and I enjoyed some quality time and got to know each other better. There were the dinners in Quincy and Braintree so as not to let anyone from Jefferson see us outside the college campus. We always fought over who would pay.

"Craig, I got it," I said as I clenched the bill at Bertucci's restaurant the other night.

"No, I got it. I want to pay. You always pay," Craig fired back, his hands holding the other end of the bill.

"Seriously, this is my treat, Craig. You can buy me dessert."

"If you don't let go, I'll make a scene!" Craig said with a devilish look in his eyes, as we pulled back and forth on the bill in a tug-of-war. He wasn't going to give up this time, and the other customers were looking at us, so I caved in. It reminded me of my playful arguments with Papi at Don Shula's restaurant in Miami Lakes.

"Fine, you can pay this time. I wouldn't want you to make a scene or anything. It's not as if we're making one right now," I said.

Then Craig extended his right hand and squeezed mine. "You always pay for the wine and drinks. This dinner's on me," Craig said before leaning over the table and kissing me. He didn't care who was watching us. I like Craig's carefree spirit and how he doesn't concern himself with what others think—unless they are his viewers on *Jefferson Today*.

Besides fighting with me over the dining bills, Craig also sleeps over once or twice a week when schoolwork allows him to. When he does stay over, we wake up and share a two-mile run along Wollaston Beach. At night, we continue watching various classic *Star Trek* episodes and then engage in heavy discussions about them. But then we start kissing, which always leads to hot sex. Every time we mess around, we continue boldly going where our bodies haven't gone before. Craig thinks that joke of mine is pretty cheesy, but he laughs anyway because he likes me.

And whenever Craig leaves my apartment to catch the subway back to his dorm after a night together, I stand on the cement balcony where the cool, nippy air brushes against my face.

The other morning when Craig left my apartment, I observed him as he dashed across the street toward the Wollaston subway stop. Just as I was about look away, he waved back to me and blew me a long-distance kiss. I returned the wave and smiled before heading back inside to the warm heat, where I counted the days for his return.

Sitting here at the bookstore, I realize that the more time I spend with Craig, the more attached to him I become. Being with Craig has been like finding a rare treasure. You weren't necessarily looking for it, but now you're glad that you found it. You can't help but admire it, hold it, and appreciate it.

I try to recall how I spent my time before I met Craig. Those days look somewhat like today so far—sitting in a bookstore having coffee or tea and watching the world pass by from my window perch. I didn't realize how lonely I was on the weekends until Craig became a part of them. Pre-Craig on a Saturday or Sunday afternoon, I ordered takeout from the Cheesecake Factory in Braintree or I stopped at the nearby Wendy's for those tasty grilled chicken sandwiches or headed to Dunkin' Donuts for my iced caramel coffees. I browsed the shelves at the video store and usually rented a romantic comedy with Sandra Bullock and Julia Roberts, or I stayed home and watched my favorite *Star Trek* episodes even though I've seen each episode several times. Or I came here to the bookstore and rummaged through the entertainment and news magazines and graded papers.

I always had Nick to hang out with, but I usually saw him on Thursdays or Friday nights after a long week of teaching. Those empty Saturdays and Sundays remind me how alone I was until Craig. He's like a beautiful new hue adding color to my otherwise black-and-white palette.

On my commutes to the college or on my walks back to my condo from the subway stop, I have questioned what exactly my situation with Craig is and whether this invisible connection between us can survive our age difference. What am I getting into? Just as I'm getting to know to him better and appreciate the person he is and is growing into, I also feel like I'm running out of time. What happens when he graduates in May? Will I go back to my solo take-out dinners and watching Nick score at Boston bars while I stand on the sidelines?

I try and push these thoughts and doubts from my mind as I watch Nick bound into the bookstore. He quickly glances around the store until he spots me in the corner. I wave to him.

"Well, look who it is, my long-lost amigo!" Nick greets me with a strong hug and some slight sarcasm.

"And look at what the cold weather dragged in!" I say, returning the embrace. Nick unwraps his scarf and peels off his puffy green ski jacket, which he places on the back of his chair. He's wearing a tight black long-sleeved shirt that beautifully defines his lean body and biceps. His jeans are just as snug and outline his Portuguese-Irish bum. I offer him a drink, but he quickly turns me down.

"GG, I got this one. I think I can afford a low-fat hot chocolate. I'm not that broke!"

"I didn't say anything, Mr. Public School Teacher!" I say, cupping my hot tea.

A few minutes later, Nick returns with his drink in hand, and we settle into our seats and some good conversation. All around us, early holiday shoppers rummage through the tables of new books and holiday cards, while some other people sit in the plush sofa chairs and read the celebrity gossip magazines without paying for them.

"So what's the latest on your hunt for your students' hot fathers?" I say. My nose accordions at Nick.

"Nah, the one hot dad, the Tom Cruise look-alike, turned out to be really straight. I did my best, using my gifted charm and swagger, but he wouldn't agree to meet me off campus to, ahem, discuss his son's progress in class. Whenever I looked into his eyes, he'd immediately talk about his girlfriend, a publicist for a local department store. You win some, you lose some. But hey, I still think he's a closet case or has some BT, bisexual tendencies. He'll come around. You'll see. One day, we'll see him out on the dance floor at Estate."

Nick loves a challenge. After all, he teaches middle schoolers in Somerville, which has a growing Latino population because of all the Mexican and Central American families that have migrated there. Sometimes, I help Nick with his Spanish when he needs to talk to a student's parent. I don't envy Nick's job, because his students are hormone-driven and adapting to their ever-changing bodies, but Nick seems to have an endless well of patience and a knack for keeping them under control. I don't think I could have that kind of patience with the Disney tween set.

"Speaking of coming around, where's your young college boy? Word is that you guys are practically married in Quincy!" Nick blurts out.

I sip some more of my drink before answering. "We're just hanging out and getting to know each other, Nick. No big deal."

"No big deal? I can't remember the last time I saw you. Yeah, I'm sure you guys are *just hanging out* and letting things *just* hang out. College boy has you whipped, slore!" Nick mimics a whipping sound. "Let me guess, *Star Trek* date nights… nice romantic runs along the bay… a secret classroom rendezvous now and then at the college?" Nick chides.

"Something like that," I demur. "At school, we just say hi and keep it on the down low."

"So, Gabriel, does this mean you guys are official, exclusive, one on one?"

"I don't know. Like I said, we hang out and have fun. The other day, when I woke up, he had a caramel iced coffee and a warm bagel for me from Dunkin' Donuts. Craig can be really sweet. Right now, I'm just going with the flow."

"Yeah, I know what kind of flow that it is—the bump-and-grind kind." Nick starts grooving in his chair, making sexual noises.

I reach across the table and playfully smack him in the arm. "Shh. Keep your voice down. There are some kids here," I say, pointing to the three kids playing with the stuffed bears at a nearby table.

"Oh, like they don't know what bump and grind is. They hear worse things on the Disney Channel or MTV. Anyway, amigo, if this guy makes you happy, I'm all for it. Just remember, the dude is still in college. He's just beginning his life, and you're, well, almost in the middle of yours."

I narrow my eyes at Nick. "Yeah, how can I forget? When he talks about his classes or complains about his other professors, I know exactly who he's talking about. Awkward! Hearing his stories remind me of my own college days. I feel ancient, and he looks so much younger than me."

"You've got that whole father-and-son thing going on." Nick jokes. "I can't relate. I don't look that much older than your students, Gabriel."

I toss my napkin at Nick. "Don't hold back, Nick. Just let it all out. You should say what's on your mind, because you never do. You're a real ego booster, I tell you," I playfully scold him.

"Sorry, Gabriel. I'm just teasing you because you always set yourself up for it. You know I love you. If anything, I'm probably projecting. My hair dye used to last me five or six weeks. Now it lasts me less than a month."

"Yeah, those grays are really coming out." I pelt him with sarcasm. "Soon, people are going to call you Old Saint Nick! I'll still hang out with you, even though you're not far off from getting annual colonoscopies and prostate exams and appearing in those cholesterol commercials."

"Oh no you didn't, GG!"

"Oh yes, I did. You'll be starring in your own Dulcolax commercials really soon," I fire back.

"Well, at least I'm not on the wrong side of thirty, GG, which now stands for Geriatric Gabe! You're closer to forty than I am."

"And you're not that far behind me. You're right on my tail!" I wrinkle my nose again. We stick out our tongues and laugh at this silly, fun banter.

As we talk, two elderly men approach the café salesgirl, and one of them asks for two drinks before pointing to the golden cheesecake in the display case. The man ordering is about my height with short but mostly snow-white hair combed to the side. He wears a red plaid shirt, a black coat, and blue jeans. He stands slightly hunched with his hands in his pockets. His friend is taller, with mostly gray straight hair that is combed back. As they wait for their drinks, they talk and laugh about something. The taller guy puts his arm around the other one and messes his hair the way Nick often does to me. The shorter man then immediately pulls out a comb and brushes his hair to the side, a lot like my father does.

My mind briefly flashes to an image of Papi riding the bicycle and fighting Parkinson's. He swears he has been using the bicycle and that he's been feeling better since the doctor boosted his dosage. I won't know for sure until I fly back for the holidays. I look again at the old men and imagine Nick and me as their younger version.

"Nick, reality check! I'm only three years older than you. We're in the same demographic, like those older guys over there at the counter," I say, casually pointing in their direction.

"Yeah, but you get to experience things first. I'm still catching up to you, you old dog!"

"You are who your friends are! Woof, woof, Lassie!" I announce with a silly grin.

With that, we start throwing our napkins at each other and laughing like two middle-school friends. The real kids nearby look at us quizzically, probably wondering, *Who are these old dudes acting so immature in the corner of the store?* The older men walk toward us and settle into the table behind us and laugh at their own private conversation.

"Let's make a coffee toast. To old men: may we laugh and act like this when we're eighty years old with walkers," I say, holding up my drink.

"To dirty old men!" Nick toasts back.

"You know it, *slore*!"

# chapter Fourteen

*WHAT... is... this?*

I'm standing in front of my bedroom mirror, getting dressed for work on Monday morning, when I notice something white, no, something gray, on my chest. I step closer to the mirror and study my chest. Oh no! It has finally happened. A gray hair has sprung up on my chest. Correction—make that two gray hairs right in the middle of my chest.

I yank them out and hold them up to the light. Each strand is scraggly and curly and... ugh! I glance down at my chest again and scan for more grays. I don't see any others. Mission accomplished. Oh wait. I'm wrong again. There's a tiny strand near my right nipple. I imagine all my black chest hairs quickly morphing into a sea of gray. Will my chest look like the top of Anderson Cooper's head in a year or two? Will I have to resort to buying chest-hair dye?

I do have some grays above and around my ears, but my hair is predominantly dark-brown. I also keep it short so the salt isn't as obvious as the pepper. But gray chest hair is a whole other matter. I instantly flash to visions of hairy old men with their tropical shirts unbuttoned to their navel, revealing huge clumps of white hair on their torso. These are the same men who walk around a cruise ship with a drink in one hand and a cigar in another while ogling every guy or girl that flounces by.

I won't let my chest turn into a white carpet. If any more grays pop up, I may have to start trimming. I can understand why so many older gay men like Harrison Ford or Mark Harmon trim their chest or shave it. They are cloaking their gray hairs. I quickly check *down there* for any others. So far, the pubic coast is clear, but it's official. I am becoming a gray gay.

I slip into my corduroy pants, a white T-shirt, a light green cardigan, and my brown shoes. I fix my hair in the mirror and grab my black pea coat. I also take a chocolate and peanut butter protein bar from my kitchen cabinet before slinging my messenger bag over my shoulder as I head to work.

As I walk to the subway stop on this chilly morning, the protein bar in my mouth, my cell phone buzzes in my pocket. I smile when I see that it's a text message from Craig.

*Hey, cutie. I have a lot of schoolwork today. I'll come over this weekend. Miss you and thinking of you. XOXO. Craig. By the way, read today's paper. There's a front-page story that will be of interest to you.*

As I power walk to the subway stop with a pack of other harried commuters, I quickly text message Craig back.

*No worries. Have a great day, smiley. Can't wait to see you, and of course I'll read the paper. :-D*

Once inside the subway stop, I wave my commuter pass in front of the entry machine, and I pass through the turnstile. A Red Line subway car rumbles to a stop, and its doors open widely, swallowing me and the rest of the passengers. I grab a corner seat in the back, where I pick up a rumpled copy of today's *Daily* that someone discarded. I scan the front page, and my eyes land on an article by Tommy Perez. It's the Parkinson's story he briefly discussed in my class a few weeks ago. The headline reads, "Just The Right Moves: Dance aids those with Parkinson's."

I read the story, which details a class for people with Parkinson's here in Boston, actually Cambridge. The class is taught by a yoga and dance instructor named Adam Smith who incorporates movements from each of those disciplines to help people with Parkinson's improve their coordination and flexibility as the disease gradually robs them of both. The story's main photograph has Adam leading several elderly couples in a series of dance moves. The students are smiling, even laughing, and clearly enjoying themselves.

My eyes shift back to Adam, whose straight, dirty-blond hair spikes up like needles in a pincushion. In one close-up photograph, I can better see his eyes, which remind me of the color of the dark-blue waters off Provincetown. He has tight and perfectly curved biceps that I would give anything to squeeze. Adam is lean, and his tanned skin remains sun-kissed by the recent summer. He looks about my age too. He sports black sweatpants that define certain body parts a bit too much and a snug white T-shirt. His smile, like his students', is sincere. But for some reason, I'm just as drawn to his image as I am moved by his quotes.

One of them reads, *"You can still dance and have fun despite this disease. Dancing is one way of fighting back for these students. When they listen to the music and start to move, they forget, at least for a little while, that they have the disease. In this class, they are not patients. They are beautiful dancers."* I reread the quote, and it resonates with me. It must take a special person to have the patience to teach seniors and others with a chronic condition how to dance. I find that noble.

I read the rest of the article, which says that the class is the only one in Massachusetts. The article is heavy with meaning, comprehensive, and full of colorful details as well as many voices. The students are quoted as saying that the dancing helps ease their symptoms and gives them a sense of control over a disease that often renders them powerless over their own bodies.

Tommy Perez quotes a local neurologist's explanation of the benefits of music. He also includes a brief biography of another dance student named Howard Rudavsky, a former Boston hospital executive who is funding the class with his own money and does fundraising for Parkinson's research. The story also provides the backgrounds of two students, how long they've had Parkinson's, and their struggles with the disease. One of them is quoted as saying, *"My legs and arms now follow a choreography that I did not choose…. This class moves you to do better."*

The article also explains the social component of the class, which provides a recreational outlet for people with Parkinson's. I reread the story and jot down Adam's name and the location where the class takes place, the Jewish Family Center in Cambridge. I immediately think of Papi and wonder whether there is a similar class in Miami or Fort Lauderdale. A wave of optimism rushes over me. Maybe this class could help Papi stay physically fit but also socially active. It might help him meet other people his age who are experiencing similar symptoms.

I carefully tear the article out of the newspaper and tuck it into the front pouch of my messenger bag. As I zip up my bag, the subway's automated electronic voice announces that we're approaching Park Street, my stop. I get up from my seat and clench the metal support pole as the subway slowly comes to a stop.

My mind wanders to this special dance class and when the next session might be. I want to visit the class and see for myself what Tommy Perez wrote about.

An hour or so later, at Jefferson, I finish up in my beginning creative writing class. Some of my students are slumped in their chairs, still recovering from whatever they did last night in their dorm rooms. At Jefferson, almost every night after Wednesday is a party night.

"Okay, class, that's all for today. Remember that your short story is due by Monday morning. If you are not in class, then you have to make sure I get it beforehand. You know the drill—via e-mail or leave it in my mailbox. No excuses, people!" I tell the thirteen students in today's class as they collect their books, notebooks, and papers.

"And if I don't respond to your e-mail, assume that I never got it. ¿Comprende?" I say as they begin to amble out of the classroom. "See you early next week!"

"Bye, Professor Galan," says Gina, the class's red-headed poet.

"Have a good weekend, everyone, and I can't wait to read your work!"

As the students empty the room, some still holding the Starbucks cups they brought to class earlier, I, too, gather my papers. I yawn and stretch into a giant letter T as I extend my arms out side to side, standing on my toes as I then reach up toward the ceiling. I release a big groan. I wipe the white board clean and pick up after myself so that the room is ready for the next instructor. I have a two-hour break before my next class.

I grab my messenger bag and loop it across my torso. I stroll into the hallway, where a few students linger, chatting about weekend plans or upcoming holiday trips. I, too, am looking forward to the winter break. Three weeks off! I can sleep in and spend more time at the gym. And, of course, I can thaw out in Fort Lauderdale and let my mother spoil me with her cooking.

As I round the corner of the fifth floor, I notice a young man talking to another student. I pause and squint to focus. Though his back is to me, I would recognize that buzz cut anywhere. It's Craig. Just as I'm about to approach him, I notice that he and the other guy are leaning closer to one another as they talk. I step back and retreat to a nearby corner. I'm standing a few feet away from them—close enough to watch and hear them, but I remain out of their view. Perhaps it's my inner reporter that prods me to eavesdrop, but it's one of the best ways to glean information. Like an addictive force, curiosity overtakes me. I tune in.

"So, maybe we can hang out sometime?" the guy asks Craig, whose head flirtatiously tilts to the side. He stands with one leg crossed over the other, and Craig playfully twirls his tie with his index finger.

The student, who has straight black hair spiked up and gelled, blue eyes, and thin eyebrows, flirts right back. The guy also has endearing dimples that can probably hold a dime in each cheek. Tiny jabs of jealousy poke me. I don't like this feeling, but it hits me in small waves as I watch the scene.

"Sure. I have some projects I need to finish up, but I'll be around before the holiday break," Craig responds cheerily.

"Great! I know this great little restaurant in Cambridge by Central Square that serves great Chinese food. I want to pick your brain about the college newscast," Mr. Blue Eyes says to Craig. I imagine my eyes shooting invisible laser beams at the student and pulverizing him.

"Yeah, sure. We can talk about the newscast. You'd be a shoe-in for the team when we have auditions in the spring. It would be better if you had a mock reel to show the staff what you can do, but I can tell you all about that over dinner. "

"Deal! I can't wait," the guy says.

Craig then scribbles something on a small piece of paper and hands it over to the guy. "Or just add me on Facebook, Tony!"

They shake hands and hug. Tony—so that's his name—lets his hands fall to Craig's lower back before pulling away from the embrace. The guy then walks with Craig to the south-side elevators. Their laughter and chatter fills the hallway.

More jealousy burns in my gut, but it's now mixed with disappointment. I process the scene. They were just talking, right? How can I compete with that dapper younger guy with eyes the color of skies who also wants to be a TV reporter? This is exactly why I hesitated for so long to do anything with Craig. Dating a younger guy, especially a college student, can only lead to complications and those lingering bouts of doubt. The entire student body is my competition, and I'm the Socrates among the contestants. As these thoughts swirl inside me, I hear a familiar voice behind me.

"Gabriel, good morning! What are you doing standing here in the hallway? Are you lost?" teases Alisa, my Journalism Department head.

I turn around and try to think of something plausible to say. "Um, I… was… just, um, I dropped something. One of my contacts popped out, but I can't seem to find it. The floor is white, which isn't helping," I say, suddenly blinking repeatedly in my right eye to make the story sound more believable.

"Oh, let me help!" Alisa says, tucking her straight brown hair behind her ears. She places her purse on the floor and then bends down and looks around. I bend down too.

"I looked right here, but it's hard to see with just one contact in," I say, feeling embarrassed over this silly lie. I'm acting like one of my students trying to weasel out of an assignment. "Alisa, seriously. You don't have to look. I would have found it by now. Someone may have stepped on it. I have a pair of glasses back in my office. I can just wear those to get back home."

Alisa is now on all fours, looking within a five-foot radius of where we are. I cringe at the sight. "I don't see anything, Gabriel. Sorry," she says, rising back up and wiping her hands. "Well, I gotta get going. Mr. Contreras asked me to cover one of his classes because of jury duty. See you later this afternoon."

"Thanks, Alisa. Talk to you later," I say as I continue blinking with my right eye and waving good-bye to Alisa, whose heels echo down the hallway. When she walks, her hips sway from side to side as if she wants all the young men here to admire her bombshell physique. Alisa is one of the most attractive educational department heads I've ever encountered, and a lot of the male students have crushes on her.

As Alisa disappears from sight, I turn around and return to my own office, where I plan to make some phone calls to see when the next Parkinson's class will take place. I want to see the class in action. As I walk, I carry with me a mix of confusion and disappointment. I try to make sense of what I witnessed between Craig and Tony. Is he about to cheat on me? Perhaps it's time we define what our situation is.

# chapter **Fifteen**

I'M AT the front lobby of the Jewish Family Center, where Doris, the receptionist, greets me with a warm grin. "Welcome to the JFC, how can I help you?"

"Hi! I'm Gabriel. I had called about the dance class for Parkinson's. I wanted to check out the class and see if maybe it might be something for my father. I read about the class in an article in the *Daily*."

"Oh yes, I remember. We spoke on the phone. Just sign in right here, and I'll show you where the class is. It starts in a few minutes, so you're right on time," Doris says as she hands me a clipboard and pen.

I scribble my signature on the sign-in sheet.

Doris then directs me to the elevator. "The class is on the third floor. Ask for Adam Smith, the instructor. You can't miss him," she gushes. "Have fun, and hopefully, this will work out for you and your father."

"Thanks, Doris. I appreciate it." I wave good-bye as I walk toward the elevator.

Once I'm inside, the elevator gently lifts for a few seconds and then halts to a gentle stop.

When the elevator pings, I know that the dance adventure is about to begin.

Stepping out of the elevator, I walk into a bright conference room where tables have been pushed to the side to make way for a big carpeted dance floor. As I survey the room, I notice a blond blur coming into focus. Correction, it's a blond god. This must be Adam Smith.

"Hi there, and welcome to our class! I'm Adam Smith, and I'll be your instructor today," Adam greets me. I'm paralyzed, stunned by his beauty. He looks even better in person than in the photos and video from the article. His short, spiked-up hair seems blonder, his eyes more cerulean. A smattering of freckles dots his arms. I want to touch each freckle with my finger. Speechless, I flash a wide smile and extend my hand.

"Are you ready to get your groove on?" he teases. "You're a little younger than our typical student, but I'll take care of you. You're in good hands here," he says with a warm grin.

I finally regain the use of my vocal cords. "Oh... I'm not dancing, although I love to dance. I'm here for my father. He has Parkinson's, and I read about your program in the paper. I wanted to check out your class and see whether this might be something for my dad, although he hates to dance. I'm Gabriel, by the way." I realize that I'm babbling. Inner butterflies feel more like birds soaring in my stomach. *Why am I nervous?* Maybe because I'm transfixed by Adam's California surfer looks. Or it could also be that he's wearing black sweatpants that outline his sculpted figure and a snug blue T-shirt emblazoned with the image of a two smiling stick figures dancing together.

Adam's smile—dashing with pearly white teeth—radiates sincerity. Now that my nerves have calmed, I feel comfortable around him, yet I don't know why. But I digress. This is class is about Papi, not about me finding Mr. Right in tights.

"Nice to meet you, Gabriel. Are you sure you don't want to dance? I can probably convince Doris to be your temporary dance partner. I don't think she would mind busting some moves with you."

*Oh my God, is he flirting with me? I think he is.* I start to laugh. I also like the way he sounds younger than he is. "Thanks, but I just want to observe. I don't want to hurt anyone with my break dancing or crunking," I joke. "Just pretend that I'm not here. I'm a nice fly on the wall. I won't get in the way."

"Well, in that case, then, come with me and we'll get you a name tag and find you a place to settle in." As he talks, Adam places a comforting hand on my upper back and escorts me to the registration table as if we're old friends. He writes my name down on a sticker and gently places it on my upper chest. I feel an instant tingle. *Pat me again, por favor?* He then hands me some brochures about the class.

"We'll be forming a circle in the middle of the room for the class, but you can sit right over there," he says, pointing to a corner by the window. "You'll have a great view from there." Little does Adam realize that I have a great view of him from right where I stand.

"If you'd like, we can talk after class about the program and your father and see how far along his Parkinson's has progressed. But the best way to understand what I do with my students is to simply participate or, in your case, just watch."

"Thanks, Adam. I really appreciate you and the JFC for letting me being here."

"You're welcome, Gabriel!" he says with the warmth of sunlight.

I settle into my designated corner of the room and watch the doorway as the students trickle in. Some have walkers. Others have canes. One gentleman is in a wheelchair. Many students are accompanied by their loved ones.

As I watch everyone approach the registration table, I overhear one woman in her sixties talking to a younger clone of herself, most likely her daughter. They chat a few feet away from me.

"Do you think this will really help your father?" says the elder woman, who has a bush of strawberry-blonde-and-gray-streaked curly hair just like one of the infamous *Golden Girls* characters.

The daughter, with matching blonde hair, tilts her head and offers a closed grin. She looks at her mother with affection. "I hope so. It can't hurt. Studies have shown that music sparks coordinated movement. At least he'll feel better and he'll meet other people with Parkinson's. He'll see that he's not alone, and that we're not alone in dealing with this."

The elder woman cranes her neck to plant a kiss on her daughter's cheek and then loops her right arm in the crook of her daughter's arm. The mother taps her daughter's hand as they walk. "It's up to us to take care of your father. He always took care of us. Now it's your turn to help your pop," the woman says as the man they're talking about takes a seat in one of the chairs that forms a circle in the room. He is hunched over, and his left hand and leg shake. He reminds me of Papi.

As I take in the scene, beautiful Adam bends over the table to scrawl some other students' names on white rectangular stickers. He clearly enjoys what he does and takes the time to greet everyone with a big smile. He exudes a positive energy that I can feel from across the room.

I manage to peel my eyes off Adam for the moment and survey the room. The place features wall-to-wall windows overlooking a lush forest in Fresh Pond Park across the way. Tree tops have shed their rust-colored and golden-yellow leaves. I can see a pond flanked by a running trail where joggers and dog-walkers trek despite the frigid thirty-degree weather.

A few minutes later, people finish signing in and settle into the seats that form a giant circle. Some folks are hunched over but share in laughs with one another. Two seniors drool, and their caregivers quickly and lovingly wipe their faces with handkerchiefs. My heart aches at these scenes.

Dressed in sweatshirts and pants, the more active seniors stretch their arms to warm up as they wait for the class to begin. They all have different stages of Parkinson's.

Although I know Papi has had the disease since he was seventy, it never became a disruptive issue until this past year, or perhaps I never really noticed until recently. Papi never complained about his condition. Whenever I visited, he seemed strong, positive, and active. He exuded a strong front so I wouldn't worry.

When I saw the photos and online news video that showed elderly dancers doing their best to move to the beat, something awakened within me. The image gave me the feeling that this could help Papi somehow. Maybe the class would help him smile more. I've noticed that he doesn't smile as much as he used to. The article served as a personal wake-up call for me to do something—anything—to help Papi.

And so here I am, a voyeur who hopes that this class won't just help my father move a little faster and ease his symptoms but will also help us bond better as father and son, a relationship that has always been partially strained by what he did to my mother, and by his silent discomfort with my homosexuality. I hope this class might give me a little more time with Papi as the disease slowly takes him from me and the world.

"Welcome to the Dance Away Your Parkinson's class!" Adam announces as he stands in front of the twenty students in the half-moon of chairs. One woman in her late fifties sits near me and says a silent prayer with a rosary in her right hand.

Gorgeous Adam plays some soft music by Enya, and the class begins with some gentle stretching exercises. The students' caregivers fill the role of dance partners for the class, so they grab their dance partners' shaky hands to get started. They look at each other and exchange small smiles. The proverbial curtain is raised, and the students dance. I sit back and watch everyone follow their own beat to the foxtrot, jazz moves, the tango, the Macarena, and the Hokey Pokey.

An hour later, the class ends and the room bursts with chatter and laughter. The students who had walked in slowly at the beginning of the class now appear energized, reinvigorated, and animated. I like what I am seeing.

"So, what did you think, Gabriel?" Adam's voice suddenly jolts me from my concentration on the class.

From my seat, I look up and stare into his blue orbs. "Um, I'm impressed. Everyone looks like they have more energy. They seem... happier," I say, rising from my seat.

"Isn't it amazing? The music and social interaction is the best medicine for these students. That's why they keep coming back. You should bring your dad sometime."

"I'm definitely going to try and get him here, even if I have to drag him, but he has this whole Cuban macho-guy thing. I'm not so sure I can sell him on the dance class."

Adam playfully pats my shoulder. "Oh come on. I bet you can talk anyone into doing anything, Gabriel." *Was he just flirting with me again? That's twice in a row.* I know why this class is so popular: Adam.

"If it helps, I'd be happy to speak with your father," Adam offers. "At first, the class may be somewhat daunting for someone who has never danced in a group, but everyone is in this together. If someone falls or loses balance, we all step in. There is nothing for the student to be embarrassed about. It happens to all of us at some point," Adam says reassuringly.

I take in everything he says and nod as he speaks.

"Why don't you come back for the next class and dance with one of the students with Parkinson's? It may give you an idea of what to expect with your father. I'm sure we'd have a lot of volunteers who'd want to dance with you, Gabriel."

I'd rather do the tango with Adam, but his idea agrees with me. "Deal. I'll come back for the next class and actually dance!"

Adam's face lights up. "Your dad must be so proud," Adam says, putting his hand on my upper back as we follow the rest of the students toward the elevator.

"Why do you think that? You don't even know me," I say.

"Because of what you did today. You must love your father a lot."

"Yeah, I do. I don't see him as often as I'd like to because he's in Miami. I am hoping I can get him to visit and take the class."

The elevator is packed with the other seniors who are gabbing about the class and music. Their laughter is music to my ears.

"Well, you know where to find us. You and your father are always welcome," Adam says as we step into the next elevator, where we find ourselves alone. As we descend to the first floor, I glance down and grin. Shyness suddenly envelops me.

"What, are my pants too tight?" Adam says mischievously, adjusting the dangling string on his sweatpants. Flirtation número three.

"Umm, no. I just get giddy in elevators. My mom and I used to always laugh in elevators or doctor's offices." I look up and our eyes lock.

"Oh, you're one of those. A perpetual giggler, huh?" Adam says with a playful expression.

"Yeah, something like that," I answer, suddenly giggling. "I can't help it sometimes. I even do this in front of my class once in a while."

Adam looks at me with surprise. "Class? Do you teach dance too?" he teases.

"Nah, I teach journalism and writing at a college downtown."

Adam nods, a small smile forming in the corner of his mouth. "I figured you were a TV reporter or something. You could easily be on any of the news channels here."

Flirtation, flirtation, flirtation! I could listen to him all day. "Why, thank you, Adam. That is very sweet of you to say," I say. My cheeks suddenly warm.

With my ego boosted, we arrive at the ground floor, and we step out of the elevator. I extend my hand to shake Adam's, but he surprises me with a friendly small hug. "See you next week, Gabriel."

"Thanks for everything, Adam," I say, my gaze lingering.

"Oh, and one more thing," Adam says. "Save the last dance for me."

"Ha! I bet you say that to all your students!" I say as I walk toward the front entrance of the center. Adam waves good-bye before turning around and reentering the elevator to return to the dance area.

A few minutes later, I traipse back to my Nissan with an extra spring in my step. I also carry the brochures that Adam gave me earlier. The whole way, I positively float on the excitement of meeting Adam and seeing the class up close. As I hop into my car, my thoughts remain on Adam and the effect he had on me in such a short time. I felt good around him but also inspired—a feeling similar to the one I had when Craig and I began hanging out. I'm looking forward to returning to the class and getting a better sense of the class—and Adam. I wonder if this is how Craig felt when he talked to Tony in the hallway the other day.

# chapter Sixteen

"HE WAS that hot? How big was his sausage?" Nick says as I spot him on the bench for a set of curls. Nick is sitting down, and I'm standing right next to him in this basement-level gym on the Cambridge/Somerville border, not far from where he teaches middle school.

"*Shhh.* Keep your voice down. We don't have to announce to the world that we're horny gay dudes!"

"Sorry, *Gay-briel*," Nicks declares louder so that the nearby pack of brawny Italian guys at the upper-body machine can hear us.

"So, how big was this dancing queen?"

"I saw an outline of it, so I'm not completely sure, but—"

"Oh just say it, Gabriel! The dude was hung. Stop dancing around it, so to speak," Nick interrupts me. He lifts the thirty-five-pound dumbbell and gently lowers it. His bicep tightens into a ball with a bulging vein in the middle. He performs five more reps before stepping aside for my turn.

"Yes, he was *huge*! There, you got me," I say, picking up the twenty-pound dumbbell to begin my set of reps.

"I knew it. Now the bigger question is, is he bigger than Craig? Remember him? Your student, er, I mean former student but current student at your place of employment nonetheless."

"Thanks for reminding me of whom I'm dating or spending time with or whatever. What would I do without you, Nick?" I sigh and place my free hand over my chest.

"See, GG, without me, you'd be completely clueless. At least with me, you are just semi-clueless."

I hold up the dumbbell to Nick's face and widen my eyes. "You know, I think it's the other way around. I could just drop this right now if I really wanted to, since I'm so, you know, clueless."

Nick tilts his head to the right and offers his most charming sexy smile. "But you wouldn't because I'm your best friend and you love me," Nick says, now leaning his head on my upper right shoulder like a little kid. He's endearing. I don't think I've ever been mad at my friend. He always seems to know what to do to defuse a situation.

"You always know what to say when your life is threatened," I joke.

"Whatever you say, *slore*!" Nick fires back.

We each perform three sets of reps before moving on to the military press machine. As we continue chatting, the chorus of weights clank in the background. Overhead, small speakers blare the latest dance music. The gym is packed, mostly with students from nearby Harvard and Tufts universities, and their muscular young figures are reflected on the wall-to-wall mirrors that adorn this place. These guys are easy to spot because they wear T-shirts with their school logos. That's why Nick prefers to come here: fresh young faces—mostly straight, though—that you wouldn't see out and about in a bar.

Nick is up first at the military press machine. The fluorescent lights glisten against his naturally tanned Portuguese skin. His tight-fitting black tank top sports some sweat spots below his nipples.

"So have you spoken to the future Brian Williams lately?" Nick says, squaring his back, pulling the bar down to his chest and then releasing it. On the ride here, I told Nick what I had overheard between Craig and Tony in the hallway at Jefferson.

"We exchanged some texts today and yesterday. I should see him tonight, and I'll ask him then about his *new friend*."

After Nick finishes his set, I swap in to work out. I adjust the weight from a hundred pounds to eighty. I'm not as strong as my good friend here, who is scanning the entire gym like the beacon of a Cape Cod lighthouse.

"You don't have the whole story yet with Craig. This is exactly why I like being single. No drama! You don't have one guy saying he's doing one thing while making plans with another. And this is exactly why I don't get too serious with young dudes. They are so fickle."

"Um, like you, Nick?" I zing him.

"Exactly, old buddy. Look, all I'm saying is don't get too serious or attached to Mr. Wannabe Anchorman. But now this dance instructor, hmmm. That's another story. Tell me why you didn't just grab him right there in class and make out with him?"

I complete my set and Nick slides in again. "Because I was there as an observer for my dad, not to hook up."

"Yeah, I could tell that you *observed* a lot. I want to see what this guy Adam looks like. Can I come with you the next time you visit his class? I'll be your dance partner—or Adam's," Nick says, pulling the bar down.

"Actually, that might be a good idea, but hands off Adam. I saw him first."

"Hey, but you're already seeing someone else, so Adam is up for grabs."

I narrow my eyes at Nick. "He's in his mid-thirties, Nick. Oh, did I forget to mention that?"

Nick smirks. "Fine, he's all yours. Besides, I like younger guys, not dudes older than me. That's your department, Professor!"

For that, I playfully punch Nick in the arm. Then he suddenly grabs me into a headlock and starts shouting, "Who's your daddy! Who's the man!"

The group of Italian guys just stares at us as if we're new oceanic life forms that just washed up on shore.

"Oh you are, master. You are, master!" I tease. Nick and I start laughing as we head to the locker room to change. The entire way there, the inescapable stench of sweat and gym shoes follows us like a smelly shadow.

"Seriously, buddy, it sounds like you have a lot of things to figure out, especially with Craig. This could be the beginning of a never-ending series of complications. And since you're not officially dating Craig, I'd take this opportunity with the dance classes to get to know Adam better. He sounds like quite a catch. I bet your dad might even like him if he were to take the classes. This dude sounds like he enjoys helping people with Parkinson's, and that says a lot about his character," Nick says as we step inside the locker room. Inside, the place is filled with a dozen shirtless guys, who are mostly lean, sculpted men in their early twenties. They hunch over as they change in and out of their shorts and sweatpants. Some douse themselves with their sport body sprays, which thankfully temporarily cloak the sweaty stench.

As we open our red lockers, I consider Nick's advice, which is reasonable and well-intentioned, as always. My mind immediately wanders back to the class and how Adam assisted his students. I remember how much care and time he took to make sure the participants enjoyed themselves, and yet he made sure that they didn't overextend themselves, either. His eyes were filled with tenderness, and that moved me.

As I slip on my blue jeans, something vibrates in my right pocket. It's my cell phone. I pull it out and notice a text message from Craig.

*"Are you around tonight, cutie? I want to see you. Miss you."*

I turn to Nick, who is putting on his red sweatshirt. I hold up my phone to show how him the text message.

He grins. "Tonight's forecast calls for some drama with a little sex, but that can change. More to come at eleven," Nick says, mocking a news anchor.

"Thanks, weathergirl!" I whip Nick gently with the end of my towel.

"Just for that, you get another headlock. Who's your daddy! Who's the man?" Nick blurts out loud as he grabs my neck and tousles my hair. All around us, the other gym rats stare quizzically. Some laugh at the sight of two old friends horsing around, while others probably wonder if we're rowdy gay lovers.

ON THE drive back to Quincy, I dial Papi. When he answers the phone, his Spanish-TV newscast blares in the background as usual.

"Hola, Gabriel! You're calling earlier than usual. Are you okay?"

"Yeah, Dad. I'm just leaving the gym and heading home. I have plans tonight, so that's why I'm calling earlier. How are you doing? How's the Parkinson's today?" I ask. As I drive along Memorial Drive, I notice Cambridge's low-rise canyon of brick buildings on my left across the Charles River and the string of Boston University buildings ahead on my right.

"I'm fine. Don't worry about me."

When Papi says "don't worry about me," it usually means the opposite.

"Papi...."

"Gabriel...," he responds, mimicking me.

"Did something happen that I should know about?

"Nada, chico. How are your classes?" he says, trying to change the subject. I lower my radio's volume to better hear what he has to say.

"Papi…."

"You're not going to give up on this, are you, Gabrielito?"

"I'm just as stubborn as you are. We can do this all night. What happened?"

Papi takes a deep breath before he begins to explain. "I was driving to one of the apartment buildings that I exterminate here in Miami Lakes. At the traffic light, I tried to accelerate, but my right foot wouldn't move."

"Has that happened before, Papi? Are you okay?" I ask with alarm.

"Every now and then that happens when I drive or walk. My legs freeze. I can't move, but it only lasts for a few seconds."

I suddenly imagine Papi sitting stuck at a traffic light in his Chevy Impala while all these drivers behind him honk obnoxiously. I see him alone and scared, trying to retain control of his legs. My heart aches at the imagined sight. But I also feel a rush of anger at myself for not being down there.

"But I was able to move and drive home. It's okay now. You don't have to worry, son."

In my research on Parkinson's, I read that some patients shuffle as they walk, taking short steps, while others find themselves temporarily frozen and unable to move, as if they're suspended in animation. "Papi, I don't think you should be driving if these episodes keep happening. Why didn't you mention this before?" I say, descending into the tunnel traffic under downtown Boston toward Interstate 93 south.

"I didn't want to worry you. It has happened to me when I exterminate or when I go shopping for food."

Again, my mind flashes to images of Papi being alone and helpless. *Why is this happening to him? Why did God pick my father to inflict his cruel disease upon? Why does anyone have this vicious disease, anyway? It slowly robs the patient of any independence and strength.*

"I am going to call Dr. Steinberg and let him know what you just told me. This is serious, Papi. What if you were trying to slow down in traffic and couldn't move your foot? You could have seriously hurt someone."

"I know, Gabriel. I know," he says in a defeated voice.

"Papi, we'll figure this out, okay?" I say reassuringly. "In the meantime, I would rather you not drive, but if you have to, keep your hand on the emergency brake in case your foot locks up again. Or ask Aunt Cary to drive you around if she can."

"I only drive on my good days. Today was a complete surprise," he confesses. The words replay in my mind—*my good days.* What else hasn't my father been telling me? This reminds me of those sitcom episodes when a child only reveals information to his parents when cornered or put on the spot. The more I press with Papi, the more he opens up. I thought I had gleaned everything I needed to know on my last visit. But with this latest episode, I realize I am going to have to press Papi more from now on. I have to be the reporter that I used to be and ask all sorts of direct questions that he will have to answer one way or another. And maybe it's time I push him more on the possibility of retiring.

As I pull off my exit to Dorchester/Quincy, I tell Papi, "I'm almost home. I'll make some phone calls and talk to you tomorrow, okay?"

"I'm fine, Gabrielito. Now go have fun tonight with your friends."

With that, I hang up.

On the short drive to Wollaston Beach, my mind is fixed on Papi. I grow frustrated as I realize this disease continues its forward march to erode my father's body. The boosted medicine dosage seemed to help a little at first, but now we have another set of problems with Papi's legs freezing up.

As I pull into my parking lot, I notice that Craig's little Mazda is parked outside. I spot him standing by the front entrance of the building. He smiles at me as he leans against the wall. One of his legs is casually crossed over the other. He looks like an Abercrombie model posing for a picture. As I walk toward him, I realize that I would rather be home alone than deal with whatever Craig has to tell me or hide from me.

# chapter Seventeen

UPSTAIRS in my condo, Craig plops himself on my sofa and props his feet on my coffee table. I'm in the kitchen dropping off my gym stuff. I empty my keys, wallet, and loose change into a basket that I use for such things. I offer Craig something to drink, and he asks for wine, but not before he playfully shoots me with my *Star Trek* toy phaser, which sits next to my TV remote control.

"Resistance is futile, Gabriel!" Craig announces from the living room.

I fake being shot to the heart.

"Captain… you… got… me!" I cough, pretending to drop to the floor. "Seriously, though, put the phaser back on stun and I'll get you some wine. I want to talk to you about something."

"Uh-oh. That sounds important, serious," Craig says as he places the toy phaser in its place and returns to his spot on the sofa.

I make myself a vodka with Red Bull and top off his wine glass and then join him in the living room. As soon as I sit next to him, Craig rubs his hand through my hair and kisses my cheek.

I close my eyes and enjoy his physical touch. "What is that for?" I tease, handing him his glass of wine.

"For being you. I haven't been around as much lately because of school and the morning newscast, but I have been thinking of you."

"Oh yeah? Sounds like you've had a lot on your plate, Craig," I say, with a hint of disbelief.

He catches my tone and studies me with a perplexed look. "Yeah, I've been busy, but I'm here now, with you, the hottest professor in Boston. No, correction, make that the Commonwealth." He gently strokes my inner thigh and smiles.

I place my hand on top of his and squeeze it. "So, anything new? Did you go out with classmates or anything this week?" Craig's touch tingles, running through me like liquid heat. I try to stay focused.

Again, he looks at me quizzically. "Um, not really. I've been doing a lot of schoolwork now that the end of the semester is nearing."

I pull away. "Craig, either you hung out with people or you didn't. It's a simple question," I say, looking away.

He takes a sip of his drink and looks at me with surprise. "Where is this coming from? What's with all the questions? Are you suddenly a reporter again?"

"I guess reporters don't like to be pressed for answers when all they do is fire away. I just want to be clear on something. You didn't have dinner or plans with someone this week?"

Craig begins to stutter. "Um, I, um," he says before taking another sip.

I have my answer already. I finish my drink and realize I could be making phone calls on behalf of my dad or doing more research on Parkinson's or reading one of my romance novels instead of playing these little games.

Craig finally answers the question. "Well, there's this freshman who wants to be a correspondent for the school newscast. He asked me for advice, and we grabbed a bite to eat in Cambridge. I was just being helpful. I remember what it was like trying to break into the tight clique of student reporters here, so I was trying to help him out."

"Over dinner? You couldn't talk about this in school? Was he cute? Is he gay?"

Craig leans over and rakes his hands through my hair again. "He has nothing on you. Besides, you have my heart. He's just a kid. He looks up to me because he sees me on the morning newscast every day. No big whoop."

"See, this is what I don't want to deal with—secrets! You couldn't have told me this earlier? I had to press it out of you."

"Because it wasn't a big deal. I almost forgot about it."

"You have dinner with a cute gay guy from school at a restaurant in Cambridge to talk about journalism. Sounds like a date to me, Craig."

"It wasn't," he fires back. "And he's not *that* cute."

"I think it was a date. This is why I was stupid to get involved with a younger guy. I can't compete with guys who are practically half my age," I ramble on.

"You don't have to compete. They have to compete with you, Gabriel," Craig says with a small smile. He squeezes my right hand to reassure me. "You are mature, smart, successful, and sexy as hell. Who wouldn't want that, Gabriel? Besides, you give great blow jobs!"

I laugh a little. The last comment caught me off guard. I do think I'm pretty good at doing that. "Why thanks, I think. Maybe you can write me a recommendation on my oral presentation. But seriously, I can't stand secrets, especially with what happened with my parents years ago. Listen, if you want to date other guys, just say the word and we'll stop doing whatever it is that we're doing. This is the time in your life when you should be having fun and going out. I don't want to hold you back your senior year of college, and I don't want to look like an old fool for being with a younger guy."

Craig kisses my cheek and cups my chin with his right hand. I melt in his touch. "You're not holding me back. You're helping me grow as a person and move forward. That's why I care about you so much. I feel like a better person when I'm around you." He leans in and softly kisses my lips. Our tongues intertwine and perform their own private dance.

I pull away to continue explaining how I feel. "I need you to be open and upfront with me. I know what I'm getting myself into. The day you want to explore and be with someone closer to your age, just say the word. I can handle it."

"Deal, but I don't think that is going to happen anytime soon," Craig says as he climbs on top of me to straddle me. He plays with my hair again.

He leans back a little when he notices the brochure for the dance class for Parkinson's sitting on the top of the end table. He reaches over to pick up the brochure and starts leafing through it. He notices my notes on the brochure. "Hey, did you go to the class?" he asks. "Is this the one that Tommy Perez wrote about in the *Boston Daily*?"

"Yeah, I went two days ago. I forgot to tell you with everything going on. It's a great class, something I want to get my father involved in, if there's a similar class in Miami. I had a lot of fun watching. I'm planning on going back and actually dancing next time."

"Hmmm. I can see why you enjoyed the class so much. Was this hot blond instructor there?" Craig says, holding up the page of the brochure with Adam's smiling photo. Adam's buff arms are folded across his chest.

"Oh, that's just Adam Smith, the instructor," I say nonchalantly. "Adam let me sit in on the class and then later explained the benefits the class has for people with Parkinson's. He's a really nice guy."

Craig raises his right eyebrow, tilts his head to the right, and stares at me. "And is he gay?"

"Yeah, I think so. I didn't ask. I was there for the class, not the guy's ass, but he teaches a dance class, so the odds are low that he's straight," I joke.

"So he has a nice ass, then? Well, it looks like you definitely liked what you saw, Gabriel. You scribbled Adam's name three times on the brochure."

"Huh? Really? No, I didn't." I grab the brochure to see for myself.

Craig is right. I did write Adam's name three times in different areas of the brochure.

"Oops. I must have been taking notes, Craig," I say, letting out a nervous laugh.

Craig takes hold of the brochure again and folds it up. "Now is there something that you're not telling me, Professor Galan? Do you like this guy?" Craig looks crestfallen. He reaches over to the end table again and takes another mouthful of his wine.

"Okay, Adam is obviously attractive. I'm not blind. But I was there for my dad, and I can't help it if the instructor is nice and handsome and friendly."

"Well, that deal we just agreed to, about not having any secrets, it applies to you too, Gabriel. And if you decide you don't want to date someone younger and would rather be with an older dude, then just say the word. This guy Adam looks more or less your age, and he's obviously your type based on the, ahem, notes you took."

I pull Craig closer to me and wrap my arms around his thin, tight back. "I am interested in you. You're in my heart, Craig. ¿Comprende?"

He leans in for another kiss. "You're in mine too," he says, tossing the brochure into the corner of the living room so that Adam's smiling face isn't visible anymore. "I'm going to miss you during Thanksgiving break. I wish I could bring you home with me. Are you going to visit your family, Gabriel?"

"I'm staying in Boston. I'm trying to save money for my trip for Christmas."

"So you're going to be alone for Thanksgiving?" Craig says, massaging my head.

"Not really. Nick invited me to his parents' house in Providence, so I'll be down there. I haven't been a big fan of Thanksgiving since my parents split. The holiday lost its meaning, in my eyes. I look forward to Christmas. What I do is spend Christmas Eve with my mom and then Christmas Day with Papi."

"Well, I leave right after class on Tuesday, so at least we'll have this weekend to hang out."

"Of course, I'm all yours 'til then," I say, staring into those big Disney-deer brown eyes.

As Craig straddles me, we kiss long and deeply. I dim the light on the lamp that sits on the end table. We spend the rest of the evening switching positions on the sofa until we're finally naked and performing our own sexual dance. Every now and then, my eyes glance to the corner of the living room and they catch Adam's smiling photo poking from the brochure. Despite the incredible sexual chemistry I have with Craig, my mind temporarily flashes to Adam and the way he danced with the students. I try to will him out of my thoughts, but he appears when I close my eyes. I focus on Craig and his sinewy arms and soothing eyes and savor him the rest of the night until we collapse into a deep, peaceful sleep.

# chapter Eighteen

"EVERYONE, pass your stories forward. I can't wait to read them," I announce as I begin to collect their news stories. Students shuffle their papers and chat about their holiday plans. Some of them talk about catching trains to New York and New Jersey, while others discuss their trips to Connecticut or Rhode Island. Like a deflating balloon, Boston empties out during Thanksgiving week. A mass exodus takes place, leaving the city with vacant parking spaces and less traffic on Interstate 93. I wish I could be on a plane going somewhere, but I need to save my cash for Christmas break.

"So when you guys come back, I'll have your papers graded, and we'll discuss some of your common grammar and style mistakes. And with that, class is over. Your break begins now," I say, counting the papers in hand. On days when assignments are due, class attendance is full, at least in my journalism classes. I have a strict no-late-work policy, and the students know that. "I hope you guys have a great Thanksgiving. Don't party too hard, capisce?"

My students gather their things and funnel out of the class.

"Bye, Professor!" says Alex, Mr. Anchorman, as he applies some lip balm.

"See you next week," says Jenny, a red-haired student with thick black-framed glasses.

I'm leaning over the podium and waving as everyone leaves when Angie approaches me. She slowly walks up to me and tucks her straight, dark-brown strands behind her ears. She clenches her notebook against her chest. "Um… Professor Galan…," she says meekly.

"Yes, that's me. What's up, Angie?"

"Um, like, I really want to ask you something?"

I gesture with my right hand for her to spit it out. "That's what I'm here for, Angie. What can I do for you?"

"Well, there's this opening for a resident advisor on campus and, like, I wanted to ask you for a recommendation, because I love your class and look forward to it even though it's at 8 a.m. and I have a hard time getting up so early." She shyly smiles, looks away, and continues tucking her hair behind her ears. "You're the first professor I wanted to ask. So will you write one for me?"

I'm flattered that she asked, but sometimes I don't know why my students or former students really want me to write a recommendation. Do they really like me as their instructor? Or is it because I usually say yes, if I like the student? I like to help out whenever I can, even though it brings me extra work. I've written three recommendations in the past few weeks. It's become a job in itself. Nick was right, I am a slore, after all. "Sure, Angie. Just send me an e-mail explaining why you want this job with the recommendation form and I'll put something together for you."

"Really? Oh my God!" she squeaks, bouncing up and down with excitement. "Thank you so much, Professor. I really appreciate it. I need the money from this job to help pay my tuition," she adds, playing with her hair. Angie is one of my better journalism students and one of my few Latina students. A native of Dallas, she attends Jefferson on a partial scholarship, so I am glad to help her pay for school.

"Are you heading off to Texas for Thanksgiving?" I ask as I neatly slip the assignments into my messenger bag.

"I can't. The flight is too expensive, so I am staying with a friend in Cambridge. How about you, Professor Galan?"

"I'm in the same boat. I'm staying in town, but at least I'll be in South Florida for Christmas."

"Well that's great, Professor. You can come back with a tan. You're kinda pale for a Latino. Anyway, thanks again."

I smile and wave.

WITH an hour break between classes, I saunter to my tiny, dimly lit windowless office and call Papi's doctor. As I leave a message with his assistant, I boot up my computer, which is topped with framed photos of me with Mom, Dad, and my Aunt Cary. To the left of the monitor is a funny photo of Nick carrying me in his arms during our summer road trip to Provincetown. I remember I couldn't sleep at all that weekend because Nick kept sneaking guys in and out of our hotel room and their sexual moans kept me up, but that's another story.

My office is small, so there's not much decorating to be done. It's a picture of organized clutter. A small bulletin board bedecks the back wall and features some notes and letters from previous students. In the corner, a small bookshelf brims with several journalism and writing textbooks. At the edge of my desk is a bumper sticker that reads "Don't Mess With Writers!" Years ago, one of my former students in Fort Lauderdale gave that to me as a gift. My pencil holder is a repurposed Dunkin' Donuts mug.

There's only enough room in this office for a desk, a chair for myself, and a chair for a visitor, usually a student looking to discuss a paper. In a nutshell, my office is akin to a retooled closet. Small college means small office. That's why I prefer to grade papers at home or in the expansive school library downstairs.

As soon as my computer cranks up, I start researching Parkinson's symptoms and frozen movements. I study the articles, and again, I'm surprised how aggressive this disease can be. Just when I believe things have settled down with the disease, another symptom or complication emerges for Papi. It's as if the disease knows how to outsmart the medicines. The condition has its own trajectory, a mission that it won't abandon until completed, leaving in its wake a small population of people who can no longer care for themselves. *I hate you, Parkinson's.*

I square my shoulders and exhale in frustration. I continue reading additional articles on patients whose muscle movements freeze or are slow to respond, as if they suddenly stepped in puddles of crazy glue. The articles echo the same thing: this symptom is one of the difficult and most distressing struggles of people with Parkinson's. About one out of every three Parkinsonians has issues with freezing or a sudden loss of mobility. It can happen when the person is about to say something, when they store laundry, or when they attempt to climb out of bed. Researchers suspect that freezing occurs when something in the brain interferes with the person's normal flow of movement, but they don't know why that is. The article goes on to state that patients become extremely agitated and frustrated when these episodes happen. As a result, they tend to become depressed, isolate themselves, or avoid crowded social settings in fear of a public episode. Again, my mind flashes to Papi stranded somewhere alone, unable to move, as if his feet are trapped in blocks of cement.

As the computer bathes me in its luminous blue glow and lights up the rest of the office—again, it doesn't take that much lighting to do the trick—I place my right hand under my chin and use the mouse to scroll down the article with my left hand. Just when I decide to give up the search as fruitless, I stumble across a list of helpful tips that other Parkinson's patients have shared with their doctors. Maybe these can help Papi.

I stare at the photo of us, which was taken outside the college when he helped me move to Boston a few years ago. We stand with our arms around each other's shoulders by the entrance of Jefferson on Tremont Street. In that photo, he looks stronger and healthier, with his head up high, posture confident. He also looks at least seven pounds heavier. The disease has slowly ravaged him, and for some time, I have been oblivious to the emotional toll this has exacted on him. My father has never been one to express his emotions, the way Mom does. She wears her heart on her sleeve (preferably a peach or pink color), while Papi has Teflon emotional armor.

When I visit for the holidays, I am going to sit down with Papi and ask him how he *feels* about the disease. I want to hear his frustrations, his fears, and what pulses through his mind. Does he feel less independent knowing that he sometimes struggles with buttoning a shirt or holding a glass without spilling it? Perhaps this might be as awkward for him to share as it is for him to ask about my *personal* life? I would feel somewhat uncomfortable revealing to Papi the details of my trysts, my drinking adventures with Nick, and most of all, my tangled feelings for Craig. It's hard enough for my father to wrestle with my being gay. I don't know how he would react knowing that I am dating or semi-dating a student at the college.

My focus shifts back to the web site on my monitor, and I continue digesting some of the story's tips. One of them involves marching like a soldier. The article explains that when patients find themselves locked in a frozen stance, they need to imagine themselves marching in the military or to music. The mental image can help trigger movement. Sound also helps. Some people can unfreeze themselves by thinking or speaking out loud in a rhythm, such as shouting, "One! Two! Three! Four!" or, "On my mark, get set, go!" I never thought about that. I can imagine Papi yelling on the street or at the supermarket, "*Uno, dos, tres, cuatro!*" and scaring nearby customers.

Other tips from the article include adding floor strips in areas where a Parkinson's patient often finds himself freezing. People can unfreeze themselves by aiming their next step at a particular spot on the floor, as if they imagine there's a fly on the ground and they want to squash it. *Take that, mosquito!* The research says that it gives the patient a target, a command for the patient to keep moving. With Papi's line of work as an exterminator, this could be helpful in getting rid of roaches.

I print out the tips so I can share them with Papi later tonight. As the printer spits out the research, I notice the brochure on the dance class poking out of my messenger bag. I pull it out and notice how I scribbled Adam's name in the top corner, then down below and again on the back. I'm like a schoolgirl with a crush on her teacher. I look at the schedule of classes and realize there's another class coming up right after Thanksgiving. I note the date in my organizer.

My hope is that I can get a better sense of the class by actually participating and then ask Adam about the freezing symptoms. A small smile forms at the corner of my mouth as I picture Adam working with the students. I can see him coaching Papi on how to stay fit and active.

As I prepare to head to my next class, which is a creative writing one, there is a quiet knock on my door.

"Come in!" I log off my computer and click on "Shut Down." Looking up, I notice Craig poking his head through the door.

"Professor, I have a complaint about my grade, and I want something done, *now!*" he teases.

"Oh yeah? We'll have to see about that."

He turns the lock on the door and drops his bag on the floor. He twirls me around in my chair and then straddles me. "I'm going to miss you. I won't see you for a week," he says, frowning. I softly rub the back of my right hand against his cheek.

"It'll fly by. Before you know it, you'll be back in Boston, Craig. It's only a few days."

"I know. I know. I just thought it would be fun if we could spend Thanksgiving together and you can meet my mom and sister and all my cousins."

I imagine the look on his mom's face if he were to bring me home. How would he introduce me? *Hi, Mom, this is my former professor at Jefferson and my current lover. Oh, and he's thirteen years older than me, but he looks great for his age. Cool, huh?*

"That's very sweet, Craig, but you should enjoy this time with your family. You never get to see them. Besides, I'll be here grading some assignments and hanging out with Nick."

Craig smirks. "Yeah, that's why I'm worried. Don't you refer to your friend as 'Nick the dick' because he likes it so much?"

I look away, stifling my laugh. "He is boy-crazy, but I'm not. I'm just crazy about a certain boy, and his name is Daniel," I joke.

"Daniel? You better be kidding," Craig fires back. He cups my face in his hands and smushes my cheeks. He pulls me closer to his chest, and I rub my hands against his firm back. "Correction, I mean Craig, who will break hearts all over the country when he becomes the next network evening news anchor."

"That's what I like to hear! I'm leaving for the airport after my last class, so I wanted to see you before I took off."

We kiss some more, and my body grows aroused. I could have this guy right here, right now. I begin to lose myself in Craig's long, wet kisses when a knock on my office door interrupts us. Our eyes widening like saucers, Craig and I suddenly stop and stare at each other in panic.

"Professor, it's Angie. Are you in there? I thought I saw you walk in earlier," she says from the other side of the door. I glance at the bottom of the small rectangular window by the door and see Angie's brown boot tapping against the carpet. Before the semester, I had covered the top half of the window with wallpaper for privacy, but I never considered filling the bottom half, because who would really peek into the office for a cat's eye perspective except for my mother's cat, Clara?

Craig immediately leaps off me, straightens his shirt, and grabs his bag.

I silently motion for Craig to open the door as I wipe my mouth and groom my hair by running my hands through it.

"So, Professor, thanks for the advice on the internship," Craig says as he opens the office door and walks out. "And Happy Thanksgiving!" He passes Angie standing in the doorway.

She offers him a small smile.

"Thanks, Craig. You too! Don't eat too much turkey!" I casually wave.

Angie looks at Craig and then at me as if she knows that she just interrupted something. Well, she did, so I can't blame her for the probing, suspicious eyes. I glance down at my desk and notice that all my papers are brushed to one side and some of the framed photographs have toppled over. This mess must have happened after Craig and I became frisky.

"I didn't mean to interrupt your time with another student." She sits down, crosses one leg over another, and pulls out some forms from her notebook.

I lean forward from my chair. "Not at all. I did him, ah, I mean, I was done with him," I stutter, trying unsuccessfully to regain my composure.

Angie laughs at the bumbling. She then gladly hands me the recommendation forms for the resident-advisor job. "I thought it would be easier if I printed them out and gave them to you right away. So here you go," she says, tucking her hair behind her ears.

"Thanks, Angie. I'll get these back to you after the break."

"Fantastic!" she says, her eyes now focusing on the dance-class brochure sitting at the corner of the desk with the rest of my shuffled paperwork. She picks up the brochure and studies it. "What is this for? Are you looking to take dance classes? I think that's so cool, a professor who can dance," she says, leafing through the brochure.

"Why thank you, Angie. I'm sure I'm not the only instructor who can bust a move or, perhaps, crunk here and there. But the class isn't for me. It's for my dad." I point to the photograph of Papi on the corner of my desk.

"Professor, you look just like him. Is he okay? This brochure says that the class is for people with Parkinson's." She looks up at me with her big, black, soulful eyes. Her face softens as she listens.

"Yep, you're right. This was the class that our guest speaker Tommy Perez was talking about a few weeks ago. I checked it out, and I'm trying to see if it's something my dad would want to do. Do you dance?"

Angie's eyes light up, and her voice rises in volume at the sound of the word. "Oh... my... gosh! Yes! I studied ballet for years in Dallas. I still carry my ballet slippers wherever I go. Whenever I feel down or homesick, I slip them on and dance. It lifts me up, so I bet this class will do wonders for your dad and other people with Parkinson's. Dancing and music have magical qualities," she says, pressing her notebook against her chest.

"Thanks, I'm hoping so." With that, I wish Angie well, and she gets up and wishes me a happy holiday in return. As she leaves, she forgets to close the door behind her. I hate when that happens.

I grab some of the articles from the printer and place them inside my messenger bag, where something bulges from the right side. I wonder what that could be. I fish into the deep abyss of the bag and am surprised to pull out a black rectangular box with an attached card. I immediately recognize Craig's handwriting. Now I know why he turned my chair around before he straddled me. He was trying to distract me so he could slip in this gift as a surprise. I prop open the smooth box, and there's a pin of the Starship *Enterprise*. I hold it up and admire the tiny flat ship glimmering in the light of my office. I attach the pin to the right side of my blue polo shirt, just over my heart. I peel open the envelope and read the card.

*Gabriel, thank you so much for coming into my life. You've taught me in so many different ways, and I'm not talking about journalism. Because of your warmth and kindness and the way you see the world, I feel that I am a better and wiser person. I hope this gift reminds you of me, of all our Star Trek nights, and this wild and crazy journey we've embarked on, Captain!*

*Always, Craig.*

I reread the card a few more times, and my heart melts. I was stupid to doubt Craig. He cares about me deeply. I carefully fold the card and place it in my bag. I sling it over my shoulder and lock up my office as I head to my next class. On the way there, I glance down at the pin and let my index finger graze over it. The little ship sits near my heart, which Craig has.

# chapter Nineteen

"YOU drive so slow, GG! Can you pick up the speed a few knots? At this rate, we'll get there, oh, sometime this century?" Nick taunts me.

We're in my Nissan Sentra barreling south on Interstate 95 toward Providence for Thanksgiving dinner with Nick's family. At times, my driving can frustrate Nick, because I'm not the world's biggest speed demon, and you can't really speed in downtown Boston or Somerville because of the narrow, dense streets and traffic lights at every turn. Besides, it snowed earlier this morning, and I would rather drive safely than be splattered along the highway with my amigo by my side. I don't want to be one of those roadside memorials with flowers and teddy bears that read, *Gabriel and Nick, RIP. They were killed because Nick was so impatient with his slore friend's driving.*

"We're only half an hour away. Be patient, Nick. We'll get there before you know it!" I reassure him. I lean over and flick his earlobe. He does the same to me, and that leads to some playful, girly slapping.

"I might as well get comfortable, then. This is going to be a *looong* ride." Nick reclines the passenger seat and folds his arms under his head. He props his right foot on the dashboard.

"You're just cranky because you're either really hungry, you don't want to deal with your family, or you're really horny and can't wait to get laid!"

"All of the above, my friend! You win the daily double, GG. The sooner we get there, the faster we can get our night started back in Boston. I want to go out and play this long weekend. I can party and sleep in with a cute guy," he says.

I shoot him a sidelong look. "Doesn't your dick ever get tired, Nick?" I say, turning my head to my right to momentarily face him.

He props himself up. "Um, no. My dick isn't dead!" he says, grabbing his crotch and raising his thick black eyebrows. "I'm single and I like to play. Nothing wrong with that, especially after a long day of teaching middle-school kids."

"Well, don't worry. We can't stay at your parents' all night. They know we have an hour's drive back. But if I had a big family like yours, Nick, I would love these gatherings. I would treasure them. Do you realize how lucky you are?"

Through my swishing windshield wipers, I notice the upcoming exit sign for Foxboro, where the New England Patriots play at the giant bowl-shaped stadium. The red taillights from the flowing traffic dot the interstate like blinking Christmas lights. A mix of melted snow and rain mists my windshield, and my car whips up some slush from the snow-covered roadway. Naked trees hug the highway's shoulders from both sides. Like a small light bulb, a full moon hangs over New England and casts a luminous glow over the interstate.

"Sorry, GG. Sometimes, I can be insensitive. I know you'd probably prefer to be back in Florida with your mom and dad for Thanksgiving, but my family is your family. In fact, you can have my family, if you like loud, lovey-dovey, in-your-face relatives," he jokes.

"No worries, Nick. I love your family, no matter how loud they can get. I think it's endearing, especially the way your mom pampers you and your sister."

"Well, get ready to be pampered. My mom has always liked you. I hope you fasted today, because they're gonna have to roll us out of Providence with the feast my family is preparing." Nick pokes my stomach with his index finger.

"I'm always game for a good home-cooked meal, no matter how fattening it is! It beats my usual take-out dinners from the Cheesecake Factory or Wendy's."

"Well, my mom made a special dessert just for you, Gabriel."

"Really? Like what? Inquiring Cuban minds want to know!" I say, briefly turning my gaze to him again. My eyes widen with curiosity.

"You'll see. Just get us there already, will you?" Nick says. Then he points at the road, noting, "Look! We're approaching North Attleboro. We're almost out of Massachusetts!"

And with that, I activate the cruise-control option and punch up the speed by four miles per hour. Well, for me, that's speeding.

"Oh Gabriel, you are going sooooo fast! Watch out, you may get a ticket—for driving too slow!"

I shake my head, turn to Nick, and stick my tongue out. He does the same to me.

Almost half an hour later, after driving through the winding lanes of Interstate 95 through Pawtucket, we descend Exit 22 C into downtown Providence, New England's mini-Boston.

We drive on small, narrow, bright-green ramp panels that loop along this cute red-bricked residential development before the roadway deposits us and a few other drivers along the Pleasant Valley Parkway. We pass the backside of the stacked cement parking garage of Providence Place Mall and then drive along the river on the wide Memorial Boulevard, where the bright red glowing sign of the Biltmore Hotel beckons in the distance. We navigate the brief, steep-inclined streets that flank the Rhode Island School of Design and Brown University's sprawling low-rising academic buildings, which have always reminded me of the crimson-hued Harvard University campus. We pass bustling Thayer Street, a one-way thoroughfare packed with a variety of restaurants, coffee shops, bookstores, and clothing boutiques. An old movie theater sits there with a vintage marquee that seems to feature independent films. College students and urbanites like to hang out and meet up here, including Nick and myself for our day trips to Providence.

A few minutes later, we pull into a charming middle-class neighborhood of one- and two-story Victorian homes. I drive to the end of the block and park in front of Nick's childhood home, a two-story cream-colored house. A small statute of the Virgin Mary greets us from the front yard.

As we walk up the five wooden steps to the front door, Nick turns to me. "Gabriel, are you ready for this?" He puts his hand on my right shoulder.

"Sure… I think." I gulp loudly. My stomach rumbles at the smell of the roasted turkey wafting in the air.

Just as Nick is about to open the front door with his key, it swings open.

"Nicholas! My baby!" squeals his mother, Alexa Dias, before embracing him at the entrance. She squeezes him tightly and peppers him with kisses.

"Um, hi, Mom. Good to see you too!" Nick says, trapped in the embrace.

As she hugs him, she leans over and gives me a kiss on the cheek. "Gabriel, so good to see you. Thank you for bringing my son back to Providence. He never visits anymore. We never see him!" Nick's mom is a female version of him, with thick black hair that flows to her shoulders. She has the same Egyptian-green eyes and plucked and shaped black eyebrows.

We finally make it inside, where an intoxicating smell of mashed potatoes, stuffing, and bread rolls greets us. I wipe my feet on the welcome mat, which reads *Bem-vindo*, Portuguese for "welcome." Although Nick was born in Providence and so were his parents, they retained their cultural ties to Portugal because Nick's paternal grandparents were born there, while his late maternal grandparents hailed from Ireland. Nick is quite a mutt, which explains his tanned skin and green eyes. He grew up speaking Portuguese and English, although Nick never speaks Portuguese in Boston unless one of his Brazilian students needs help.

Deeper inside the house, the rest of the family welcomes us in waves. Nick's paternal grandparents hug me, and Nick's little sister Vickie, who is a senior in high school, gives me a peck on the cheek.

"Hey, Gabriel. Welcome back to our dysfunction junction," she says, rolling her eyes and twirling one of her permed dark-brown curls with her right index finger. I've always thought Vickie wore too much mascara. Her eyelashes are so long and curled up that if they could, they would reach out and touch me. But I guess that's her look. She's sweet, though, and reminds me of what it might have been like to have a younger sibling. When she sees Nick, she simply punches him in the arm.

"Oh no you didn't, you little slut!" Nick says before he begins to chase her.

They run through the house with Vickie squeaking up and down the stairs. The clomping of their feet drums against the wooden floors upstairs. When Nick finally catches her, she giggles and shouts, "Nooo. *Stop!* You gaylord!" Nick and Vickie's laughter fills the house.

I smile at the scene.

"Will you two calm down? You're like two dogs in a park!" yells Nick's father, Paulo, as he rises from his leather recliner in the living room. He shakes my hand firmly, gives me a hearty hug, and welcomes me to the family's Thanksgiving.

"We are happy that you can share the holiday with us, Gabriel. We don't see enough of you—or our son. Thank you for coming to our house," he says.

Like Nick, he also has short black hair combed up, but he has a receding hairline. Nick's father also has a beer belly and soft brown eyes. He runs the family restaurant nearby in Federal Hill, which is also home to many Italian restaurants and bakeries.

From the kitchen, Nick's mom rings a miniature cowbell, signaling for everyone to gather in the dining room, which sits between the kitchen and living room. We gather around a long rectangular table where I'm sandwiched between Nick and Vickie. Ceramic plates painted with fruits and vegetables decorate the dining room's walls.

On the east wall hangs a large picture of the infamous last supper. Nick has told me how religious his mother is, hence the Virgin Mary in the front yard, yet she embraced Nick when he came out to her in college. The rest of the family doesn't seem to have an issue with him being gay, either, from what I can tell, because they've always embraced me as a long-lost member of their family. They've been extremely warm and welcoming to me since Nick and I have been friends. Nick's family reminds me of how every family should be—loving, loud, and loyal.

When I'm around Nick's family, I imagine my parents still together, like Nick's. I picture Papi and Mami acting all lovey-dovey the same way Nick's parents do whenever we visit. I fantasize about coming home to one house instead of two homes. As I sit at the table, I envy Nick for all that he has. I don't think Nick realizes how lucky he is, but I do. If I were Nick, I'd be here every weekend, at home.

I'm snapped out of my train of thought as we begin to say grace. As we eat, Nick's father talks about his restaurant and how business has been slow because of Rhode Island's weakening economy, one of the worst in the nation. The grandparents complain about the hoodlums at Providence Place Mall, where they go to walk each floor of the towering mall for exercise.

"That place is a zoo sometimes," says his grandmother, whose gray hair is pulled into a bun, as she slowly slices the turkey on her plate.

"Kids these days! No offense, Vickie. You're not like them," the grandfather pipes in, taking a pull from his beer and winking at Nick's sister. "I remember when that mall wasn't there and it was just a vacant old lot. You know, they moved the river to make room for that monster of a mall. It was that NBC TV show that ruined everything."

Nick and Vickie both roll their eyes as they stifle their laughs. They've heard this rant before.

"That old TV show on NBC called *Providence?*" I say in between bites of stuffing. I remember the show fondly and how the three adult siblings return home after their mother dies. They take care of their father, a local veterinarian. The theme song, a cover of the Beatles song "In My Life," has always been one of my favorites.

With his eyes, Nick signals for me to switch subjects. He leans over and whispers, "Don't get him started on that TV show. He hated it and blames it for the regentrification of downtown."

"That TV show—" Nick's grandfather begins before Nick's mother jumps in, saying, "We've heard that story before, Papa Dias. Gabriel, tell us about your family. How are your father and mother doing in Florida? What do they do for Thanksgiving?"

With my fork, I pick at the white tender slices of roasted turkey and take a mouthful before answering. "They're good. My dad is with my aunt and cousin tonight for dinner. My mom is at a friend's house. I'll be down there for Christmas. Thanks again for allowing me to share this holiday with you and your family," I say to Nick's father and the rest of the family at the dinner table.

"You are always welcome here, Gabriel. You're one of the Dias family."

"Like, totally," says Vickie, leaning her head on my right side and gently rubbing my upper back.

Nick looks at me and winks. "Trust me, you don't want to be a Dias. You'll end up like us, all crazy and nutty," Nick says, holding up his fork. But deep down inside, I wouldn't mind being a member of his family. I'd be honored.

As we finish dinner, everyone passes their plates over to the next person until they all arrive at the end of the table where Nick's grandmother sits. She piles the plates into one neat stack with all our knives and forks on top. She carefully hands the plates to Nick's mother, who carries them into the kitchen. Nick's father follows her. Through the opening of the doorway from the dining room to the kitchen, I catch them exchanging a sweet, tender kiss. They quietly mouth to each other, "I love you!" I watch the scene unfold as I sink into my chair and pat my bulging stomach.

Nick pours me another glass of white wine and clinks his glass with mine. "To Boston, to Providence, to good friends!" he says.

"To impatient backseat drivers!" I say.

And at the same time, we bust out and say, "To slores!," laughing at our inside joke.

As we drink our wine, Nick's parents emerge from the kitchen with two pies: a golden pumpkin pie and a dome-shaped flan topped with dark caramel syrup like the one my mom makes.

"In honor of Nick's friend, I made a special flan the Cuban way," she says, holding up the plate with the flan as if it were a gleaming jewel on display. "I hope this tastes just like your mother's, Gabriel. Nick has told me how you miss your mother's cooking and her sweet flan."

I put my hand to my heart, and my eyes mist slightly. I look over at Nick's mom, whose eyes beam with love. I then look around the table and everyone stares back at me, their eyes full of kindness.

She didn't have to do this for me. I'm not even a blood relative, yet she went out of her way to make me feel welcomed in her home on a holiday when families gather and celebrate.

I blink back the tears in my eyes and look down briefly. I don't know what to say because I am so moved by the gesture. "Mrs. Dias... wow... that is really nice of you. Thank you, or as you would say, *obrigado*!"

She tilts her head and smiles as she carefully places the plate down in the middle of dining table. Nick's father plops down the plate with the pumpkin pie and begins to serve slices for everyone. Nick's mom tops off each slice of pumpkin pie with a dollop of whipped cream. Immediately, the sounds of forks scraping against the plates fill the dining room as everyone chows down, savoring every spoonful of the delicious pie, flan, or both. (I have both.)

After a round of seconds, our plates are empty and our stomachs are full. We gather in the living room and watch some of the corny holiday specials that usually air on television this time of year.

IT'S just past nine at night, and Nick and I decide that it's time to return to Boston. We hug everyone good-bye, which takes about fifteen minutes because with each hug, there is some talk about the weather (it's supposed to snow this weekend again), driving safely (I always do, and my Nissan has new all-weather tires), and everyone asks when we'll be back in town. (Who knows! I never do, because Nick prefers to hang out in Boston.) Nick's mother and grandmother also delay us: they prepare leftovers for us to take back to Boston. We each leave with slices of the desserts and extra turkey in Tupperware containers.

"Please tell your parents that we wish them a happy holiday," Nick's mom says as she hugs Nick and nearly squeezes him to death.

Nick's father shakes my hand and gives me one of his strong hugs, which smushes the leftover boxes against my chest. Once he releases me, I brace myself for the onslaught of Nick's Mom's hug. I manage to squeak out, "I'll tell my parents that you said hi. Thank you again for having me over."

Once she releases me and I catch my breath, Nick and I descend the steps from the front door to the front yard with our goodies in hand.

"Nick, what we are going to do with all this stuff? We have enough food to feed a small village!"

"Let's drop this off at your place before we head out to the club. That way, it won't go bad," Nick says as he climbs into the car.

With that, I make a quick U-turn on Nick's childhood street, and we begin to the trip back to the Hub. Not long after, we're weaving through Providence traffic lights toward Interstate 95. Within a few minutes, the lighted dome of the Providence Statehouse and the mall's bright lights recede in my rearview mirror. Several cars whoosh by me under a sky that looks like a dark gray blanket studded with tiny lights.

"Gabriel, can you drive a little faster? At this rate, we'll get back to Boston for Christmas!" Nick says crisply.

"Oh no you didn't!" I say, shooting one of my playful but annoyed looks, but I can't help but break out in a laugh. Nick isn't just my wingman. He's the gay brother I always wanted to have.

# chapter Twenty

IT'S just past 11 p.m., and the night is nippy, with the temperature in the mid-thirties—the standard for Boston in winter. Nick and I stand in a small but growing line congregating outside The Estate. Coming here was Nick's idea, but since he was nice enough to invite me to his family's home for Thanksgiving, the least I can do is go out with my buddy to a club, even though I'd rather be home with a drink and watching *Star Trek II: The Wrath of Khan* again. Dancing will help burn off the gazillion calories I consumed from the dinner and two desserts.

"This is so silly. I bet the place is empty inside, and they're making us stand outside to create some sort of illusion," Nick complains in front of me.

"We'll be in before you know it. There are only six people ahead of us, and it's early. People are probably still at Thanksgiving dinner."

Fifteen minutes later, we finally make it inside the club. We drop off our black coats at the coat check and climb a steep set of narrow stairs that lead us to the boom-boom-boom dance floor. I immediately survey the scene: a circus of college students and guys in their thirties and older flouncing their bodies while holding and spilling their drinks in their hands. I love it!

"We got here just in time!" Nick says, eyes widening with delight—or horniness—as a herd of cologne-wearing guys walk in front, behind, and between us as if we were invisible.

"Drinks! I'll get the first round," I offer. As we stand by the lip of the bar and await our drinks from the bartender, my mind begins to whir, roaming to the night I bumped into Craig, which was the last time I came here. In fact, I'm standing in the exact same spot as I was that night.

"Snap out of it!" Nick chides me. "You're thinking about your college boy. Tonight, it's about us hanging out and having fun."

"I know. I know. I'm just having a flashback, that's all." On that note, I turn around and pay the bartender for my vodka with Red Bull and Nick's light beer. We grab our respective drinks and refocus back to the dance floor, which looks like one giant party. The lights above flicker and temporarily suspend everyone's movements as if they were captured by a Polaroid camera. I never understood why young people sashay and jerk their bodies as if they are about to vomit.

*Did I really just think that? I really do sound like a geezer.*

"Let's fucking dance!" Nick shouts. I urge him to start ahead of me, because I want to finish my drink and not spill it all over the dance floor or myself. Armed with his high-wattage smile, Nick then disappears into the sea of club revelers, grins, and waves to me. It doesn't take long before he finds a dance partner, a young studly Irish boy with a crew cut and a tight white T-shirt and blue jeans.

I remain at the bar and watch the scene unfold like an MTV video. Again, I feel old, like an uncle standing on the sidelines of his nephew's or niece's birthday party. I feel out of place in an establishment that sits around the corner from my employer. I'm proud of the fact that I'm not coming to The Estate as often as I did, thanks to the time I've been spending with Craig. Still, I look at everyone dancing and having a good time and I feel that I no longer belong here, that I should find other things to do on a Thursday night or Saturday night. My gay-bar expiration date has come and gone, and I keep trying to extend it.

As I silently whine to myself and mentally file the observation away, the hip-hop and pop music blares, blasting every inch of the club and penetrating my core.

I finally decide to take the plunge and stroll over to the side of the dance floor and join Nick. But he's preoccupied with the Irish boy, who dances awkwardly, with his shoulders hunched forward and his arms swaying left and right. Like a third wheel, I groove behind them and bop to the beats by myself. Nick pats me on the back now and then, probably so I won't feel so left out.

I jam and swivel my hips. My arms create giant invisible looping number eights. Catching the beat and feeling the rhythm pulse inside me, I turn around, and my eyes pause on a familiar-looking fuzzy shaved head bouncing along to the rhythm. I pause, squint, and focus some more. I study the guy's lean backside and the baggy jeans that sag at his thin waist. He's dirty-dancing with another college-age guy.

I gulp and shake my head in confusion. *It can't be! Craig?* And he's dancing with that broadcast student, Tony, with whom he had dinner the other night. My heart pounds against my chest. A small fire churns in my gut. I stand there and watch them as they laugh and sway to the left and right without a care in the world. Their eyes are locked as if no one else were in the club with them. They don't realize I'm a few feet away. I want to claw both their eyes out.

Nick suddenly taps me on the shoulder. "Hey, dudette… you okay?" Then his eyes see what mine see: Craig and Tony sucking face and embracing each other.

"Oh shit! What a friggin' douche bag!" Nick says, pounding his right fist into his other hand.

"He's a fucking asshole!" I shout as Nick pulls me off the dance floor and toward the front of the bar to get away from the scene. I reluctantly go with him.

"Forget about him, Gabriel. You deserve better. He's a young guy. He doesn't know what he wants," Nick continues his pep talk. A small vein in his forehead bulges, and that distracts me from his green eyes.

"I know, but still. He lied to me. He said he was flying to Virginia. He made this big show about not wanting to leave. I'm so fucking stupid, Nick." The whole time I talk to Nick, I observe Craig and Tony dance, kiss, and have a good time. They are lost in their own world, oblivious to the other dancers and drama swirling around them.

"Listen, maybe he has a good explanation. You never know!" Nick says, putting a comforting hand on my shoulder.

"Um, how can you explain that?" I say, pointing to Craig and Tony, bouncing in unison. Nick turns his head and looks over to the young whores making out. "What could he possibly say that would excuse that? Their body language says it all, Nick."

I shake my head and focus on the hypnotic flashing lights. Pangs of embarrassment detonate inside me like mini bombs. My eyes flare with anger, while a mix of sadness, hurt, and disappointment stews inside me like a thick emotional sauce. But none of these emotions can cloak how much of an idiot I feel. I should have known better. More than anything, I'm ashamed. I imagine the dance music washing over me and drowning out these conflicting feelings that consume me. I wish the flashing lights could wipe away the pain.

"Gabriel, let's get out of here. You don't have to see this. We can go somewhere else," Nick offers. "Let's go back to my place and eat the leftover desserts. We can even—wait for it—watch *Star Trek*... again!"

"You're a true amigo, Nick. I know how much you hate our *Star Trek* nights, and yet you put up with my love of the *Enterprise*. I really appreciate it."

"Hey, we all have our quirks. Yours are more geared to science fiction. Mine lean more toward the male anatomy."

I summon my pride and my inner strength. I'm not letting an immature college student get the better of me. I tighten my right fist into a ball and try to release all the tension building inside me, but it's to no avail.

"Nick, don't worry about me. I'll be okay. Go and have fun with the Irish guy, who keeps looking over here, probably wondering when you're going to come back to the dance floor. I think I'm going to take a walk through the Common to think things through before heading back home."

"I'll go with you. I don't want you to be alone while you're upset," Nick says, squeezing the top of my right shoulder.

I convince him otherwise. I want him to have fun, but more importantly, I want my space to process everything I've witnessed. "Seriously, Nick, I just want to be alone for now. I'll be fine. I promise. I'll text when you I get home," I say firmly.

Nick looks into my eyes. He knows that when I want to be left alone, no one can convince me otherwise. When I didn't want to deal Papi and Mami arguing about his affair, I would take long drives along A1A in Fort Lauderdale, where the beach breezes soothed me. Sometimes being alone comforts me. It's what I know best. No one can hurt you when you're alone. It's become a protective armor in my life.

Nick swings his right arm around me. "Okay, but call me if you need anything, even if it's five in the morning. Remember, you're not alone. I'm here for you, dude. I always have your back, amigo."

I grin tightly. "I know, Nick. I love you too. I just want to get out of here. I'm taking off. I'll text you later. And I want to hear all about what happens with you and your new friend. Your romp stories always cheer me up."

And with that, I leave the musical chaos and drama of the dance floor behind and descend back down the narrow staircase to grab my coat. The music fades away with each step I take toward the front entrance.

Once outside, I stand in the alley and smooth out my black coat in the chilly Boston air. Gaggles of young, drunk revelers, probably students at Jefferson, walk along Tremont Street. Their laughs fill the air like the soundtrack of young Boston. A pack of Jefferson smokers congregates on the sidewalk up ahead, where they shoot plumes of smoke into the sky.

I flip up my collar and button up my coat. I stroll along the cobblestone street toward the Boston Common. And then I smack into someone.

"Whoa, sorry. My bad," he says. When I step back, I realize it's Adam, the dance instructor from the Parkinson's class. I light up at the vision. It takes me a second to process the scene.

I stutter, "Um… Adam? Wow, what a surprise. What are you doing around here?" We're standing face to face. I rub my forehead to ease the pain from the collision.

"My friends were inside The Estate, and I just left. They were all getting rowdy and drunk, and I have an early class tomorrow. So I was heading to the 7-Eleven for some water and to maybe grab a slice of pizza before heading home. Want to come with?"

I beam at the offer and nod yes, even though I'm still stuffed from dinner with Nick.

During the five-minute walk to the convenience store, we pass several panhandlers who harass us for spare change, and Adam recounts his day and the various classes he teaches. As he talks, I'm mesmerized by his looks but also by his dedication to his craft. He seems to have a burning passion for what he does, and I find that inspiring. What does this mean? It wasn't like this with Craig or other guys I have dated.

"Don't you get tired from teaching two to three classes a day?" I say as we grab two bottled waters from the refrigerator at the convenience store.

"You have to pace yourself. I break up the classes so they're not back to back. But I don't just teach Parkinsonians. I also have some side gigs teaching turbo cardio classes at local gyms. There's one class I think you'd like."

"Oh yeah? What it's called?" I say as we stand at the register to pay for our drinks.

"Cardio Caliente!" he says.

I laugh at the way he pronounces the Spanish word.

"What, you don't like the way I speak en espanol, hombre guapo!" he says in his broken Spanish. He screws up his face as if to laugh at himself.

I stifle another laugh because he sounds so American enunciating the Spanish words. Adam's presence right now is comforting, a much-needed emotional balm. "No, it's not that. Just the name of the class sounds, well, funny."

"Well don't laugh at it until you try it. We do choreographed steps to Latin dance music such as Shakira, Gloria Estefan—you name it, Gabriel. So bring your father to the Parkinson's class and then come on your own for the Cardio Caliente," he says, drawing out the word into *cah-lien-te*.

We leave the bright fluorescent lights of the 7-Eleven and walk over to the small pizza place many Jefferson students flock to after a night of clubbing or smoking pot. There are only four people inside, which means there won't be a wait. After 2 a.m., a rowdy line extends from here to the park. We beat the crowd.

We each order a wide slice of greasy pizza that spills over our white paper plates. We grab two seats by the front windows that face Tremont Street and the college.

As we munch on our pizza, strings of cheese thread from our slices to our mouths. Adam says he's been good all week about his diet.

"I get to cheat here and there with pizza. Hey, after teaching so many classes, I've earned my fatty-food pick of the week," he says, his light-brown eyebrows arching.

"I love the Cheesecake Factory in Braintree!" I chime in. "In fact, the friendly women in the bakery know me by my order."

"Who do you go with?" Adam asks, the soft lighting illuminating his sky-blue eyes.

"I usually get take-out food from there and eat it at home while grading papers."

"You don't have a boyfriend?" Adam asks incredulously.

I take another bite of the pizza, which burns the top of my mouth. I'm not sure how to answer his question. I definitely don't want to date Craig after what I witnessed tonight. "You could say I'm single. I was seeing someone much younger, and it didn't turn out how I had hoped."

Adam tilts his head and puts his hand on my left shoulder. "Sorry to hear that. His loss! Besides, young guys are trouble."

"Thanks, I think. Anyway, what about you? Is there a special guy in your life, Adam?"

He coughs as he begins to respond. Another gooey string of cheese stretches from the pizza slice and onto his hand. I grab a napkin and dab the cheese away from his hand.

"His name is Louie. He has gray hair, big brown eyes. He's very loyal and he's been by my side for six years."

"Wow, that's great. Congratulations."

"Did I mention he loves to lick?"

"Um, I think that might be too much information, Adam."

"And he's really, *really* hairy—with curls."

My forehead folds up in puzzlement. *Why is he telling me all these personal physical details about his guy?* "What does he do for a living?" I ask, led by my curiosity.

"He's lazy. He's home all day. He waits for me to come home to hang out. I basically take care of him."

I take a swig of the bottled water. "He's unemployed? That must be hard, especially if you're living together. I can see why you teach so much."

"Yeah, I'm basically his daddy. Did I also mention he has four legs?" Adam leans back and releases a big belly laugh.

I'm such a goof. I should have seen that coming. I toss a wadded-up napkin at Adam. "So you have a dog. I got that. I meant, do you have a boyfriend?"

Adam then fishes into his back pocket and fetches his wallet. He shows me a picture of Louie, a beautiful gray poodle. "Louie is the only guy in my life right now. I just haven't met the right guy yet."

"Well, when it happens, you'll know." Our eyes lock for a second and then two before we both look away at the street scene of passing cars and late-night revelers.

As we finish our pizza, I tell him about my students and my move to Boston from Fort Lauderdale. He recounts how he adopted Louie from the pound in Somerville a few years ago because he wanted some company at home.

"Dogs have so much love to give, and you give it right back. It's nice to know that Louie is home waiting for me to walk him or run with him after a long day of dancing," Adam says.

After the pizza, we pass the club, and guys begin trickling out. It's just shy of two in the morning. Adam offers to walk me to my car, but I parked one block away.

"Gabriel, let me know when you want to visit the Parkinson's class again or when you want to do the Cardio Caliente class. I'm curious to see your Cuban dance moves," Adam says as we stand on Tremont Street under the bright halo of a streetlight.

"I'll let you know. It would be fun to do both and hang out sometime."

"I'm sure Louie wouldn't mind meeting you, hombre guapo," Adams says again in his broken Spanish. I guess that would make flirtation number five, not that I am counting or anything.

We stand face to face, smile to smile. We both lean in for a hug. He pats me on the back and wishes me a good night.

As I walk back to my Nissan, I reflect on how good I feel around Adam. My anger and disappointment toward Craig temporarily float away. The whole drive back to Quincy, I think of how I would really like to see Adam again. Maybe he can teach me something else, like how to mend a broken heart.

# chapter Twenty-One

THANKSGIVING weekend passes in a blur of errands to the grocery store, workouts at the gym, and grading student papers. I still haven't heard from Craig. After all, he's *allegedly* in Virginia. I spend my time alone in the warmth of my condo, watching reruns of *Law & Order*.

At the end of one episode, just as the jury is about to announce the verdict, my landline rings. The caller ID says it's Aunt Cary. Curled up on my sofa in a fetal position, I pause the episode (thanks to my handy DVR) with the remote control to answer the phone.

"Gabrielito, we missed you this year for Sanguiven," she says in her Spanish-accented English, using the Cuban slang for Thanksgiving. "Even your cousin Jessica was here."

I smile at the gentle scolding. She's just teasing. "I know, I know. I'll be down for Christmas for a week or so. I can make it up to you then. How are you doing?"

"Everything is the same down here. Your Papi came over for dinner, but I'm sure you already knew that."

"Yep! He's still stuffed. I spoke to him yesterday afternoon. Is everything okay?"

My aunt pauses for a few seconds and takes a deep breath. "I wanted to wait to talk to you about this when you were here down here, but I don't want this to wait a few more weeks, Gabriel."

I mute the volume on the TV and prop myself up on the sofa. "What are you talking about?"

"It's your father... I don't think he should work anymore. I know he likes his independence and he's worked ever since he was a teenager back in Cuba, but he continues to grow weaker. The Parkinson's." She exhales.

"But I just saw him a few weeks ago. He told me he's riding the electric bike and that he's been feeling better."

"He is, Gabrielito, but I don't think it's healthy for him to work all the hours he does as an exterminator, with the climbing up the stairs and bending down to spray under kitchen cabinets. Those fumes can't be helpful either."

"So what are you suggesting, that he change jobs?"

"Your papa cannot not work, you know that. But I think he needs a job that isn't as stressful on his body and doesn't require him driving everywhere. I worry about him."

"Me too," I say. "Have you told him how you feel, Aunt Cary?"

"I wanted to discuss it with you first. There are other part-time jobs he could do that would make him feel productive."

I lean my head against my right hand as I look at the framed photo of Papi and me that sits on top of the TV set. He is a proud, hardworking, and stubborn Latino. I don't want to rob him of his independence, but he won't be able to work full time forever. His body is dropping hints that it's weakening, despite the increases in his medication.

"But what else can he do? He's been exterminating since I was born," I say, recalling Papi's standard uniform: black work pants, a beige short-sleeved button-down shirt, and a matching baseball cap that reads "Galan Exterminating." I smile at the image.

"That's what I need your help with. Try to think of something. Maybe he can work the door at Costco or BJ's where he checks the receipts, or he can provide the samples to customers? I can always get him a job at my Walgreens, but I don't think he would want to work where I am. He thinks I annoy him, being his big hermana."

"You guys would drive each other crazy, Aunt Cary. I don't think he'd want to take orders from you, even if you were paying him." We laugh at the thought.

"Well, I'll put on my thinking cap and we'll figure this out. I'll also bring it up with Papi."

"Better you than me. I nag him enough as it is," she says.

"Oh really, why is that? It's not like you're a busybody," I say sarcastically.

"Hey, someone has to watch him while you educate the future writers and journalists of America. Anyway, I will let you get back to your *Star Trek* or whatever you were watching, Gabriel. I love you!" she says.

"Love you too, Aunt Cary!" I gently place the phone back in its cradle and sip some of the Peach Snapple I have leftover from earlier.

I unmute the TV back to my NBC series. As I watch the court proceedings, my mind wanders and begins to think of various jobs that Papi could do that would bring him some income but won't be so labor-intensive. I recall all the times when I was younger and I ventured out to the beach hotels and apartment buildings with Papi to help him exterminate. He would squat down, climb kitchen counters, and lie down on bathroom floors to spray under sinks. At the end of the day, his shirt reeked of chemicals and sweat. He'd remove his baseball cap and his curly, short hair would be flattened. He never complained, but I knew he was tired because he'd immediately pass out in bed with Mami by 11 p.m. After the divorce, he started falling asleep at 10 p.m. on his recliner in his Miami Lakes apartment. Whenever I visited from college or Boston, I would have to tiptoe into the living room, cover him in a white blanket, and then turn off the TV and lights.

Although I resent him for what he did to my mother, I still admire Papi for all his hard work. I'm about the same age he was when I was born, yet I can't imagine coming home after a long day of work and summoning enough energy to take care of a baby. It's hard enough just taking care of myself and getting through the day at times. Papi worked all day while Mom took care of the house and me. I wonder if he ever feels as I do, waking up and ending the day in an empty apartment. Does he hear the same deafening silence as I toss the keys into a bowl in the kitchen, the lonely echo of my shoes as I walk into the living room and bedroom? At least he has his on-and-off again lover, Gloria, to keep him company. I have—or had—Craig.

I need to confront and resolve things with Craig instead of letting the situation linger. I remember I read somewhere that if you have a mess in your home, you clean it up immediately. You don't allow trash to sit in the corner of your kitchen for too long because it will stink. Once I hear from Craig, I'll handle the situation once and for all and move on.

My focus returns to *Law & Order*. Just as the episode ends, I pass out on the sofa.

Just before midnight, my cell phone vibrates on my end table in the living room and wakes me up. I rub my eyes and stretch my arms out like a cat on the floor. I pick up the phone, and the screen displays Craig's name. It's a text message from him.

*I'm back in Boston. Have classes tomorrow. See you in school and later tomorrow night. Missed you!*

The text message disgusts me. Who does he think he is? I immediately delete it as I force myself to get up and trudge to my bedroom. On the way, I delete all my other old text messages from Craig. I wish I could delete him from my life. I slip under my covers and set my alarm for my early morning class. As I begin to fall asleep again, I wonder what I am going to do when I see Craig tomorrow. Chances are that he will stop by my office or at the end of one of my classes. He knows my schedule by heart.

School is not the proper place to have the conversation that I need to have with him. I created this mess, and now I have to clean it up.

I temporarily will away the thoughts. I just want to sleep and forget about the other night at the bar—and Craig.

# chapter Twenty-Two

THE day flies by uneventfully, class after class. Students with questions about their stories and papers. Discussions of current events and news, as well as the lack of Latino authors in Boston, at least until Tommy Perez publishes his first novel. I am secretly jealous that he is doing that. I can never say that my job is boring even though I recycle the same syllabus year after year. But the students are really the subjects of the class. I find them more interesting at times than the stories we discuss. Their probing questions and enthusiasm for journalism and writing inspire me to come to class every day. I owe it to them to make the class as engaging and fun as possible.

At the end of my last class of the day, a beginners' creative writing course, I scoop up my messenger bag from under the classroom podium. I wipe away my notes on the white board. I'm done for the afternoon.

I sling my bag around my torso and begin to walk back to my office. I maneuver around the throngs of students lingering in the hallway and chatting about their holidays with their families, the latest pop-singing diva's bad behavior, and their upcoming weekend plans. Some students wave or nod to me. I offer a small smile and keep walking.

As soon as I arrive at my office, I spot Craig smiling and leaning against my door. His eyes light up when he sees me.

I don't return the expression.

"Hi, Professor Galan!" he says.

I grin tightly. "Hey, what are you doing here?" I say gruffly.

Craig's eyebrows furrow in confusion. He doesn't know that I know about what he did the other night. About the lies. The disappointment.

I jiggle my key into the lock and open the office door. The whole time, I can feel Craig's eyes studying me.

"Are you okay?" he asks, locking his eyes onto mine, but I look away. His dreamy expression won't work on me anymore. It doesn't matter how much he looks like James Franco. I'm now immune to it.

"Um, no, I'm not, and I can't talk to you right now, especially not here." I plop my bag on my chair, toss my keys on my desk, and settle in front of my computer.

Craig closes the door behind him. "Gabriel, what's wrong? You seem upset."

I glance up at him and squint. My mouth forms a big letter O. I imagine my eyes shooting a spray of needles at him, but I keep it cool. "Craig, listen. I can't talk to you here. In fact, I don't want to talk to you right now. At all! I need you to go… *now!*"

"But… but… what's going on?" he stammers, approaching me. "Did something happen while I was away?"

I roll my eyes and shake my head side to side in disbelief. *"Did something happen while I was away?" I can't believe him. Was I blind this whole time?*

"Yes, something did happen, and this is not the appropriate place to talk. Craig, you gotta go," I repeat, raising my voice.

Craig backs up and holds up his hands as if to deflect whatever I am about to throw at him. "I can see you had a bad day, so I'll leave you alone, but we're going to need to talk at some point. When you calm down, call me, okay, baby?" he says, trying to win me over with his puppy-dog eyes.

"Yeah, sure. Okay!" I blurt out, exhaling loudly.

Confusion swimming in his eyes, Craig finally leaves. I get up, shut the door behind him, and lock it. I lean back in my chair. I prop my feet up on my desk and rest my hands on my stomach. *How am I going to defuse this situation? How do I extract myself from this relationship without damaging my career? What if Craig tells someone about our affair? What if he reports me to the administration?*

I rub my fingers against my forehead and try to think of the best way to have a civil conversation with him. I don't want to set him off, not that I believe that he's violent or psychotic. But you never know what people might do. I'm sure my mom never thought that her first love would have cheated on her, but look at what happened to them.

As soon as I get home, I toss my messenger bag on my small wooden kitchen table and empty my pockets. It's an unusual fifty-degree December day. It's only 4 p.m., and there's still some sunlight left, although it's quickly fading. It won't be long before the sky fades into a grayish gloomy blanket.

To release some tension, I decide to go for a run. I change out of my professorial attire and slip into navy-blue sweatpants and matching sweatshirt. I put on my baseball cap and twirl my scarf around my neck like a strand of pasta around a fork. I pop in my white headphones and clench my iPod with my right hand.

I dash down the two flights of stairs, where a small gust of cold air greets me. Standing in front of my building, I kick my legs up and down to warm up. Puffs of breath mark the cold space before me. I then jump up and down to pump up my energy. I glance at my watch and set my timer. I'm set to go.

I play some Tim McGraw as I sprint along the choppy gray-bluish bay water. I'm one of a dozen runners in sight as cars zip by on the coastal boulevard. With each pounding step, I strive to stamp out my thoughts of Craig. I want to run away from the situation as fast as I sprint along the seawall toward Marina Bay.

Mixed thoughts swirl in my head. *Am I unlucky in love? Maybe Nick has the right game plan—stay single and just have fun. No commitments. No broken heart. No drama. Just spontaneous hot sex with random young guys.* This seems to work for Nick. He never complains about being single. He enjoys his space and solitude. *If it works for him, why not me?* But I'm not like Nick, who is emotionally constipated. I'm a romantic at heart.

Six minutes into the run, and I've already reached my mile mark, which is the entrance to Marina Bay. I run and run, my breath labored as I will away these conflicting thoughts. I think of my ideal guy: about my age, a professional, passionate about his craft, a good person at heart, attractive, someone who can make me laugh. I can overlook if he has different tastes in television and movies. Not everyone is a *Star Trek* fan.

As I mentally tally the qualities I desire in an ideal partner, an image suddenly surfaces in my mind. It's Adam, smiling and sharing pizza with me. I smile at the memory. *Adam. Adam! Adam?*

The more I run along the outskirts of the marina, the more my thoughts drift to Adam. I barely know him, yet from the little that I've seen of him, I've been moved. My heart has also raced the times I've seen him. I can easily imagine taking Adam to Fort Lauderdale to meet Mom and Clara the cat. Another image surfaces—Adam talking to Papi about the benefits of exercise, particularly dancing, for people with Parkinson's. More thoughts flood my mind. I temporarily forget the cooling weather as my adrenaline streams through my body. Sweat trickles down my face.

A montage of images unfolds in my mind like a movie trailer. Adam and me cuddling in bed as we wake up on a Sunday morning and fight over the newspaper. Us running along the Charles River or here in Quincy. I imagine him beating me in a race (he's in better shape, from what I can tell) and then pulling me into a big embrace that lifts me off my feet. I surrender my body to his as we dance in sync at a club, a party, or in the privacy of my home. I picture meeting his dog Louie and walking him in Cambridge as if he were my own. The thoughts are comforting and reassuring to me. *Adam!*

As the sun dips like a dimming golden bulb in the horizon, I turn around and begin to head back to my condo before it gets too chilly. I slow down to catch my breath and walk with my hands resting on my hips. The flowing traffic whooshes by.

I'm glad I took this run. It released some of the physical and emotional tension that has built up since Thursday night. The adrenaline courses through me like a feel-good elixir.

With my condo two blocks away, I drag my feet and breathe in the cool air. I finally catch my breath; the warmth of my sweaty body continues to invigorate me. I glance skyward and see the belly of an American Airlines plane as it prepares to land at Logan International Airport.

When I walk up to the entrance of my red-bricked building, the cause of my recent disappointment comes into full view. Craig sits on the front steps with his legs folded and his arms leaning forward. He smiles when he spots me. Whatever physical and psychological comfort I gained from my run quickly blows away with the bay breeze.

Craig rises to greet me and approaches with his arms open for a hug, but I pull back.

"What's going on, Gabriel? Talk to me!" he says with a pleading look in his eyes.

"That's just it. I don't want to talk to you or see you."

Craig steps back as if an invisible force has just shoved him. Confusion fills his face. "What did I do?"

I furrow my eyebrows and let out a long sigh. "You know what you did! I saw you with Tony the other night, dancing the night away."

Craig looks stunned.

"Is it coming back to you? You, Tony, The Estate, Thanksgiving night? Oh wait, weren't you supposed to be in Virginia with your family? You can't explain yourself out of this one, mi amor!"

Craig's eyes well up with tears. He frowns. His shoulders slump. His body language just confessed. He's caught. "Gabriel, you're the one I want to be with. Tony doesn't mean anything to me. We just had fun that night. It's not serious."

I look to my left in disbelief as if looking for a hidden camera, and I think, *What the fuck?* "I thought you were different, but you know what, Craig? You're twenty-two. You're young. You're doing what you should be doing, and that's having fun. But you did it at my expense. I don't even blame you. I blame myself. I'm the older one with more experience. I should have never let this go as far as it did." I fold my arms and rub the underside of my right arm. I look down, feeling ashamed for knowing better yet not doing anything about it early on.

"I'm so sorry. I wasn't thinking. I ended up not going to Virginia after my flight was delayed. I knew you were going to Providence with Nick, and I didn't want to interrupt that. I know how much family means to you, and Nick is like your brother. Tony had called me to hang out, and we decided to get some drinks and dance at Estate. And things got out of hand. We got carried away with the alcohol. It's all my fault, Gabriel. I never intended to hurt you."

"But you did, and what's done is done. You can't undo this."

We stand in front of my building and stare at each other in a long, uncomfortable moment of silence. The gravity of the situation sinks in for Craig as well as for me. Although I'm sad and disappointed, I'm also somewhat relieved. I know what I want in a partner, and Craig doesn't match those qualities right now. He needs some more life experience.

I take a step back, tilt my head to the right, and study Craig some more. I realize he's still a… boy. Not an anchorman. An anchorboy. I was probably just a hot fun story for him to explore and research. But after seeing how badly he feels, I know he did care about me in his own way.

"Let's just part ways. No bitterness, Craig. I'm not mad at you, okay?" I reassure him. I place my right hand on his shoulder and pat it. I try to act like the responsible mature adult that I should have been months ago.

"But… I care about you. We can work this out," he says with misty eyes.

"I don't think that's a good idea. I don't think you're ready for a serious relationship. You have another semester left. You have future internships, and you'll be a great anchorman somewhere in a big market. You have so much ahead of you. This is your time to go and have fun. I've already done that. I'm looking for something more long-term and stable."

Craig leans in, and I offer him a friendly hug. His embrace feels good and yet so bad at the same time. I need to let go in more ways than one.

"Trust me on this. This is for the best. Listen to your professor, will you? He knows what he's talking about."

A small smile forms at the corner of his beautiful mouth. He rubs his right hand through his fuzzy brown crew cut as he turns away.

"It's going to be okay, Craig. I promise. Now if you don't mind, I need to go upstairs and change. I'm a sweaty mess!" I say, using the back of my right sleeve to wipe the sweat off my forehead.

Tears continue to roll down his face. "I guess I'll see you at Jefferson," he says, his body hunched over.

"I'll see you in school, Craig."

He walks away toward his car. I hold back my tears until I saunter into my building. As I walk up the stairs, I can't breathe. A knot forms in my throat. Tears roll down my face as I climb the stairs.

A sadness deepens within, but I am comforted by the fact that I did the right thing. I just have to remind myself of that. I know I will get over this. Time will help heal the hole in my heart. I need to find ways to stay busy for a while. I should use this time to revisit Adam's Parkinson's dance class. I could use him as a friend right about now. And, of course, there's Nick. If he's not a great distraction, I don't know what is.

Once back inside in my condo, I peel off my clothes, leaving a trail of them along the way to the bathroom. I turn on the hot water in the shower. Once the vapor rises, I step in. I let the rush of the water soothe my body. I luxuriate in the shower and pretend that the cascading water is washing away the hurt. I imagine that the beating water is replenishing my heart and my soul. I lean against the white-tiled bathroom wall. Some more tears pour out. I'll be okay. I know I will.

# chapter Twenty-Three

"HOW is Boston's best writing professor?" Papi greets me over the phone.

"I don't know. If I see him, I'll ask him," I tease. "How's South Florida's best exterminator?"

"He's fine," Papi says, laughing on the other end. "Is it snowing up there?"

I look out the window of my balcony, and the sky looks gray, just as it was two days ago when I last saw Craig. The gloomy sky reflects my mood. "It hasn't snowed in a few days, Papi. It doesn't snow every day here in winter."

"I was just wondering, Gabrielito. In Chicago, there is una tormenta," he says.

I exhale a long sigh. We've had this conversation before. The never-ending weather conversation. Mom and I have similar exchanges. "Papi... Chicago is in the Midwest. Boston is northeast. New England. Nueva Inglaterra. It's like asking if Miami has the same weather as Dallas."

"Bueno, it could. Both cities are south," he says.

I prop my legs on my sofa and just smile at the mindless but good-natured conversation. It temporarily lifts my mood. "Okay, you win, Papi. How are you doing with the Parkinson's?" I know he hates when I bring the subject up, but if I don't ask, he won't discuss it. I can't help it. I have noticed that he has been more open in talking about it since I forced him to go to the doctor's appointment, but again, I have to instigate the conversation.

"Ah, it's okay. I have my good days and my bad days. I've been feeling more tired at night."

I lean my head against my right hand. "Papi, can I ask you something?"

"Of course, ¿qué te pasa?"

"I know you like to work, but do you think it's a good idea for you to keep exterminating? I remember how labor-intensive that job is. It can't be healthy for you, especially as the Parkinson's progresses."

"I have to work, son. I have bills to pay."

"I understand that, Papi, but maybe you can work and do something that doesn't exhaust you so much. You are taking *a lot* of pills for the Parkinson's. You can't exterminate forever."

"And what do you suggest I do? Retire? It won't be enough to cover my expenses…. Estoy solo. I am alone."

The last two words resonate with me. Sometimes, I feel just the same way.

"No, you're not, Papi. You have Aunt Cary. I'm here up here. All I am suggesting is that you can still work, maybe part time in a job that is less stressful."

"Like what, Gabrielito?"

"Maybe at Publix helping with the groceries? I know you always liked going to Costco to get the free samples. That's an easy job, and you get to interact with the public. I see people your age sitting behind serving counters and offering shoppers samples of juice and pieces of fruit and desserts. And hey, you can give me some free food when I visit," I joke.

"Oye, thank you for your concern, but I can exterminate a little while longer. When I can't anymore, I won't. I'll apply for Social Security." His stubbornness rears its ugly head.

"Whatever you feel comfortable doing, Papi. I just want to help."

"Yo sé, and I appreciate it."

The conversation moves on to more lighthearted fare. As Papi talks about the Miami Dolphins (I just listen, since I don't follow sports), I hear some catchy dance music playing in the background.

"Is that Chayanne I'm hearing, Papi?"

"Sí, the Puerto Rican singer, and his real name is Elmer. He has a new album out."

"Papi, he's not Puerto Rican. He's Mexican American, and I don't believe his name is Elmer."

"Gabrielito, he's Puerto Rican. I know my Spanish music."

"No, he's not."

"Yes, he is."

As we verbally toggle back and forth, I quickly crank up my laptop on my coffee table and search for Chayanne's Wikipedia page. The first line reads, *Elmer Figueroa Arce (born June 28, 1968), best known under the stage name Chayanne, is a Puerto Rican Latin pop singer.*

"Okay, you win again, Papi. You're on a roll today."

"I may be un viejo, but I know who sings the music that I like."

We share a laugh. I feel better already. When I hang up the phone, I watch the local news station until I pass out on the sofa in a deep sleep.

The next few days float by with school, the gym, walks around the Boston Common and the Quincy shore, plus some late-night *Star Trek* episodes. I've managed to dodge Craig at school. Before we dated, I rarely saw him in the hallways or on campus. I have also changed my routine in entering the school (I am using a side door) and exiting through the back of the main building, which spills out into the alley of clubs and restaurants. I would rather keep my distance and avoid any awkward moments where I might see Craig with Tony or chatting with classmates. I do think about him often, but keeping busy has helped me get through the week. So has Nick, who wants to surprise me with a dinner this Saturday night.

He left a message on my cell phone while I was in class.

*"Gay-briel! Don't make any plans for Saturday and Sunday. I want to take you somewhere different for dinner. Talk to you later, slore!"*

I replay the message. *Saturday and Sunday? What is Nick getting me into?* Whatever it is, I'm sure it will be fun. Life is always an adventure with Nick by my side.

# chapter Twenty-Four

IT'S early Saturday evening, about 6 p.m., and I'm spritzing myself with my Cool Water cologne when Nick obnoxiously sounds his horn downstairs. I pop my head out the balcony and shout, "I'll be right down."

I imagine Nick sitting in his truck and fixing his spiky black hair in the rearview mirror.

A few minutes later, I'm riding shotgun in Nick's truck as he makes a swift U-turn on my street.

"Where are we going? What's with all the secrecy?" I turn to Nick.

"You'll see. It will be fun. I promise," Nick says with a conspiratorial glean in his eye.

"We have different interpretations of 'fun' and 'different', and that's what I'm afraid of," I say, buckling my seatbelt.

Nick playfully punches my left shoulder. "You can't always be in control, Professor! You have to let loose sometimes and have fun, and I'm the perfect guy to do that with."

"Oh brother!" I say as Nick steps on the gas. My body jerks back as we zoom over the Neponset Bridge that connects Quincy with Dorchester. In the darkening sky, the twinkling lights of downtown Boston beckon against the bay.

Fifteen minutes later, Nick pulls into Boston's Jamaica Plain neighborhood, where I sometimes like to run around the big pond during the summer.

"Are we going to the lesbian bar here?" I turn to Nick, who unveils his trademark devilish grin.

"Now why would I want to torture you like that, GG? What fun could we have in there?" he says as he drives along Centre Street, the spine of the neighborhood. We pass the dimly lit independent mom-and-pop convenience stores, beauty salons, and auto garages. Shortly, Nick pulls up in front of El Oriental de Cuba, Boston's most famous Cuban restaurant.

"We're here!" he declares as he cuts the ignition. "We are going to have some good old Cuban food to cheer you up. It's time to strip you of your 'Saddest Gay of the Week' title."

I tilt my head and smile. "I haven't been here in a while. This is perfect. Thank you, Nick," I say, squeezing his upper right shoulder.

As soon as we climb out of his pickup truck, the succulent aroma of cooked Cuban food immediately greets us. Above the front door is a yellow sign that says, *"Un pedacito de Cuba en Jamaica Plain"* (A little piece of Cuban in Jamaica Plain). Once inside the restaurant, a friendly young ponytailed waitress with long black hair greets and seats us by the window mid-way into the restaurant. She hands us our menus before returning with two ice-filled glasses of water.

Pulsing Latin music softly plays in the background as other patrons eat and chat. The click and clack of forks, knives, and spoons echo throughout the room. The sounds mix with the steamy sizzle of steaks against a grill. As I settle into my seat, I hear two guys toast, "Oye, to Beantown Cubans. Whoo hoo!"

I peek over the rows of diners and notice that the toast came from two guys with dark brown hair. I wonder what that toast was all about. They must have had too much sangria or something.

"I'm hungry already! I can eat everything off this menu," I say, my eyes scanning the menu images of shredded beef, breaded steak, and tostones.

Nick rubs his flat stomach. "I fasted all day for this. If this doesn't make you feel like home and cheer you up, I don't know what will," Nick chides.

When the waitress returns, we place our orders. I ask for the breaded-chicken sandwich with a side of black beans, rice, and a mamey shake, the creamy and sweet tropical fruit drink of my childhood. Nick orders the grilled chicken, also with black beans and rice, plus a Corona.

"Now, this is only part one of our weekend. There's more to come," Nick says, his eyebrows arching and eyes widening with excitement.

"Oh yeah? What else is on our dance card? Inquiring Cuban minds want to know!" I say, leaning forward like a curious little kid.

"You'll see. Before you know it, you'll forget what's-his-face, he whose name shall not be mentioned tonight or any other night."

I raise my right eyebrow and sip the chilly water. "We'll see about that."

"Are you feeling any better since Thanksgiving, dude?"

"I'm taking it day by day. The whole thing was doomed from the beginning. Deep down inside, I knew that." I look down as I fold my arms across my chest.

The waitress returns with our drinks and a red basket of bread rolls and butter.

"But at least you gave it a shot, and that's what counts. I wouldn't have gone that far with such a young dude. You took a risk, and you're growing from it," Nick says, munching on a piece of bread, which rains crumbs on his shirt. He immediately wipes them away with his right hand.

"I guess I was schooled, so to speak, by this experience."

"Nah, I wouldn't put it that way. You put your heart on your sleeve, Gabriel, and that's one of your best qualities. You'll find someone out there who will appreciate you for the great guy that you are. I believe that."

I lean over and tap Nick on the hand. "Thanks, amigo! And maybe we'll find someone for you too."

Nick grimaces. "Um, not! No relationships for me. Just cute bums to tap. This is a drama-free, relationship-free zone," he says pointing to himself.

It doesn't take long for the waitress to return with plates bulging with our food. Nick and I immediately chow down and discuss our plans for Christmas. I'm headed to Miami for a long-overdue break. Nick is planning to visit his family in Providence and then do whatever he does when I'm not around—grade homework, work out, and drink and meet up with young men.

It only takes us twenty minutes to wipe our plates clean. The waitress offers us the dessert menu, but we pass, patting our bulging stomachs.

As soon as Nick pays the bill—he wouldn't let me, even though I tried—we get up and gather our coats from behind our chairs. As we put them on, I hear a familiar voice.

"Gabriel Galan, the subject of a fabulous article in the *Boston Daily* newspaper?" the voice asks.

I turn around. It's Tommy Perez, standing with his big happy-go-lucky smile and a Diet Coke can in his hand. He's with another cute Spanish-looking guy who reminds me of Orlando Bloom, but thinner.

"Tommy Perez, the one and only!" I say, greeting him with a hug.

"Good to see you, Professor! What are you doing around here?" Tommy asks as he wraps his red scarf around his neck while his friend zips up his black coat.

Introductions are made, and everyone hugs and shakes hands. When Tommy introduces his friend Carlos Martin, Nick simply greets him with a big, "Woof," which makes Carlos grin with a puzzled expression.

I roll my eyes. "Don't mind my friend here. He sometimes turns into a wolf during a full moon, which may be tonight. But he does more than bark at cute guys… he humps them," I joke.

To that, Nick playfully barks, "Woof, woof," toward Carlos, which makes him smile sheepishly.

"We were craving for some good old Cuban food, just like you guys," I say, standing face to face with Tommy. To my side, I notice Nick and Carlos staring at each other, their eyes locked, with Carlos turning away every few seconds or so with a shy smile. He is taller and leaner than Nick, while my friend is more muscular. An obvious mutual attraction flickers between them.

"Well, this is where Carlos and I meet up each week. We're the Beantown Cubans. Carlos moved here a year ago from Miami. Does that sound like déjà-vu, Gabriel?"

I can't help but laugh. We all share a similar migration pattern from South Florida to New England.

I turn to Carlos and explain. "I'm from Miami Lakes and Fort Lauderdale. My parents still live there, and I visit often. I've been in Boston for a few years."

"I know all about you, Gabriel. I read Tommy's article. I have to read all his articles. He gives me a pop quiz each week to see whether I've actually read them. It's a requirement to be friends with Tommy," Carlos says with humor in his eyes.

As Nick undresses Carlos with his eyes, Carlos seems excited to have made another Cuban connection in Boston.

"Oye, how many of us are there here in Boston? Have we started a northward migration trend?" Carlos says, his grin broadening into an infectious smile. Carlos has the lightest and prettiest brown eyes I've ever seen, even nicer than what's-his-face's.

"The more, the merrier," Nick jumps in, resting his right hand just above his belt buckle. Nick probably has a boner in his pants right about now.

"Carlos, my friend Nick here is from Providence, but he's a middle-school teacher in Somerville. I still like to consider him an honorary Latino."

Tommy jumps in. "What a coincidence! Carlos lives on the Somerville-Cambridge border, but he teaches at Dorchester High. So we've got two schoolteachers, a professor, and a reporter extraordinaire here. What does that make?"

"An orgy?" Nick blurts out loudly as he and Carlos just smile at each other.

"Well, maybe we can all come back here for dinner sometime," Tommy suggests as he plays with one of his long dark-brown curls with his free hand while taking a sip from the Diet Coke.

"Sounds like a plan," I say as I finish buttoning up my jacket. "By the way, Tommy, I really enjoyed your article on the dance class for people with Parkinson's. We discussed it in class, and I attended one of the classes out of curiosity."

Tommy's forehead creases. "Oh yeah? That's great. Do you know someone with Parkinson's, Gabriel?"

"My dad. I thought I could check out the class and see if this is something he may want to do."

"That class would be great for him. I remember how animated the students were during and after the class. But one thing I left out in the article because of space is that similar classes are being organized in South Florida because of the large elderly population and interest there among families with Parkinson's. You also have the Bob Hope Center for Parkinson's near Jackson Memorial Hospital, so the resources are available. If I had known your dad had Parkinson's, I would have mentioned that to you early on. I can get you the contact information if you'd like," Tommy offers as we stand by the entrance of the restaurant.

"Please, that would be terrific, Tommy. ¡Muchas gracias!" I say.

"Hey, anything that can help a fellow Cuban in Boston, I'm there," Tommy says, moving in for a hug.

"Well, we have to get going. Carlos and I are going to attend a book reading by a Latina radio psychologist that we both know—la doctora Bella Solis. We don't want to be late, but let's keep in touch and make plans to hang out again."

"Deal!" I say as Carlos and I hug good-bye, followed by Nick and Carlos and then Tommy and Nick.

Before they leave, Nick pulls out his cell phone and asks Carlos for his number.

"I'm in Somerville most of the time. Maybe we can grab a drink or coffee," Nick offers, punching Carlos's name into his phone.

Carlos lights up at the idea, leaning closely over Nick as he recites his phone number. As I watch them, I can't help but think what a cute couple they would make, if Nick allowed himself anything beyond a simple hook-up.

And with that, we all say good-bye.

Tommy and Carlos hang a left, heading south and walking toward a white Jeep Wrangler parked toward the other end of Centre Street. As Nick and I walk back the opposite way toward his truck, laughter erupts in the distance. We hear, "To Beantown Cubans! Whoo hoo!" That must have been Tommy and Carlos, our new friends. Nick and I look at each other, laugh, and wrap our arms around each other as we continue walking.

# chapter Twenty-Five

"AND now we begin the second half of the night," Nick announces as he navigates his truck off of Jamaica Plain's service roads before following signs to Interstate 95.

I fiddle with his CD player and pop in some of Lady Gaga's best hits before I lean back in the passenger seat. I prop my right foot on his dashboard, and my foot taps along to the music. "There's more? I thought we were just doing dinner!" I say, folding my arms behind my head as my bulging stomach rocks side to side.

"And since when do have such an early night, GG? The night is still young, and so are we, sort of. Maybe not as young as the so-called Beantown Cubans, but we look good for mid-thirties," he says, fixing his hair with his right hand in the rearview mirror. He turns to me and says, "I would try to get comfortable. We have a bit of a drive."

"Can you at least give me an idea of where we're going, Nick?"

"We're going to one place where no one will know us, well, at least not you, GG. We're heading south!" Nick then hops on I-95 following the traffic signs for Providence.

"To Providence?"

Nick glances at me with his trademark devilish look and wiggles his eyebrows. "Maybe."

I roll my eyes and relax in my seat for the trip.

Forty-five minutes later, Nick parks his truck in downtown Providence, where the giant mall and the Westin Hotel hulk over the city. We get out of the car and pass several college-age students walking by on a pub crawl. We mosey along the collection of redbrick buildings that anchor almost every city block. We pass the arching windows that decorate the brick home of the state's biggest newspaper, the *Providence News*. As we make our way to—well, I don't even know where we're headed—the city pulses with the sounds of twenty and thirtysomethings as they traipse along the grid-like downtown streets.

"Are we meeting up with your family down here?" I ask as we stroll toward a corner bar.

"Not tonight. We're going to The Dark Lady, Señorita Galan," Nick says, pointing to the bar that has a small figurine of a black horse above the entrance. A small line of men forms outside. Some smoke cigarettes. *Eh.* Others eye each other in line and look at Nick and me—the out-of-town fresh meat for the night. *Ugh.* None are cute, but that shouldn't be my main focus of the night. It just feels good to be out and about with my good friend.

"I thought we could use a night away from Boston to get out of your element. I doubt you'll bump into what's-his-face or any of your students here. And besides, you always seemed to like coming down here to visit my family, so I thought we could have a boys' night out in my hometown. A lot of the Brown University students and RISD art students are out and about getting hammered before finals week. We have them all to ourselves," Nick says, his eyebrows shooting up.

We stand in the back of the line.

"Thanks, Nick, for doing this. I really appreciate it."

"You're my bro. Anytime. I love you, man!"

"I love you too, chico," I say as he suddenly grabs me, puts me into a headlock, and rubs his knuckles against my hair. I burst out in giggles.

When I look up, the bald bouncer wearing a leather jacket and an unflattering V-neck shirt that reveals a carpet of hair stands before us with his arms folded like a prison guard. He doesn't look amused and stares at us stoically as if to say, "These snobby Boston queens! Go back to where you came from."

But instead, he politely says, "IDs, gentlemen!"

Nick and I turn to each other and grin. We pull out our licenses. "Gladly!" we shout at the same time, handing the bouncer our IDs. Nick and the bouncer have made my night. The last time a doorman asked me for ID was the night I met Craig at The Estate two months ago.

A few minutes later, Nick and I are inside the bar, which has sweeping Victorian ceilings. Once we arrive at the main bar, we bob our heads and dance in place. We immediately order our drinks. We groove to the pop music blaring in this rectangular bar, which has a small dance floor on the other side. My head sways to the left and right, and Nick and I sing out loud—and off-key—to some of the songs that dominate this bar. Small crowds of young and middle-aged men clog the lip of the bar, while streams of men flow to and from the dance floor. When a few pass us, they leave a trail of their heady colognes in their wake.

"See, look at all these young guys here. Who needs cute journalism students when you have all these Ivy League studs and twinky art students?" Nick shouts into my left ear.

"Now I know why they call this place The Dark Lady, Nick. It's dark, and the guys here walk very ladylike," I say, laughing at my own joke. "Yeah, there are some cute guys here, but we did see two cute guys tonight at the restaurant. I think you made a connection with Carlos."

"Woof!" Nick barks before taking a swig of his drink, and he moves his eyebrows again in a cartoonish way.

"So does that mean you'll hang out with Carlos Martin sometime soon?"

"We'll see. Carlos seems like a nice-enough guy, and he's very lean with some hair on his chest. You Cubans tend to be hairy. I'm curious to see what's underneath his cardigan… and jeans and underwear. Me likes me some Carlos."

"Well, don't traumatize him or anything with your Portuguese-Irish dick or your manwhore ways. I really think we could all hang out one night as friends. It would be nice to have a little social group," I say.

"And what should we call ourselves? The lady and the tramp?" Nick says into my ear as he takes another sip from his beer.

"If I were one of the two, that would work, but I'm not. So seriously, Beantown Cubans is taken, and you're not Cuban, so that doesn't work anyway." I place my finger under my chin and consider some names.

"Hmm. I got it! Let's make a toast, Nick!"

"To what?"

"Boston Boys On Top!"

"Not a bad name. It'll do, but aren't you a big Cuban bottom?" Nick cajoles me before continuing, "For a second there, I thought you were gonna say Dumb and Dumber."

"Nah, that would only be half true."

Nick unleashes his trademark high-wattage smile and sticks out his tongue. We clink our glasses and toast.

We spend the rest of the night dancing, drinking, and having fun. We may be men in our thirties, but deep down inside, we're still as young and free-spirited as the college students here tonight. I don't believe that the soul ever grows old, despite our physicality. A little bit of Cuban food and Providence was exactly what I needed. Correction—spending time with a good friend has been the best medicine for a broken heart. I'm blessed to have a great amigo like Nick by my side.

# chapter Twenty-Six

IT'S just past 5 p.m. on Thursday as I walk into the Dance Away the Parkinson's class, which has already begun. I practically tiptoe in and take a seat in the back of the class. There are sixteen people who are gathered near the large glass windows that overlook the small forest in Fresh Pond in West Cambridge. Adam spots me and winks. I grin and wave as I scoot into my chair.

"Look around the room, everyone! Look at the beautiful people we have here. They are going to be your dancing brothers and sisters today," Adam tells the class as he extends his arms out and back toward his heart.

"I want you guys to really enjoy this time, relish it. Reward your bodies," he says as everyone follows his lead.

The students, who are seated in their chairs, extend their arms out and fold them toward their torsos. Soft, comforting music by Enya plays in the background.

I look around the room, and everyone's eyes are fixed on Adam. I can't blame them. Today he wears black sweatpants and a snug, light-blue T-shirt that matches his eyes, which are framed by small crow's feet. His blond hair is spiked up as usual.

Several walkers and canes are propped up against the windows. They must belong to the elderly couples here, most likely one partner afflicted with Parkinson's. There are mother and daughter pairs, and one son with his elderly mother. Some wear sweatpants. Others wear shorts. One couple sports matching black headbands that say "His" and "Hers." I imagine Papi sitting here performing the exercises with me at his side.

"Heels together, toes apart," Adam continues, asking the class to repeat the sequence five times. I lean back in my chair and study everyone's reactions. Smiles form. Spirits are lifted.

"Wiggle your fingers toward your neighbors and extend your arms like beautiful wings," Adam says, performing the moves. "Wiggle your fingers at the ceiling. Your arms are like wet noodles, loose and free. You're in control."

The pace of the music gradually picks up, and the class is soothed by the jazz sounds of Nina Simone.

Adam walks around the room and compliments the students. "Good job, Esther," he tells a woman who has white cotton hair and sports a pink T-shirt and matching leggings. Next to her is a sun-freckled man who appears to be her husband. He sits hunched over in his chair and gently lifts his arms.

"I see people moving in ways that honor their bodies," Adam says as he continues to circle the room. Whenever his eyes meet mine, he grins or winks. "We are rewarding your bodies."

I just nod at him like a happy bobblehead.

Gradually, the pace of the class accelerates some more. Students follow a series of exercises that involve twisting their arms left and right. Then, they cup their hands as if they had water in them and then throw their arms backward, tossing that imaginary water over their shoulders. At the same time, they jut a foot outward. They bring their arms and hands together before their faces, part their hands, and lean forward, arms dropped toward the floor and dangling.

"If you have any tension or anxiety, release it. We are dancing in defiance of the disease to take back control of our bodies. We are dancing to celebrate our bodies and spirits," Adam cheers as he leads the students into another song, "Ob-La-Di, Ob-La-Da" by The Beatles. I can't help but tap my right foot along to the beat and snap my fingers in rhythm.

"Now you can do this standing up or, if you feel more comfortable, remain seated in the chair. Either way, we are going to get our groove on to The Beatles."

Some students get up, but a third of the class remains seated. Two students are in wheelchairs. Every now and then, the wife of the bald elderly hunched man dabs his chin with a handkerchief to wipe his drool. Arms sway in the air as if the class is creating big, invisible circles.

"*Happy ever after in the marketplace....*" Adam sings along to the song and encourages the students who are standing up to march in place. Those who are sitting down move their feet as much as they can. My own feet bop to their rhythm.

More smiles break out, and some students begin to clap to the beat. Me too.

"You're doing a great job, everybody! And don't mind that handsome gentleman sitting in the back. He's our guest. Everybody, please say hi to Gabriel!"

The class turns around and welcomes me. I'm so embarrassed that I look down. I sheepishly grin and wave to everyone. My eyes widen like saucers as I look at Adam.

"Gabriel is a local writing professor and a good friend. He is checking out our class for his father, so let's show him what you guys can do. We want to see him and his father in our class someday."

After The Beatles medley, which also included "In My Life," begins the tribal dance-pop sounds of the Pussycat Dolls. The Pussycat Dolls? ¿Que cosa?

Suddenly I hear the lyrics: "*Don't you wish your girlfriend was hot like me...*," and I can't help but laugh. My head bobs to the beat. The students also get into the groove and move in their own sexy ways.

Adam announces that the class is now going to tango—*to the Pussycat Dolls!* Okay, Adam gets an A for creativity in my grade book. I would have never thought of dancing the tango to the slutty pop group. Those students who feel comfortable standing up grab their partners and lead each other in cheek-to-cheek dances. Their arms are pointed like arrows about to be deployed. Rows of students gently glide forward toward the mirrored wall and then back as if they were floating to the music.

Laughter and giggles fill the room, including my own. This looks fun. Everyone is animated and having a good time. I feel the energy and the spirit of the music as well as the camaraderie of the class. I am also feeling closer to Adam. To see someone passionate about his or her work is to see that person shine. And right now, with the way he inspires and leads the class, Adam is a big bright star in my eyes—and my heart!

Distracted by the rows of dancers, I don't notice Adam approaching me. He grabs my hand and pulls me onto the makeshift dance floor.

"Wait! Hold on… I'm just here to watch," I say, resisting Adam's pull.

"Why watch when you can dance, guapo?" he says, overpowering me. It doesn't take much. "It's your turn to dance! Everyone, let's welcome Gabriel to our class," he says, locking my arms in place.

"Um… I," I say, not knowing what to say. Adam has completely blindsided me.

"Do you want to lead?" Adam offers, his eyes one inch from mine. Tiny freckles dot the tip of his nose. I want to reach out and touch them with my tongue.

I begin to stutter again, partly from the dance-floor ambush, but also because something about Adam makes my tummy flutter. My heart flips inside my chest whenever I see him or think about him. My heart just melts around him.

"Um… well… you can take the lead," I say. And with that, we march toward the end of the mirrored wall, passing the other dancing pairs.

A middle-aged blonde woman with her elderly mother, who could be her older doppelganger, passes us.

"What do you think, Gabriel? Having fun?" says the daughter in a thick Boston accent.

"You ain't seen nothing yet," the mother pipes in with her crimson cheeks.

As Adam and I glide back and forth on the carpeted dance floor, I turn to him, narrow my eyes, and mouth, "I am going to kill you!"

He grins tightly and then suddenly dips me. *Whoa!*

I break out in laughter as he props me back up.

"You were saying?" Adam says.

"I just wanted to"—I say before he dips again in mid-sentence—"watch today."

"But now you have a better idea of the class, right? Dancing is basically a conversation between two people. I'm just trying to get everyone to talk and have fun and reward their bodies," he says before whipping me back up like a rag doll. I can completely relate to how Jennifer Grey's character felt while dancing with Patrick Swayze's in *Dirty Dancing*. In fact, I don't want to stop dancing with Adam. I feel safe and warm in his strong arms. I want to wrap my legs around his waist and spin around the room. I just want to be with Adam.

"If you want to turn up the spice a little, put some hip into it, Gabriel."

I just nod my head and smile, shuffling like an amateur on the dance floor with him. I do my best to keep up, but I butcher the first few steps. Then I catch on and manage to match Adam's every step. He seems impressed.

After the tango, Adam finally allows me to return to my seat in the rear of the room. For the next half hour, the class shimmies to "Runaround Sue," struts to "The Lion Sleeps Tonight," and grooves to other songs by Lady Gaga and Tina Turner. Everyone scoots and shuffles at their own pace to the various dance styles. All the exercises emphasize balance and stretching the muscles.

Before the class ends, Adam winds everyone down by repeating the same arm-extending exercises from the beginning of the class.

At the end of the class, everyone seems invigorated. They chat as they gather around a rectangular table that has small plastic cups of juice and soda on it. I remain in the back of the room and watch everyone banter and talk to Adam. The students really look up to him. Some hug him good-bye.

As people leave the class and pack into the elevators, I walk up to Adam.

"So what do you think, Professor? Is this something your father would want to try out?" Adam says, leaning close to me. No one else is here, and our voices echo over the mechanical hum of the heater.

"I think this would be a wonderful class for my dad. I really think the social aspect of it would get him to talk about his condition and meet others like him."

Adam puts his hand on my right shoulder. "Parkinsonians are so often isolated. The tendency for them is to stay home and watch TV because they are embarrassed to have people see their hands or bodies shake uncontrollably in public. This helps them break out of their shell. There's no cure for Parkinson's, but we see this as something that can sustain them."

"I hope so," I say, offering to help clean up the room. Adam gladly accepts my help.

It takes us ten minutes to clean up and then stack the chairs in the corner of the room.

"I think we're all done!" I say, placing my hands on my waist as we survey the room.

"Actually, there's one more lesson," Adam says as he dashes to his CD player and pops in a disc.

He slowly walks toward me and takes my right hand.

"Gabriel, will you dance with me?"

I grin and look at this beautiful man with such a kind heart and accept his invitation.

As he leans in closely, Michael Buble's cover of "Save The Last Dance For Me" begins to play.

Adam gently pulls me toward him and then pushes me away. When he spins me around, he twirls me like a strand of pasta. We laugh and sing along to the song. We skip around the room as if we were waltzing on ABC's *Dancing with the Stars.*

After each turn, he stands behind me and grooves to the beat, singing softly into my ear.

And just as the song ends, he spins me around one more time, but this time, we're face to face; our legs are intertwined. He leans in, and we kiss slowly, softly, and deeply. Even after the music fades away, we continue to slow dance and kiss to our own imaginary soundtrack. I taste his strawberry-flavored lip balm as my tongue tickles his.

Adam did save the last dance for me. And somehow, I become the student who fell for his teacher.

# chapter Twenty-Seven

I APPLY a glop of pomade to the top of my head and comb my hair from left to right, smoothing it down. I touch up some spots I missed in my earlier shave in the shower and then smear on moisturizer evenly. I pluck some longer strands of my black eyebrows to look more groomed. Holding the tweezers in my right hand, I stare at myself and think, *What am I doing? Why am I trying so hard?*

The answer is Adam. I'm nervous, okay? After visiting Adam's dance class the other day where he literally swept me off my feet, he asked me out on an official date.

And of course, I said yes. If he asked me to have a colonoscopy, I'd probably say yes to that, as well. I'd be crazy not to go out with this handsome, sweet, and passionate guy, but why am I overdoing it and trying so hard to look good and young for this guy who is my age and obviously likes me?

In the brief time I have known Adam, he has never given any indication that he cares whether I'm thirty, forty, or fifty, whether my crinkles are pronounced when I smile or that I might not know all the latest dance moves from the pop divas. I don't think he'd care that some random gray hairs salt my hair. I sense that Adam likes me for me, Gabriel Galan, and not so much for what's on the surface. So I decide to stop right here with all the vain cosmetic applications. I look fine. I spritz some of my cologne. Hey, a guy's got to smell good, at least.

As I slip on my navy-blue corduroys and my brown long-sleeved thermal, I wonder where we're going tonight. Adam wouldn't say over the phone, adding that it was a surprise. He did say to dress for the cold weather because we were going to be outdoors. He also asked for my shoe size. *Hmm. I wonder if he thinks it's true that one's shoe size has a direct correlation with penis size. Either way, I should be okay. I hope!* He should be here any minute now to pick me up.

As I step into my black winter boots by the front closet, the intercom's buzzer goes off. "Hi, Gabriel, it's Adam. I'm downstairs," he says into the box.

I press the "Talk" button and say, "I'll be right down in a second."

Before I leave, I quickly spritz on some more cologne around my crotch area—hey, it can't hurt—and say good-bye to the large poster of the original *Star Trek* crew in my hallway. "Wish me luck, Captain Kirk!"

I grab my ski cap and jacket before bounding downstairs to the front of the building.

The moment I see Adam, a warm tingling sensation overwhelms me, and my breath catches in my throat. My cheeks redden. Adam is standing there holding a big bouquet of pink and white carnations. His grin widens into a big sincere smile. "For you, hombre guapo!" he says, handing me the flowers. He then gives me a strong embrace followed by a soft kiss.

I take the bouquet and inhale its sweet fragrance. The scent of fresh flowers. *I could smell these all night.*

"Thank you, Adam. That's very sweet." I step back and my eyes drink him in. I want to etch this vision into my memory. I want to remember this moment and all the brief memories I've shared with Adam. Tonight, he wears a bulky light-blue jacket, a brown scarf, comfortable blue jeans, and brown winter boots. His blue eyes glisten under the building's lights. His lips are red, probably from his strawberry-flavored lip balm, which I am now savoring on my own lips. I stand mesmerized at the sight. More so, I'm more moved by the flowery gesture and the fact that he has a special night planned for us. It also doesn't hurt that he offered to pick me up. I haven't met a lot of guys who own cars in Boston. Most people walk or take the subway to get to school or work.

"You ready, guapo?" he says, his gaze lingering for a long moment.

"I don't know. You haven't told me what we're doing. I don't know if we're staying in Boston, jumping out of a plane, or hunting for deer—who knows! And what do your plans have to do with my shoe size, or were you just being nosy?"

Adam laughs and wraps his arm around my shoulder as we walk to his rugged old black Jeep Wrangler, which is parked outside my building. "It's a surprise. I thought we could get some exercise and do another kind of dancing. It'll be fun. I promise," he says with sincerity as he opens the passenger door for me.

"As long as we're not doing Zumba, the Macarena, or square dancing, I'm up for anything," I say, cradling the bouquet of flowers and sniffing them again in the passenger seat. I smile at the gift as Adam darts around the Jeep and climbs into the driver's seat.

And with that, we go to—well, I don't know.

Twenty-five minutes later, Adam pulls into a parking space alongside the Boston Common. It's a chilly night, about thirty-five degrees, and the air is crisp.

"We're here!" he announces with laughing eyes.

"Um, the Common?"

"Yep, we're going to the Frog Pond," he says, pointing to the rear of the park.

"To watch little kids skate?" I say.

"No, silly. *We're* going to ice-skate. I brought a pair of skates in your size. I thought it would be fun to skate in the middle of downtown Boston in one of the oldest parts of the city. It's something different to do than going to a gay bar or club. If you don't know how to skate, I can teach you, but I have a feeling you can skate as well as you dance."

"Nah! I'm a Cuban from Fort Lauderdale. We're not designed to skate. Swim, yes. Build cool rafts from old Chevy and Ford car parts, yes. Skate, no," I tease.

"Oh, you're not happy about this. I screwed up, didn't I?" he says, a slight frown forming.

Now I feel bad. He went out of his way to make this a romantic, memorable evening, and here I am raining on it like a dark cloud with my playful teasing. I try to clear this up. "It's very sweet, Adam. I just don't want to kill you, myself, or any innocent kids or squirrels that come into my path. It's been a while since I skated. I'm a really, *really* bad skater. I have two left feet."

Adam puts a reassuring hand on my left shoulder, which makes me feel all goose-bumpy. "We don't have to do this. I wouldn't want to make you feel uncomfortable. I just thought it was, well, romantic."

"It is, and I'm up for the challenge and spending time with you. Let's do this, but don't say I didn't warn you! I may end up in the emergency room at Massachusetts General Hospital. Good thing it's nearby," I say, pantomiming falling.

Before I know it, we're lacing up our skates tightly by the edge of the Frog Pond, which is bathed in the bright white light from the city's decorative street lamps. Behind the rink, along Beacon Street, sparkling holiday lights decorate the red-bricked brownstones common in every Boston neighborhood. The lights of downtown skyscrapers and hotels beckon in the distance and overlook the park like celestial steel guardians. In one skyscraper, two office lights flicker and make me think that they are winking at me in approval.

Tourists snap photos as little kids circle the rink, their laughter echoing in the park. Their parents watch like them, hawk-like, from chairs at the Lily Pad Café by the rink's entrance. Some younger couples slowly skate hand in hand, lost in their own private moments. I watch an elderly couple also glide and smile secretly to themselves, and I am immediately reminded of my parents. I imagine them taking strolls along the infamous seawall in Cuba when they were younger and in love.

The older couple seems oblivious to the hockey-wannabe speed demons who whip and weave inside the rink as if they're members of the Boston Bruins.

As everyone skates, holiday songs play overhead. This is a Boston holiday greeting card come to life, and Adam and I are the characters on the cover.

Adam enters the rink and immediately spins like a professional skater. He calls me over, the cold weather marking his breath with small puffs.

Like other cautious skaters, I carefully inch my way inside and grip the handrail that ribbons the rink.

"See, you're doing great, Gabriel. There's nothing to it," he says, skating backwards. "You got this!"

I narrow my eyes at him. I *pretend* to stumble. Adam immediately scurries over toward me. He holds my left hand and patiently teaches me to glide with my left foot and then shift with my right repeatedly.

We slowly skate together. My legs wobble, and I clumsily move forward. I almost fall, but Adam quickly props me up. "See, you're skating, Gabriel. You can do this."

I laugh nervously. "Okay, so I think I've got the hang of this. Let me try skating alone. You and the elderly skaters will be safer this way."

"Are you sure, Gabriel?" he says, his eyes full of concern as they bore into mine.

I am loving this. "Yeah. I have to learn somehow. But just watch me, okay, in case I—gulp!—fall," I say.

With that, I decide to stop acting like such a novice. I confidently lunge forward and pick up speed. I cross my right leg over my left as I turn. I quickly loop around once and then start skating backwards. I dash between the hordes of little kids and the other couples. I pass the aspiring hockey players. I perform another loop and hide my smile whole time. When I approach Adam, I abruptly stop using the side of my skates, sending small shards of ice onto Adam's skates.

"Is that how you pros do it?" I tease with a wink.

"You dork! You had me going all this time! You already knew how to skate."

"Yeah, I grew up skating in Fort Lauderdale during the summers, if you can believe that. We had a youth center with a big skating rink. I wanted to get back at you for making me dance in front of everyone in your class."

Adam puts his hands on his waist and cocks his head to the right with a crooked, sweet smile. "You're full of surprises, Professor!"

"So are you, Adam!"

"Since you can actually skate, let's see what you're made of!" Adam pulls away and takes the lead.

I bolt forward and carefully navigate between the other skaters. I quickly catch up to Adam and spank him on his butt before I pull ahead of him again. "Catch me if you can!" I dare him.

I accelerate, my blade scraping the ice with each step. Adam hits his inner fast-forward button and quickens his pace. When he's on my tail, he grabs my waist and starts tickling me.

"Noo!" I belt out with a full-on belly laugh.

He hangs onto my waist, and we become a human choo-choo train. I can't contain my laughter, which fills the rink. And then suddenly, I lose my balance and fall, dragging Adam down with me. The traffic of skaters flows around us.

"You okay, Gabriel?" he says helpfully but with a big smile.

"Yeah, I'll live. Can you give me a hand?"

As Adam gets up and tries to pull me up with him, I leverage my weight and pull him back down. He falls on top of me. We break out in hysterical laughter.

Being with Adam is so effortless, natural, and fun. It's a chilly night, but Adam's presence makes it feel like spring in my heart.

After we get up on our feet, we continue skating laps around the frozen pond. Sometimes we glide hand in hand. Other times, he skates backwards in front of me and holds my hands to tow me forward. Every now and then, we exchange kisses, his warm lips soothing mine.

After an hour, we decide to warm up by taking a break at the café, where he buys us some hot cocoa. He won't let me pay.

"Having fun, Gabriel?" he says, sitting down next to me in the café.

"This has been great, Adam. Thank you for bringing me out here. It's a nice change of pace. It's been a while since I've skated. On TV, I see people skate at Rockefeller Center in New York and wish I was there with someone special doing the same. It's not fun to skate alone, so I usually don't," I say, cupping my drink which warms my hands.

"Well, I don't think you'll have to worry about that, guapo. Whenever you want to skate, I'll be your partner, if you let me," he says, leaning in for another kiss.

I place my head on his shoulder, and he links his arm through mine as we watch the parade of skaters flow by. A light snow begins to sprinkle the city as if it were inside a snow globe.

After we finish our drinks, we skate for another half hour and work up an appetite. As we remove our skates by the bleachers, Adam tells me that part two of the date is about to begin.

"Is this another surprise?" I say.

"Yep. I want to take you to a special place to eat. It has really good food, and the chef is *superb*!"

"Is his name Chef Boyardee? What's with the mystery? You can't keep a former reporter in suspense. It's like the ultimate gay tease, Adam."

"I know, but you love it, don't you?"

I nod my head with a little grin. I do like surprises, and my imagination has been running on overtime wondering what this special guy has in store for us.

With skates in hand, we walk through the park on the way back to the Jeep. We stroll along trees bedecked with holiday lights as if they were jewelry. The whole way, Adam holds my hand. I like this picture and the comfortable feeling that envelops me whenever I am around Adam.

As we walk near the bulky mounds of snow piled up along the sidewalks, I look up at the sky, which is sequined with bright stars. I wonder, *Where did this guy come from? Has Cupid finally used his GPS and found the correct map to my heart?* I look to my left and admire the man beside me, so full of life and heart. He is smart, compassionate, sweet, and centered. He also keeps me guessing with his spontaneity. He has gone out of his way to make this a great first date, which shows how much he cares about me. I hope it's the first of many dates.

Fifteen minutes later, Adam pulls up to a small three-story clapboard building just outside Harvard Square in Cambridge. Down the street, a small pizza place scents the air with the succulent aroma of baked bread and pasta.

"We're having pizza?" I ask as we climb out of the Jeep.

"Nope. We're having dinner upstairs," he says, pointing to the second floor.

"Is there a restaurant in this building? It looks pretty residential."

"Yep, it's called Chez Smith."

Then it hits me. We're at Adam's apartment.

"I thought you could use a good home-cooked meal. I made us some pasta and chicken. A simple, nice dinner at home. I just need to reheat it."

"Really? You cooked for me? Adam, that's so, wow, sweet. I don't know what to say."

"Don't say anything. Just enjoy the food and company. But we have another dinner guest waiting inside," he says as he opens the front door of the building.

We climb the creaky wooden stairs to the second floor.

"Another dinner guest?" I say, wondering who it could be.

"He's been wanting to meet you, Gabriel. He's heard a lot about you."

I remember during our night at the pizza place after The Estate when Adam said that he lived alone and was single. Maybe he invited a neighbor for dinner, or perhaps a student from the dance class? *There goes the rest of our romantic night.*

As Adam jiggles his key into the front lock, I hear scratching sounds coming from the other side of the door. When he opens it, the most adorable gray-haired miniature poodle leaps into Adam's arms and licks him as if he's ice cream.

"This is our other guest. Louie, meet Gabriel!"

I'm so clueless. Of course he was talking about his beloved dog. Adam places an excited Louie on his weathered hardwood floors. The dog immediately places his paws on my right knee and looks up at me with his wet, warm black eyes. He happily wags his tail. I squat down and hug Louie. His tongue licks my right cheek and ear, which tickles.

"I think he likes you. You passed the test, Professor."

"What test?" I say as I rub Louie's back and ears before scooping him into my arms like a big baby, the same way I do with Clara the cat.

"If Louie likes you, then you've earned membership into our small private club."

As I hold Louie, I look up at Adam, and hope continues to bloom in my heart.

# chapter Twenty-Eight

"PAPI, it'll be painless and fun. I promise!" I reassure my father.

"Ay, Gabriel, I am not sure this is a good idea," he says in his Spanish-accented English.

"Trust me, you'll be moving in ways that you haven't in a long time."

"Bueno, we'll see about that."

My father isn't buying my sales pitch even though it's my tenth one since I first learned about this class. He looks slightly terrified, or perhaps annoyed, as we walk through the glass doors of the Jewish Family Center in Cambridge. I brace him tightly by his frail right arm as he takes small steps forward. His right leg drags a little because it has grown weaker in the last seven months, so he leads with his left and shifts more of his weight there.

I continue my *rah-rah* words of encouragement, exude my positive attitude, and flash my big smile. I know that he'll enjoy this if he just gives dance a chance. "Papi, listen to me. I wouldn't do this if I didn't think it would help you. I did my homework. Dancing will help you move better. Just trust me."

"Ay, this is you and your mama's way of getting back at me for not dancing at all those weddings and fiestas," he says like a passive-aggressive annoyed child. "You are getting back at me for not buying you a new car when you were sixteen," Papi continues. His forehead wrinkles.

"If you say so…." I raise my thick black eyebrows to underscore my sarcasm. "Besides, I loved my used light-blue Nissan hatchback with the missing muffler. Who wouldn't?"

Papi sticks his tongue out at me. I twitch my nose at him. We exchange loving smirks.

At the front lobby of the center, Doris the receptionist greets us with a warm grin. She recognizes me from my previous visits. Today I am here as a student and dance partner.

"Welcome back. I see you brought a special visitor. My, my… he's one handsome man," Doris flirts, patting herself on the chest as if fanning invisible flames.

"Yeah, this is my dad, Guillermo Galan."

They exchange smiles.

"Have fun, guys!" she says with a wave.

We leave Doris and gradually walk toward the elevator. I don't want Papi to take the stairs. I wouldn't want him to overexert himself by climbing the steep wooden steps. Sometimes, he gets vertigo and loses his balance, a symptom that he's not proud of, but it's a reality of Parkinson's. He has his good days.

In the past few months, he's had more bad days. Papi does his best not to show it. That's my father, Mr. Independent Macho Man, but I love him regardless.

Just before the elevator doors slide shut, I catch sight of my mom scurrying into the lobby, her heels echoing with every rushed step. Looped around her right arm is a purse pregnant with napkins, crackers, a bottled water, and whatever else she can miraculously squeeze into a bag the size of a small dog. She catches her breath and uses her fingers to tuck her hair behind her ears. She notices that Papi is having second thoughts, which are etched all over his sun-wrinkled face. She scolds him like she used to when they were married.

"Now, Guillermo, you promised Gabriel you would take this class, *so ya*! Stop complaining to Gabriel, and don't say you weren't, because I know you better than anyone else, hombre. This was his idea. Let's see what happens," Mami says as we ride the elevator. She clenches my left arm, and I slide my arm through the crook of Papi's right. The three of us stand together in solidarity like the family we once were.

The elevator gently lifts for a few seconds and then comes to a gentle stop.

When the elevator pings, I know that the dance adventure is about to begin. "You ready to get your groove back, Papi?

"Do I have a choice?" he says with a tight grin. "But for you, I will do anything, son." He softly grabs the back of my neck and squeezes it with his trembling hand.

So here I am, trying to make my father dance, and we are well on our way. It may look and sound awkward, and it might be for him at first, but dancing can save his life, or what is left of it. We—what is left of the Galan family—certainly hope so.

As we step out of the elevator, we walk into a bright conference room.

"Welcome to our class. I'm Adam Smith, and I'll be your instructor today," Adam greets Papi. I flash a wide smile toward Adam, who has been my boyfriend the past four months. I like the sound of that.

Adam is as gracious and sexy now as he was the first time I visited the class.

I enjoy squeezing his biceps whenever I spend the night at his place, with his dog Louie sleeping at our feet. Adam is lean, and his tanned skin remains sun-kissed despite the fading winter. I know every freckle on his face and body. He's wearing black sweatpants that define certain body parts a bit too much and a loose white T-shirt. His smile is sincere, and I can tell that Papi likes him and feels comfortable around him. Who wouldn't? But I digress. This is class is about helping Papi, not about describing my own McDreamy.

With his right, sun-freckled hand, Papi shakes Adam's hand and unveils his pearly white teeth and dashing smile, the same one that hooked my mom more than fifty years ago when they were teen sweethearts in Havana.

"Thank you. I am Guillermo, but you can call me Gil, and you already know my son, Gabrielito," Papi says, shooting me a sidelong look. I told Papi all about Adam over Christmas, and he seemed happy that I was so excited about meeting someone so special.

"I know Gabriel, but Gabrielito? That's a name I haven't heard," Adam teases.

"Um, yeah, that's my family nickname. Forget you ever heard it."

"How can I, Gabrielito? It's so cute, just like you." Adam winks and then stares at me intently, just like he does when we're alone in the car, at a restaurant, or in his bed.

I then introduce him to my mom, whose cheeks blush upon greeting him.

"Great. We've got the whole family here! Nice for all of you to come to our class. Come with me, Gil, and we'll get you a nametag and find you a chair. Gladys, you can take a seat over there by the windows, with the other guests."

Adam places a comforting hand on Papi's hunched back and slowly escorts him to the registration table as if they were old friends. As they walk away, Papi looks back and raises his right arm and waves slowly with a half-grin.

"We'll be right there, Papi. You're in good hands." I stand in front of the doorway where other students are trickling in. Like me, they are adult children or spouses and loved ones of people with Parkinson's.

As we watch everyone walk toward the registration table, Mami turns toward me. "Do you think this will really help tu Papa?" she says.

I tilt my head and offer a grin.

"I hope so. It can't hurt. Studies have shown that music sparks coordinated movement. At least he'll feel better and he'll meet other people with Parkinson's. He'll see that he's not alone, and that we're not alone in dealing with this. And besides, he's in great hands with Adam."

Mami cranes her neck to plant a kiss on my cheek. "It's up to you to take care of your Papi. He always took care of us and, of course, that woman he cheated on me with, but this isn't the time or place to bring up that sucia's name. Now it's your turn to help your Papi. I am here to support you helping your Papi. Thank you for bringing him here, Gabrielito," she says.

Despite her bitterness toward Papi, I know she still cares for him, or she wouldn't be here helping me help him. He was her first love, and they know what goes on each other's lives because of me and our tight Cuban family in South Florida. I invited her to Boston to spend time with me and Papi. Besides, I wanted her to meet the other man in my life, Adam. I can't wait to hear what she thinks of him. I can tell by the way she marvels at his profile that she is smitten just as I was when I first met him.

"I will find a way to pay you back for the flight, hijo."

"Don't worry about it, Mom. Paying for this was the least I can do. I haven't been down to Fort Lauderdale as much since I moved to Boston. This is my way of helping out in the best way I know how. By the way, you were the best thing that happened to Papi."

"No, Gabrielito, you are the best thing that happened to him." She caresses the side of my cheek with the back of her sun-spotted hand. I offered her the same gesture whenever I caught her crying alone in the kitchen of our old house after the divorce.

As Adam, my beautiful and kind Adam, bends over the table to scrawl Papi's name on a white rectangular sticker, I glance around the room.

After people sign in, they settle into one of the seats that form a giant circle in the middle of the center's second floor. Just as in the previous classes, some people are hunched over, but they share laughs with one another. The more active seniors stretch their arms to warm up as they wait for the class to begin.

The class is one of two in Massachusetts for people with Parkinson's, and there are two more being developed in South Florida. I credit Tommy Perez's article in the *Boston Daily* for introducing me to this class, which also led me to Adam.

I'm hoping that Papi will want to take these classes down there once they start up in the spring. I plan to take the classes with Papi in South Florida whenever I visit.

And so here we are, about to take our first step together in a program that won't just help my father move a little faster and ease his symptoms but will also help us bond better as father and son, a relationship that has always been partially strained by what he did to my mother and by his silent discomfort with my homosexuality. I hope this class will give me a little more time with Papi as time and Parkinson's slowly rob me of him. I know that there is no cure for the disease, but this class may help boost his spirits and help him stay active in my life a few years longer.

"Welcome to the Dance Away Your Parkinson's class!" Adam announces to the twenty students, who include my father and myself as we sit in a circle of chairs. Mami sits nearby and says a silent prayer with a rosary in her right hand. I commend her for willingly flying up here to help her ex-husband, but she promised that she would always do anything for me if I asked her, and that includes helping me get Papi to take this class.

Adam begins to play some soft familiar music by Enya, and the class begins with some gentle stretching exercises. I grab Papi's shaking right hand. We look at each other and exchange a soft smile. Adam looks at me and smiles as well. I'm so glad that Adam is finally meeting my parents. They are three of the most important people in my life right now, along with Nick, who has a boyfriend. Yes, he does.

Remember Tommy Perez's friend, Carlos, half of the so-called Beantown Cubans? They met up for coffee after our weekend in Providence. Nick thought Carlos would be another one of his many hookups, but Carlos resisted Nick's advances. (Good for Carlos!) They continued having dates with Carlos not putting out, which surprised and impressed Nick. In the process, Nick realized he really did like Carlos, and he got to know him as a human being and not just as an orifice or body part. Feelings developed. Who would have guessed? They've been dating for the past few weeks. Papi, Mami, Adam, and I are meeting up with them after class at the Cuban restaurant in Jamaica Plain for dinner as soon as the class is over. I also invited Tommy Perez. The more friends, the better.

Remember how I was trying to get Papi to retire? We reached a compromise. He retired from exterminating, but he still works part-time to supplement his retirement checks. So when I visit South Florida, I always make sure to stop by the Costco warehouse near Miami Lakes, where Papi gives me extra samples of cheesecake, fruit juices, or whatever he is serving that day. I beam with pride when I see him gladly help shoppers from his serving station.

Adam's voice snaps me out of my thoughts and back to his instructions. Papi and I begin the stretching exercises and a new journey together as father and son—and as dance partners. The proverbial curtain is raised, and we begin to dance. And to my surprise, Papi takes the lead.

JOHNNY DIAZ is a Business staff writer for the *Boston Globe* where he writes about local TV news, radio, print, and advertising. Before that, he was a Living/Arts writer for three years where he wrote about pop culture, style trends, and Hispanic-related arts. He was also a reporter at the *Miami Herald*, where he shared in the 2000 Pulitzer award coverage of the federal seizure of Elian Gonzalez and the chaos that erupted in Miami afterward. He also covered some of the biggest breaking stories in South Florida, such as the Gianni Versace murder. He was a featured contributor in the first *Chicken Soup for the Latino Soul* book.

Johnny is the author of *Boston Boys Club*, *Miami Manhunt*, and *Beantown Cubans*. He lives in Boston.

Visit his web site at http://www.beantowncuban.com.